Praise for *The Strange Courtship of Abigail Bird*

"John Blumenthal has created in his narrator Ishmael Archer a character who is at once charming, entertaining, and thoroughly original. Archer's courtship of the beautiful Abigail may indeed be strange, but it is also poignant and heart-meltingly romantic. A delightful read."

- Lindsay Maracotta, bestselling author of *Dead Hollywood Moms Society* and *Adorably Dead*

"An original, featuring delightfully eccentric characters, literature, and the pursuit of true love."

- Cherise Wolas, author of *The Resurrection of Joan Ashby* and *The Family Tabor*

The Strange Courtship of Abigail Bird

John Blumenthal

Regal House Publishing

Published by
Regal House Publishing, LLC
Raleigh, NC 27612
All rights reserved

ISBN -13 (paperback): 9781947548862
ISBN -13 (epub): 9781947548879
ISBN -13 (mobi): 9781947548886
Library of Congress Control Number: 2019931631

All efforts were made to determine the copyright holders and obtain their per-missions in any circumstance where copyrighted material was used. The publish-er apologizes if any errors were made during this process, or if any omissions occurred. If noted, please contact the publisher and all efforts will be made to incorporate permissions in future editions.

Interior and cover design by Lafayette & Greene
lafayetteandgreene.com
Cover art © by Shutterstock/Everett Collection

Regal House Publishing, LLC
https://regalhousepublishing.com

The following is a work of fiction created by the author. All names, individuals, characters, places, items, brands, events, etc. were either the product of the author or were used fictitiously. Any name, place, event, person, brand, or item, current or past, is entirely coincidental.

Printed in the United States of America

To my mother and father

PART ONE

One

Call me Ishmael.

Kindly pardon this disgraceful act of plagiarism, but that is indeed my true given name and one that I carry with unflinching pride, not because of its Biblical origin but rather for its literary renown, although I must confess that it is an appellation which frequently inspires considerable drudgery whenever I am compelled to spell it innumerable times for pseudo-literate mid-level bureaucrats and similarly challenged dunderheads. In my youth, when I was less than overjoyed by this unconventional moniker, more than a few people, my parents not included, dubbed me *Ishy*, a sobriquet that bore an unfortunate resemblance to the word *itchy*, thus providing sufficient ammunition for derision, most often delivered by my less imaginative grade school colleagues in spite of the fact that I was seldom afflicted with rashes, insect bites or similar maladies of the epidermis that required the application of fingernails upon the skin to provide relief. Even today, there are certain people, no doubt eager to engage me in amusing repartee, who will occasionally deliver a remark such as, "How is Captain Ahab, hahaha?" to which I habitually respond, "Obsessive."

You see, my mother and father—both of whom were employed as English teachers at our local high school—had a profound fondness for Mr. Herman Melville's transcendent novel and thus considered the name an *homage* of sorts although, for reasons that defy logic, I believe it caused me to develop a strong distaste for all things maritime. I have, for example, always been vulnerable to seasickness and thus abhor boating; aquariums terrify me; I find the costumes worn by sailors to be a sartorial travesty; I am unable to successfully engage in the art of staying afloat in water. And so forth. Ergo, when I was but a lad, I would have preferred a title that was less

3

unseaworthy and more conventional, such as Jake from *The Sun Also Rises,* Amory from *This Side of Paradise,* Holden or even Dorian, although I am greatly relieved that Mother and Father did not choose to saddle me with the likes of Huckleberry, Fitzwilliam, Ebenezer, Humbert or Quasimodo. Given their fascination with *Moby Dick,* I feel blessed that they refrained from selecting Queequeg, a name fraught with an infinite variety of daily mortifications.

Nevertheless, one might say that my childhood, if not idyllic, was more than agreeable. Our domicile, which was not dissimilar in style to a British row house, was situated in Forest Hills, New York, where I attended the local public school, as my mother and father lacked the resources for a private education or a tutor, either of which would have been their preference. As they had given birth to me late in their lives, I was not required to endure the companionship of a sibling and, as a result, received their full attention, a status quo that I found most satisfactory. My father bore an uncanny resemblance to Nicolai Lenin, although his demeanor was considerably less confrontational, while my mother was somewhat portly and prematurely gray. Sartorially, both were given to frumpiness, although Father was somewhat obsessive about the state of his shoes. They were sociable people—all manner of intellectuals frequented our house and I recall with great vividness, the scintillating banter that resulted from said associations, although I did not participate in it for, as a young fellow, I was somewhat intimidated by their philosophical depth. On occasion, they played a parlor game known as charades, but it was not until I had reached the age of ten that I was allowed to participate.

Fortunately, according to the recollections of Mother and Father, I required very little in the way of discipline or punishment. My only household duty as a lad was to shine my father's shoes every other day, a task for which I received monthly remuneration in the form of two dollars, often rewarded in coinage. To the disgruntlement of my parents as well as my dentist, I frequently utilized said financial bonanza to purchase all manner of confections from a gentleman known as Claude Finkleman, the proprietor of a quaint candy store located six blocks from our residence.

Yet most significantly, my parents instilled in me a deep affection for literature that commenced shortly after I had achieved the age of six, at which time I eagerly consumed *The Mayor of Casterbridge* by Mr. Thomas Hardy. Thoroughly enchanted by this captivating tale, I would remain awake throughout the night, a brazen violation of my parents' bedtime decree (which they seldom enforced), my fingers flipping madly through the book's magical pages, my head covered by a blanket emblazoned with images of barnyard animals, my sole source of illumination provided by a miniature flashlight. Yes, this was the book that first awakened me to the wonders of fiction. I adored the sensuous feel of a book, the glorious musty smell of an old hardcover, the heft of a lengthy tome, the colorful symmetry of a regiment of volumes standing side by side on my bookshelves, the very act of turning pages. Thus I have always eschewed the use of flat, aesthetically barren electronic devices. From that point on, I devoured the works of Austen, Trollope, Dickens, Thackeray, and the Brontë sisters, eventually moving on to noted American scribes and those of other nationalities—Stendhal, Hugo, Dostoevsky, Mann, Marquez, Proust, Kafka, and all the rest. My gluttonous reading of the nineteenth-century British classics during my formative years resulted in my somewhat stilted and admittedly verbose manner of speaking which, in my youth, was nearly incomprehensible to most of my young classmates and often considered snobbish, although that was never my intention. Simply put, I have always harbored a distaste for the vernacular as well as all manner of slang, both of which I find somewhat pedestrian.

Yes, I was a precocious lad, beloved by my grade school teachers for my superior intellect, flawless grooming (I customarily sported a starched white shirt and bow tie to class), and admirable behavior (I was a quiet, brooding sort of young man who caused no disruption in class). Yet to my dismay, my mostly gushing report cards (written in a loopy cursive mode of handwriting and frequently containing a few minor but egregious misspellings or questionable grammar), always included a sentence or two regarding my profound lack of social skills—*Ishmael would benefit from more interaction with his schoolmates. He seems to be quite shy.* Having consumed many of the classics, I found it somewhat absurd that in grade school I was expected to read and discuss a thirty-page, poorly illustrated, ineptly plotted book involving the insipid escapades of various dimwitted characters and their equally insufferable pets. Simply put, I was entirely devoid of friends, as my schoolmates and their activities held no interest for me. The only connection I had to those in my age group consisted of a passion for such delicacies as Snickers chocolate bars, Black Vines Licorice Twists, Twinkies, Cheese Puffs and other items one might describe as unhealthy victuals, but that was the full extent of my shared interest. As this was insufficient to inspire a true connection with my colleagues, I remained virtually friendless during those early days of my education. And so I invariably ate alone in the school cafeteria, my briefcase by my side, consuming the repast (which usually consisted of a ham and cheese sandwich) that my mother had hurriedly prepared for me the night before, and filling the remaining time with the perusal of a book.

Although I later made several acquaintances during my teenage years in high school—most notably Arthur Poindexter, my teammate on the chess squad—it is true that my solitude as a child disturbed my parents, who had been called in to discuss this matter with my teachers on more than one occasion. After much discussion, it was suggested by the principal that engagement in athletics might be a suitable solution to this handicap.

Unfortunately, school athletics did not appeal to me—football struck me as perilous to one's skull and I was unable to comprehend the mysteries of baseball. But had there been a croquet team, I might have participated, simply to eliminate that last annoying sentence from my report cards, a failure that so displeased Mother and Father. Besides, croquet seemed like a simple, civilized pastime, one that would require an economy of movement and an inconsequential risk of injury, not that I would have excelled at it. It was an abysmal waste of time of course, but perhaps a strategy with which to improve my woefully inadequate social skills.

"I hate to tell you this, Ishmael, but I'm afraid croquet will not become part of the school's athletic curriculum," Mr. Ramsey, the school's gym teacher, said one afternoon as I sat quite alone in the school cafeteria. I had by that time submitted a formally written request that a croquet team be organized. In spite of my aversion to sports I had a fondness for Mr. Ramsey, who took a great liking to me and thus violated school regulations by allowing me to abstain from gym class activities, mostly because I was so pathetically inept at them. He, too, was an avid reader but I had no idea what sort of literature lined his bookshelves, not that it mattered, for Mr. Ramsey was my sole friend.

"I am not surprised to hear that, Mr. Ramsey," I said. "Truth be told, I held out little hope for the acceptance of my application, but I am most thankful that you were kind enough to propose it for me."

"Well, I'm sorry," he said, with sympathy in his tone. "Principal Thorndyke didn't think standing around hitting wooden balls through hoops was good exercise."

Although this was the precise reason I had suggested that the school adopt the sport, I did not address his citation of Principal Thorndyke's reasoning.

"*C'est la vie*," I said. "But I fear my parents will be quite displeased by this news."

"Why is that?"

"Because, alas, it appears that I have no friends," I said.

"Well, you're not the only one."

"Oh?"

Mr. Ramsey glanced around the room and I followed his gaze until it fell upon a young bespectacled fellow who sat at a nearby table. I observed that he was quite alone as he consumed his lunch with great concentration, his eyes squarely fixed upon a yellow cupcake as if it were an ancient relic from an archaeological exploration. It appeared that he was myopic as he held said cupcake two inches away from his visage.

"That's Jerome Duckworth," Mr. Ramsey told me. "He's a loner too. Maybe you two could eat at the same table. He doesn't talk much."

"Hmm," I said. "Perhaps this suggestion is worthy of consideration."

I placed a bookmark in the novel I had been perusing. Mr. Ramsey peered over my shoulder. "What are you reading today, Ishmael?"

"*Dead Souls* by the Russian author Mr. Nikolai Gogol."

He nodded. "Sounds like a hoot."

I chuckled at his witticism. Just then the first warning bell rang signaling the end of the lunch hour, so I folded up the remains of my lunch in the tin foil my mother had wrapped it in and placed the novel in my briefcase.

"You sure do a lot of reading, Ishmael," Mr. Ramsey said. "Every time I see you, you've got your nose in a book."

"Reading is my primary form of gratification, " I said. "Yet I also do it for inspiration."

I glanced around at my schoolmates as they sucked noisily through the straws in their miniature milk cartons and then proceeded to unload their trays into the trash receptacles.

"Inspiration for what, Ishmael?"

"For my work."

"You mean your homework?"

I hesitated. Should I tell him? Would he laugh or make a condescending remark? After all, I was only eight.

"No," I said. "A slightly more formidable project."

"And what would that be, if you don't mind me asking?"

"Do not inform a soul, but I have recently commenced writing the Great American Novel!"

He raised an eyebrow. "Is that so? I must say, I like your ambition, Ishmael. It's very admirable for a young fellow like you to think big. I look forward to reading it."

"Thank you," I said. I had yet to inform my parents of my lofty goal for fear that they would find it a trifle too ambitious and there-fore discourage me from undertaking it at such an early age. Mr. Ramsey's encouragement was most welcome.

"What's it about?" he asked. I looked at Mr. Ramsey. In some ways he reminded me of Charles Bingley, Miss Jane Austen's delightful fictional character, in that he was a cheerful fellow, although the whistle that resided around Mr. Ramsey's thick neck was not a fashion accessory Mr. Bingley would have sported.

"I am not entirely certain of that yet, Mr. Ramsey," I said. "Perhaps a memoir disguised as fiction. Something along those lines."

"A memoir, huh?" he said. "But you're kinda young, Ishmael. Have you had a lot of memorable adventures?"

I gave this some thought and said, "Well, I once purloined a package of Hostess Ding Dongs from a convenience store."

He appeared to be stifling a chuckle. "Why?"

"I had just completed reading *Oliver Twist* by Mr. Charles Dickens and I wished to experience the art of theft, although I did not possess the derring-do to attempt the picking of pockets. Please do not tell anyone as I do not wish to be taken into custody by the local constabulary."

"I won't," he said. His expression told me that he was being truth-ful. "So how far have you gotten in this book you're writing?"

I removed my spectacles and wiped them with a napkin. "Alas, at the moment I have written only two words."

"And what might those be?"

"The word 'Chapter' and the word 'One.' I have not yet decided whether or not to pen the words 'Part' and 'One,' but I may do so, thus doubling my word count."

"Well, you're off to a good start," he said with a smile. As the second warning bell sounded, he put an arm around my shoulders and together we ambled out of the cafeteria and into the commotion of the hallway.

༄

The next day, I followed Mr. Ramsey's advice and settled myself at the table that was occupied daily by Mr. Duckworth. When I greeted him with a cheery "hello," he did not look up from his food but merely replied with a barely audible, "hey." No further conversation ensued. As he continued to examine his dessert, I read my book, hoping that he would not perceive me as an interloper who had rudely invaded his privacy. After two weeks of this peculiar relationship, I inquired as to whether he would care to accompany me to my domicile for some refreshment following school, to which he responded with the word, "sure." Thus, after the last bell sounded, we walked silently together to my house, stopping only once in order for me to purchase a few of my favorite items at Mr. Finkleman's candy shop, some of which I graciously shared with my reticent companion. When we arrived at my abode I introduced Mr. Duckworth to my mother, who beamed as if I had just won the Nobel Prize, and proceeded to offer us Oreo cookies and milk as we repaired to the living room. After we had consumed our snack from a tray, Mr. Duckworth situated himself on the floor directly in front of the television and watched, much to my approval, a quiz show known as *Jeopardy*, whilst I reclined on a nearby armchair with a notebook, engrossed in deep contemplation concerning my work on the aforementioned Great American Novel. Yet I must confess that, after a certain period of time, I enjoyed Jerome Duckworth's company, limited as it was, and commenced to call him by his given name, though he did not respond in kind to this act of familiarity. Disappointing, yes, but this weekly ritual seemed to satisfy those concerned with my unsociability, and the offending sentence regarding my solitary existence never again appeared on my report cards, thus removing the sole remaining obstacle from my path to greatness.

Two

Longfellow College, a mediocre institution of higher learning, was situated in the insufferably dreary town of Highland Falls, New York, a mere forty miles north of the magical metropolis of Syracuse. Nestled in the foothills of the mighty Adirondack Mountains, which accounted for Highland Falls' disagreeable climate, the college had derived its title from the estimable American poet, Mr. William Wadsworth Longfellow who, at least in my humble opinion, would have found it an establishment unworthy of bearing his name.

Perhaps the only civilized feature of this otherwise bleak collegiate environment was the campus's faculty lounge, which had, over the years, become my sanctuary. Designed in the style of an old English gentlemen's club, it contained uncomfortable wingback chairs, oaken tables and an oversized stone fireplace that looked as though it had not been ignited since Calvin Coolidge occupied the White House. Hanging on its walls were several rows of faded prints that depicted horses and their riders engaged in the witless sport of foxhunting.

When the lounge's dusty draperies were pulled back, which was not often the case for its inhabitants appeared to prefer a funereal ambiance, one was afforded a splendid view of the lush green meadows and forests that stretched for miles below, for Longfellow sat on the plateau above the town. In the distance, the viewer could behold the rather pathetic excuse for a waterfall (it was more of a large dripping faucet) from which the town of Highland Falls had derived its name. Apparently, the pioneers who first settled the region in 1845 were sorely lacking in imagination. From November through April, a layer of snow concealed the grassy fields, but by early June, a plethora of wildflowers provided a pleasing array of colors. Although academically undistinguished, at least the college had been placed in a scenic location, although its architecture—classic Greek Doric

11

columns, pediments, crepidoma, and porticos—gave the institution an unmerited appearance of gravity.

Thankfully, the other members of the staff who frequented the lounge were customarily silent within its walls, whispering on occasion to each other as if they were in an ancient catacomb, thus affording me the concentration required to read without being disturbed. Occasionally, a new member of the faculty, unaware of the unwritten rule of silence, would create a disturbance, which was soon silenced by the disgruntled facial expressions or muted *harrumphs* emanating from the other professors in attendance.

It was on an overcast day in April when one such newcomer, a personage of the female variety, entered the room and approached the seat beside mine. Her arms were overladen with books, papers, folders, and other paraphernalia, all of which she accidentally dropped to the floor beside the neighboring chair just prior to occupying it. The other inhabitants of the room, startled by the sudden thudding noise, looked up and grunted emphatically as she bent to alleviate the floor of her scattered papers.

"Dammit," she said in a normal tone of voice, which elicited another series of grumbling and outbursts of *shhhhh* from the others. I watched her struggle for a moment and then, as I perceived that she was not making much progress, squatted beside her on my knees in order to assist her.

"Thank you," she said. "Very kind."

"My pleasure."

"I left my backpack at home," she explained. "I do that a lot."

In a whisper, I said, "You might want to keep your voice down."

"Why?"

"An unwritten code of conduct, if you will, though its origin is reputedly unknown," I said. "Silence reigns within these august walls."

"Oh." This utterance was followed by a dismissive word that sounded to me like *pffft*.

I stole a look at her as I helped her organize the sea of papers.

In spite of her somewhat disheveled gray hair, she was an attractive woman possibly in her fifties. Her garb included several oversized silver rings and a random collection of metallic bracelets that jingled like sleigh bells whenever she moved her arms.

She extended her hand. "Constance Oswald, no relation to the assassin."

"Ishmael Archer."

She offered me a lopsided grin. "May I...*call you Ishmael?*"

"Yes," I said. "Very clever."

She wore a wry smile. "How are things going on the...hahaha... *Pequod?*"

I winced and let forth with one of my humorous rehearsed retorts, to wit, "The crew is having a whale of a good time."

She laughed, but to my relief, did not launch into any further references to my name. "My apologies," she said. "I imagine you probably get that a lot."

"I do, but it no longer disturbs me," I said. "However, most people address me by my last name, which is Archer."

"I prefer Ishmael if you don't mind."

"Not at all," I said, offering her a smile. After a moment, I inquired, "And what, if I may be so bold as to ask, is your discipline?"

"Anthropology."

"Fascinating field of study," I said. "Mine is English Literature." After a few seconds had passed, I added, "Oddly, I do not believe I have observed your presence on our beloved campus."

"I haven't been here very long," she said. "I'm subbing for Professor Potter who has been ill. I hope to stay beyond the summer term."

"Ah yes," I said. "Potter is a particular friend of mine. A lovely fellow."

Having by this time arranged her formerly scattered materials into orderly piles, we placed them on the nearby table whereupon she collapsed into her seat and wiped her brow with the sleeve of her shirt.

"Is it hot in here or is it me?" she said.

"Although I am not familiar with the normal state of your body temperature, I will concede that it is indeed quite warm."

"Well, thanks for the help, Ishmael."

"My pleasure, Ms. Oswald."

"Constance."

Then she carefully placed a pair of reading glasses upon her aquiline nose and, after shuffling through papers with an impatient growl, removed an item from her stack, whereupon I returned to my book, *The Gulag Archipelago.*

When I glanced over at her she was furiously scraping her yellow highlighter pen over a paper on her lap, a procedure that created an annoying sound not unlike that of an endangered piglet. "My God. Can't these kids spell?"

"Alas, having encountered this myself on many occasions, one may wonder whether the subject has been stricken from high school curricula."

"Certainly seems like it has."

"Fortunately, this was not the case when I attended school," I said. "In all modesty, I am proud to say that at the age of ten I was the victor in a college spelling bee. I received a trophy which currently resides in my room at the residence of my parents."

"Congratulations," she said, in a slightly droll tone. "What was the winning word?"

"Boustrophedon."

"I don't even know what that means."

"It is an ancient form of writing."

"How ever did you know this odd word, Ishmael?"

"I read a great deal and I suppose I encountered it," I said. "Are you perchance a reader of fiction, Constance?"

"I'm afraid I haven't got much time for reading except for scholarly journals," she said. "But I have read quite a few Sherlock Holmes mysteries. I do love Conan Doyle."

"A superlative author," I said. "I believe I have twice consumed

vehicle immediately—it was Eliot Altschuler's black pick-up truck. I also noticed that his spouse, Sandra, occupied the passenger seat.

It was with some difficulty that Eliot opened his car door for it was likely frozen shut, and when his feet touched firmament, he immediately slipped on the ice but righted himself and therefore did not fall. Of course, unlike me, he was attired appropriately for such weather.

"Is that you, Archer?" he said, as he grew nearer, shielding his eyes with his hand. He was wearing one of those Russian fur hats, thick leather gloves, a lined Parka, and high rubber boots. He resembled J.D. Salinger dressed as Ernest Shackleton on a polar expedition.

"Indeed, it is," I said, glancing with some irritation at my vehicle.

With an expression that betrayed a mixture of jocularity and pity, Eliot also cast his eyes at my ancient Subaru, which was now covered with snow to such a thorough degree that one could barely discern that it was in fact an automobile.

"It appears that my vehicle no longer contains petrol and I suspect my battery has perished as well," I said.

"Bad luck," Eliot said. "What year is this heap?"

"If I recall correctly, it was manufactured in 2003."

"At least Subarus hold their value," Eliot said, as if this observation would in any way brighten my day. "You could probably get a thousand for it and maybe write off the loss of value on your taxes."

I was somewhat annoyed that I was standing hatless in the midst of a blizzard discussing automobile depreciation. "Perhaps you would be good enough to drive into town and alert a mechanic in possession of a towing truck."

"Don't you have a smartphone?" he said.

"Of course, but, alas, I forgot to charge it this morning, a frequent tendency of mine," I said. "I suppose one cannot in truth call it a 'smartphone' unless its owner is actually smart, ha ha ha."

Eliot narrowed his eyes at me as if inspecting an otherworldly life form. "Doesn't matter," he said. "There's only one mechanic in town anyway, and he's probably out shoveling Main Street with his snowplow."

This complication had not occurred to me.

"Let's have a look," Eliot said. At that, he attempted to lift the hood but it was too weighted down with snow and did not budge. "Don't just stand there, Archer. Give me a hand here. This bloody thing must weigh a ton."

After much grunting, we managed to raise the hood. I held it open as Eliot inspected the car's wiry innards. "Battery's fine," he said. "Hold on a moment. Sandra knows more about these things than I do. Her father used to race cars at Le Mans."

Hugging myself to keep warm, I watched as Eliot ambled back to his truck and knocked on his wife's window, which she then lowered.

Momentarily, Sandra appeared before me. She wore a long brown mink coat and fur hat. She smiled warmly at me. "Hello, Archer," she said as she embraced me tightly. "What have you done to yourself now, you poor man?"

"The usual cock-up," I said.

"Would you like to borrow my hat? Your ears are as red as beets."

Although I did not much care for vegetable analogies, I reflexively touched one of my ears, which felt as if it might crack. "Very kind of you, Sandra," I said. "But this act of generosity would leave you hatless."

"I realize that, Archer."

"I wouldn't want to deprive you of cranial warmth, Sandra."

She ignored my response, removed her headgear, shook out her lustrous black hair and placed the garment on my head, pulling it down at the sides to cover my ears. "Now, let's have a look inside this rattletrap of yours."

As I accompanied her to the front of the car, I noticed Eliot attempting to stay upright while carrying what appeared to be a gas can from the rear of his truck.

Sandra removed one of her gloves and reached into the bowels of the car, then twisted something. It only took her a few seconds to diagnose the problem. "Loose distributor cap," she said. "Fixed. Try to start it."

Obediently, I turned on the ignition. The car burst forth with a sickening rattle but shortly thereafter the engine came to life.

"Utterly amazing!" I said, once again appearing at her side. "You are an extremely talented woman, Sandra!"

She gave me a sly look. "In more ways than one, if you catch my drift."

Before I could respond, Eliot appeared beside us with the gas can. "I see you've fixed it, darling," he said to his wife.

"Obviously," Sandra said. I detected some iciness in her tone.

"You're a wonder, my dear." Eliot smiled with pride. "Isn't she Archer?"

"Indeed, she is," I said.

"Eliot," Sandra said in a voice filled with impatience, "why are you standing there? Fill the poor man's car with gas."

"Yes, of course," Eliot said.

"I'm going back in the truck," Sandra said, mimicking a shiver. "It's fucking cold out here."

As Sandra departed, Eliot began replenishing my tank as I looked on, blowing hot air into my cupped hands. "So," Eliot said after a moment, "I assume you're aware that Dean Fletcher just appointed me temporary Dean of the English Department for the summer session."

The news left me momentarily speechless. I was reasonably certain that Eliot knew that I had not heard this discouraging tidbit of information but I did not wish to appear ignorant. "I did indeed hear that," I said.

"If I may ask, what will *you* be doing this summer?" he asked.

"Oh, this and that," I said. I stammered because I did not have an answer. "There are some exciting plans in the works."

Eliot cast me a look that combined both skepticism and curiosity but he did not pursue the topic. Then he extracted the nozzle of the gas can and screwed the top back on my tank. "There you go. All filled up. This was great fun, Archer. We should do it again some-time."

"I trust that is a witticism."

"Adieu, Archer," he said. "Drive carefully."

As he walked back to his truck and gave me a backhand wave, I pried my car door open and climbed inside. The resemblance to an igloo was uncanny. As I started the car, I saw Eliot's pick-up fly by, kicking up a puddle of slush. It was not until I had reached the Welcome to Highland Falls sign that I realized that Sandra's fur hat was still atop my head.

Three

Several days thereafter, whilst I occupied a chair in the school library, reading *Middlemarch* for the third time (one often discovers new symbolism when rereading the classics) and consuming a sodden grilled cheese sandwich and undercooked French fries from a paper plate, the dean's secretary, Ms. Anastasia Goldfine, shuffled quietly toward me so as not to disturb anyone and whispered in my ear that Dean Fletcher desired to see me and that there was some urgency attached to the matter. Ms. Goldfine was said to be in her late eighties, and several of the less comedically gifted faculty members had on occasion opined that she had once dated Grover Cleveland.

"I tried to call you on your cell phone, Professor," she said in a distinctly aggravated tone of voice. "Don't tell me—you forgot to charge it again."

"It is indeed charged," I said, "but I am afraid I turned off the sound so as not to disturb the others in attendance."

"I had to *schlep* all the way over here from the dean's office."

"An excellent opportunity to enjoy some exercise and fill your lungs with the fresh mountain air."

"When was the last time you were outside, Professor?" she said. "It's about twenty degrees. My nose hairs are frozen."

I resisted an urge to steal a look at the alleged state of her nasal foliage.

When I inquired as to whether she had any knowledge regarding the purpose of this unscheduled tête-à-tête, she merely shrugged. Although Dean Fletcher and I had dined together several times and attended the usual tedious faculty gatherings, he seldom wished to behold my presence in his office for any official reason.

Nevertheless, I hastened out of the building, placed my helmet upon my cranium and leapt on my bicycle, an unwieldy mass of metal and rubber that I had purchased recently from a student of mine. The administration building was just under a quarter mile from the library and, as I had always been fanatical about punctuality, I veered off the bike path and proceeded to take a shortcut on a diagonal path over the snow-covered grass. Pedaling furiously, I maneuvered unsteadily through the thin layer of snow, and after falling only once due to a mogul hidden in the field, arrived there on time.

Two minutes after my arrival, I found myself seated in an uncomfortable reproduction of an Eames chair in Dean Fletcher's office, trying not to appear too afflicted with boredom as he painstakingly watered one of the numerous orchids that adorned nearly every available space in his office. The dean used a miniature copper watering can and a plastic spray bottle filled with a pinkish liquid, presumably plant nourishment.

Moving across the room to tend to another plant, he said, "Archer, did you know there are twenty-five thousand different types of orchids?"

"Remarkable," I said.

"*Genus Orchidaceae genera*," he continued. "*Herbaceous monocots.* That means it has only one seed as opposed to a dicot."

"Your knowledge is most impressive."

My eyes followed him as he administered to his precious specimens, occasionally leaning in close to study one of the delicate blooms. White-haired and possessed of a black mustache and dark brows, he was exceedingly tall and displayed the bearing and slenderness of Ichabod Crane.

He finally placed the watering can and spray bottle on the side of his desk, straightened a slightly lopsided photograph of orchids on his wall and sat down.

"So how's the world treating you, Ishmael?"

I was sorely tempted to reply that the world was treating me like a cat treats a cat box but restrained myself.

"Quite well, Bob. How goes it with you?"

"Busy, busy, busy," he said. He let forth with a weary sigh. "No end to the paperwork. I am certainly looking forward to summer vacation."

"A blessed relief," I said. "And to what locale are you planning to venture, if I may ask?"

His face brightened. "Merry old Scotland. Best golf courses in the world."

"So I have been informed. I believe the Scots invented the game."

"In a manner of speaking, yes. The Romans had a sport that resembled it somewhat. They called it 'paganica' and it dates back to 100 B.C."

"Live and learn."

Bob nodded thoughtfully. "Ever been to Europe, Archer?"

"In point of fact I traveled to London some years ago to pay homage to the authors buried in Westminster Chapel." I recalled the trip and the joy I had felt. "An utterly captivating journey."

"Sort of a morbid way to spend a vacation though, don't you think?" he said.

"On the contrary. I found it most gratifying but I agree that it is not everybody's cup of tea, so to speak."

"Any plans for this summer?"

"None, I'm afraid," I told him. "As it happens, I cannot afford to travel to exotic places. Alimony is draining my bank account."

"I'm glad to hear that."

I frowned. "That alimony is draining my bank account?"

Bob let forth with a chuckle. "Of course not," he said. "I'm glad you have no summer plans."

Startled, I attempted to conceal a smile. Did this mean that he was going to appoint me to a temporary administrative position as he had done for Eliot Altschuler? "No, Bob, I have absolutely no plans at all. I am, as it were, free as the proverbial bird."

"Then you won't mind teaching a creative writing course this summer," he said. "We have nobody to fill the position—Farnsworth is on a short sabbatical as you know—and since you have written several novels..."

My face valiantly attempted to manufacture a smile but I remained silent, for Bob was well aware of my lack of success in crafting fiction.

Having been hoodwinked into teaching several summer creative writing classes in the past, I knew that the drudgery could be nearly unbearable. Summer school was a form of detention reserved for those who had achieved poor grades during their senior year and were thus required to earn the credit to graduate, although it was open to non-students as well and usually attracted an assortment of local aspiring authors.

"That sounds...um...wonderful," I said. "Truly an honor."

"There will be some extra money in it of course."

"I shall look forward to it," I said, although the pecuniary embellishment would be the only advantage.

"Good man!" he said. Then he pounded the desktop with his fist, which nearly caused his cordless telephone to topple from its cradle. "I suppose you don't know that Eliot Altschuler will be filling my shoes for part of the summer."

"I do," I said. "He informed me."

"Hmm," Bob said with a touch of displeasure in his voice. "I had asked him to keep it confidential. But I want to assure you, Archer, that his temporary appointment does not in any way mean I have chosen him for department head."

Relief swept over me. "I see."

But Bob was not looking at me. His gaze had fallen upon an orchid that sat in the corner. He was frowning. "Did I forget to water Esther?"

"Who?"

"Esther," he said. "The pink one in the corner. I have names for each of them. The yellow one by that window is called Mathilda; her neighbors are Bathsheba and Snookie."

"Perhaps you did water Esther," I said. "You were in the midst of applying water when I stepped in. Perchance you attended to her prior to my arrival."

At that, Bob rose from his chair, grabbed the watering can and headed toward Esther. "Better safe than sorry," he said.

&

Upon my departure from Dean Fletcher's office, I strolled past Ms. Goldfine who glanced up from her filing chores and gave me the thumbs-up sign, though I did not comprehend why she had performed this digital maneuver. In truth, I was not especially encouraged by Bob's assurances that I remained a contender for department head. After all, the task of conducting a mundane creative writing class was a far cry from Eliot's appointment as temporary dean. While Bob would be golfing in Scotland, Eliot would be in charge of not only me but of the entire function of the department. My task would be to assign basic writing exercises and critique them. I do not mean to appear pompous, but my prior efforts with summer classes had proved fruitless, although I must confess that the prospect of discovering at least one student possessed of some natural talent would provide a measure of gratification.

I decided to drown my sorrows, as it were, in a piece of chocolate cake and a vanilla milkshake, so I repaired to the student cafeteria, where I encountered Constance furiously typing on the screen of her smartphone. The repast that sat before her consisted of a turkey salad sandwich and an ice tea. Over the previous weeks, Constance and I had developed a camaraderie, owing in some respects to our mutual enjoyment of clever repartée.

"Mind if I join you?" Without waiting for a reply, I set down my tray.

"Please do."

She placed her cell phone down beside her plate and looked at my face. "Bad day?" she said.

"As a matter of fact, yes. How did you manage to discern this?"

"The gloomy look on your face is a dead giveaway," she said. "You look like a man who has just been spurned by his lover."

"Alas, there is no such person in my humdrum existence at the moment."

"Oh," she said. "Unfortunately, the case is the same for me. My love life has been distressingly barren for quite some time now. How long has it been like that for you?" Then she added, "I don't mean to pry."

At that, I sucked noisily on the straw that stood upright in my milkshake. Although I was aware that this was not a mannerly way with which to ingest liquid in public, the mixture that held the straw had the consistency of lava.

"I am saddened to say that I have not enjoyed a relationship with a woman since the dissolution of my marriage four years ago," I said.

She appeared startled. "Not a single woman at all since then?"

"Sadly, no. I had assignations with two women, each of whose company I enjoyed, yet when it seemed appropriate to proceed to an amorous level, I was roundly rejected by each. One of them pushed me away as I attempted to engage her lips with mine and said she would sooner kiss a fish. The other appeared shocked when I made an advance and said I was stuffy. Can you imagine that?"

"What awful women!" Then she put her hand over mine. "You are a most endearing and attractive man, Ishmael, so I don't understand their seeming revulsion. I'm so sorry you had to endure that."

"*C'est la vie*," I said.

"Well, as they say, I suppose love is complicated."

"A perceptive truism," I said. "Suffice it to say, my experience with my former wife, followed by my rejection by the aforementioned women, not to mention a high school crush and a prom fiasco, have caused me to eschew romantic entanglements."

"Understandable," she said. "So why *are* you so depressed today, Ishmael?"

I produced an audible exhalation. "Dean Fletcher wants me to teach a creative writing course this summer."

"And I'm guessing you find that unappealing?"

"Quite," I said. "It probably means that—"

I was about to further explain my dilemma, but before I could utter another word, I heard a familiar voice shout out my appellation. It was Eliot Altschuler fast approaching.

"Hello, Archer," he said.

I managed a facsimile of a smile. "Heigh-ho, Eliot," I said. "How goes it?" Before he was able to respond, I heard Constance clear her throat, and after three such phlegmy interruptions, I understood the reason. "How unforgivably rude of me," I said. "Eliot Altschuler, this is Professor Constance Oswald. She is subbing for my dear friend Potter."

"Ah yes, poor old Potter," Eliot said, conjuring his features into a brief expression of solemnity, which then immediately transformed into a smile as he turned to Constance. "Pleasure to meet you, Connie."

As Eliot was holding a tray, handshaking would not be feasible unless he put it down, which he did not. Without another word to Constance, he turned his gaze toward me. "So," he said. "Creative writing, huh?"

"And how may I ask did you discover that information so quickly?" I asked. "I myself only learned of it half an hour ago."

"Let's just say a little birdie told me."

"You speak the language of birds?"

Ignoring my witticism, he said, "Not much of a challenge."

"I beg to differ," I said with transparently false enthusiasm. "Creative writing classes can be most enthralling."

"Well, count your blessings, Archer," he said. "This acting dean position will be no picnic and I will be a slave to the office day and night, while you must simply spend six hours a week discussing the art of writing."

"Sounds ghastly," I said, my teeth grinding.

"On top of that," he continued, "I will have to water all those goddamn orchids three times a week."

"Make sure you do not forget Esther," I said.

"Who's Esther?"

"Never mind."

Our conversation was interrupted by the sound of a muffled chime that seemed to emanate from Eliot's pocket, which I surmised was not a doorbell. "That's probably Sandra." He placed his tray on our table and, with some fumbling, extracted his cell phone from his pocket. "Yes, my darling," he said. "You're on the terrace? Okay. I'll be there in a flash. Just bumped into our friend, Archer. Yes, I'll tell him you said hello."

He clicked off and said, "Sandra says hello."

"So I gathered, Eliot," I said. "Tell her hello back."

"Will do. Must be off," Eliot said. "Nice meeting you, Connie."

Once he had turned the corner into the terrace, Constance said, "Nobody calls me Connie. What nerve to assume that. You introduced me as Constance."

"I would suppose he was just attempting to exude a friendly manner. He's—"

"Shit!" Constance said. Without explanation, she leapt to her feet and hastily gathered her materials. "Fuck!" A few of the students sitting nearby turned their heads our way. "I'm late for my next class! *Fuck!*"

This lack of memory regarding her schedule seemed to be a recurring theme. After a hurried goodbye, she dashed out of the room, successfully balancing the potential avalanche of books and papers. Apparently, she had forgotten her backpack again.

Four

Summer arrived and the climate evolved into one that was oppressively humid, although now and then there existed several days that one might consider temperate. Occupying a wooden bench situated in a shady spot on the quadrangle, I watched as a stream of students, aided by their parents, scurried in and out of their dormitories and fraternity dwellings, their arms laden with all manner of furniture, boxes, and other objects necessary for collegiate residential living. It was indeed a chaotic scene reminiscent of tiny ants rushing about, dutifully carrying nourishment to their brethren.

The creative writing class that I had been assigned to conduct was to be held in the school library rather than in a regular classroom or lecture hall. Perhaps the proximity to books was the motivation behind that decision. But when I studied the roster, I immediately understood the reason, for it revealed that a mere five people—four male Longfellow seniors and one woman who hailed from the town—would be attending the class.

As I am always strictly punctual, I arrived at the designated chamber ten minutes before the class was scheduled to commence and, after fruitlessly struggling to open the windows for ventilation, glanced at my wristwatch, which indicated that the scheduled hour had nearly arrived.

The only one of my new students who had the courtesy to arrive on time was the young lady from Highland Falls. While shaking my hand, she introduced herself to me as Abigail Bird and explained that she was auditing the class. She appeared to be in her mid-twenties, quite fetching in a bookish sort of way, and except for her thick-framed spectacles, she possessed a visage not unlike my image of the fictional character Tess Durbeyfield. Her hair was piled in a lopsided bun atop her head and she wore a long dress, penny loafers, and a frilly blouse buttoned to the top. She greeted me with a charmingly bright smile and expressed her delight at attending the class, addressing me as Professor Archer with a noticeable tone of admiration in her voice. After surveying the conference table, she chose the chair closest to me, pulled a notebook and several pens from a leather briefcase, organized them in a neat row on the table, and sat down.

"Am I the only student, Professor Archer?" she said as she consulted her timepiece. I was unable to discern whether she was excited or disappointed by this possibility.

"No," I said. "But you are the only one who has demonstrated the manners to be on time for which I thank you, Ms. Bird."

"I'm a stickler for punctuality, Professor. I don't like to be late. It's rude and inconsiderate."

"And an admirable trait that I happen to share," I said. "I am proud to say that I have only once been tardy to a class and that misfortune was caused by a flat tire on my ancient bicycle, which I purchased from a young scoundrel who I believe was aware of the vehicle's faulty status when he sold it to me, but failed, most likely on purpose, to inform me of its deficiencies."

"That's deplorable!"

"Indeed."

"But an accident is probably a legitimate excuse for tardiness," she said with a nervous laugh. But then she took on a more serious tone. "Did you injure yourself, Professor?"

"Not in any catastrophic way," I said. "I merely sustained a bruised knee cap and a momentary loss of dignity as there were others nearby who witnessed the embarrassing event and, for reasons that defy logic, found it amusing. Most kind of you to inquire."

Her look of concern transformed itself into a smile. "I've been so looking forward to attending this class ever since I learned that it was open to non-registered students."

"I am flattered," I said with a slight bow of my head. I was beginning to find this woman a delight.

A moment of silence ensued but I soon filled it with words, this being the most practical method with which to combat the lack of sound during a conversation.

"Is it by chance your ambition to become a writer of fiction, Ms. Bird?" I said.

She pondered the question for a moment. "I'm not sure, Professor," she said. "I do love to write but I don't really know if I have any talent for it."

"Well, we shall soon find that out, shan't we?" I said with a smile. "What sorts of genres do you enjoy crafting?"

"I particularly like writing satire. I adore Jane Austen, Mark Twain, and Chaucer; not that I'm comparing my amateur scribbling to theirs."

"As I am sure you know, the art of effectively composing humorous prose is quite challenging," I said. "It requires a certain sort of facility."

"Very true."

"Do you read much, Ms. Bird?"

"Oh yes. Ravenously! At least two books a week, sometimes three if time permits."

This I found most encouraging. I did not mean to be condescending, but a well-read, attractive woman from Highland Falls was most likely a rarity. "Which contemporary authors do you particularly prefer, Ms. Bird?"

"I enjoy the works of Umberto Eco, Phillip Roth, John Irving, Thomas Pynchon, Toni Morrison, Heller, Cheever, Marquez, and other serious authors of literary fiction."

"As do I," I said. "And what, if I may inquire, have you read of late?"

She seemed on the verge of speaking but hesitated. "Well..." she said. "You might be interested to know that when I learned you were teaching this class, I read both of your novels."

So astonished was I by this admission that I was temporarily struck speechless. "Where ever did you find them?"

"Unfortunately, neither of them was available at the library so I purchased them at a bookstore in Syracuse last week. Actually, I had to order them."

"Alas, they have departed from the shelves of bookstores," I said. "I suppose your purchase will therefore explain the forty cents I may receive in royalty payments from my publisher."

She found this statement humorous, as it had been intended, and laughed most heartily. Although impressed by her, I must confess that I briefly suspected a possible motive behind Ms. Bird's flattery. Perhaps she was buttering me up, so to speak, in the hope that I would give her a superior grade; but anon, I remembered that she was simply auditing the class and would, therefore, not be the recipient of an actual grade. Ergo, I concluded, it was not flattery.

"I am reluctant to ask," I said, "but did you like them?"

"May I be honest?"

I cringed—in my experience those four words did not bode well. "Of course. I would expect nothing less. Fire away, as they say."

She paused as if trying to decide how to approach her response. "Well," she began. "There were some excellent parts. I enjoyed your style of writing, and your ear for dialogue is exceptional, but the characters could have been developed a bit more; the descriptions were a trifle wordy, and the endings of both books were somewhat unsatisfying. In spite of that, I enjoyed them very much. But I am hardly a critic."

I was silent for a moment, which she seemed to misinterpret as displeasure because she said, "Oh gosh, I've angered you, Professor. I'm so very sorry. I am much too critical and I have an annoying tendency to be blunt."

"Not at all. I am most pleased that you were given to honesty for it is a rarity these days. In point of fact, the reviews were not dissimilar to your opinion. I, too, am aware of their numerous shortcomings. I suppose I am not much of a novelist, which is a great disappointment to me as I had once dreamed of creating a formidable work of fiction, although I take some pride in my teaching abilities."

"I hope you don't find it presumptuous of me to say this, but I believe you have considerable talent."

Once again, I bowed my head. "Why thank you, Ms. Bird," I said, gazing into her captivating blue eyes. "You are most kind."

"I don't mean to flatter you, Professor. I speak the truth. I believe you should write another. One should never give up if one truly has the passion and it is quite clear that you do."

I was about to inform her that I had recently committed an act of arson by setting aflame the first two chapters of a novel which had resided in my desk drawer for over a year and richly deserved its transformation from paper to ashes, when two of my new students straggled in ten minutes after the appointed hour, with not so much as a greeting, and slouched into chairs at the far end of the table. Both of them appeared to be somewhat lethargic, no doubt from some late night carousing involving copious amounts of alcoholic beverages.

Five minutes later, the remainder of the class, two seniors whom I recognized as members of the football team, burst into the room laughing hysterically, and repeated the actions of the first two, abstaining from acknowledging my presence and occupying chairs at the far end of the table from whence they continued their banter. I noticed that when they perceived Ms. Bird, they both began to throw her glances that fell just short of leers. Ms. Bird wisely avoided eye contact.

I winced at the prospect of reading their future assignments, the first of which would be due two days hence.

Before I had the opportunity to introduce myself and utter a few words regarding the purpose of this seminar, one of these fellows, a gentleman wearing aviator sunglasses perched atop his head, raised his hand.

"Yes, Mr...um...?"

"Williger," he said. "I have a question, Prof."

"And what might that be, sir?"

"How long will this class be?"

"Precisely two hours," I said. "I trust that the length of this period of time will be endurable."

At that, he and the other boys groaned, but I noticed that Ms. Bird appeared peeved by their behavior and proffered them a distinctly reproachful look.

"Do not worry, Mr. Williger," I said. "If you pay attention in class and complete your homework in an expeditious way and with an acceptable level of proficiency, you will be pleased with the outcome. I will not require much of you beyond that. I do not expect to create a budding Dostoevsky or Kafka in this class. Does that meet with your approval, sir?"

A collective sigh emanated from the male contingent and Mr. Williger mouthed the word, "Awesome."

I winced, for I despised the frequent misuse of that word. "Mr. Williger," I said, "the Pyramids of Egypt are awesome. The Great Wall of China is awesome. The fact that I do not expect this class to be difficult is most decidedly *not* awesome."

"Whatever," he said.

Although this was another word that I found objectionable, as it had a dismissive quality about it, I did not voice my distaste for it. "Now, if you will kindly permit me to commence—"

"Sure, go ahead, Prof."

"Thank you so much, Mr. Williger."

"No problem."

The room finally descended into silence, punctuated only by the rhythmic and somewhat annoying tapping of Mr. Williger's pencil upon the surface of the table. I proceeded to expound upon the art of writing, explaining to them the methods used by authors to create characters and plots, and enlightening them in some detail about the employment of suitable adjectives and adverbs, illustrating my points with examples of description and dialogue taken from several classics of literature. Although only Ms. Bird took notes, I was relieved to see that the boys were at least paying attention or creating the illusion. Apparently my promise regarding the ease with which a passing grade would be achieved had succeeded in assuaging their somewhat disagreeable behavior.

"Mr. Williger," I said in the midst of my lecture. "I would be most appreciative if you would be kind enough to cease the percussion created by the point of your writing utensil upon the tabletop. I find it somewhat annoying."

His brow wrinkled, seemingly in confusion. "Say what?"

"Put the pencil down."

"Sure, no sweat," he said, promptly obeying my entreaty.

As I completed my oration, Ms. Bird crossed her legs repeatedly and I noticed that the copper coin was missing from one of her penny loafers. I was tempted to inform her of this discrepancy but did not, lest I embarrass her. Nevertheless, I must confess that the temptation was something of a distraction.

At the close of my lecture, I detailed the elements of their first assignment. "In order for me to determine the extent of your writing ability," I told them, "I would like each of you to compose an original paragraph or two that can be about anything you wish—a short autobiography, a description of something, perhaps an accounting of an experience you may have had that made an impression on you or a short discussion about things you particularly enjoy etcetera. Anything at all." I then instructed them to deposit their homework in my mail slot on the morning prior to the class so that I would be able to read and grade them before we met again in the conference room, thus leaving enough time for discussion. "Any questions?"

Yet again, Mr. Williger thrust his hand in the air.

"Yes?"

"How long does it have to be?" he asked.

I struggled to maintain my composure. "I do not require you to write a tome. Two hundred words will suffice. Please be advised that I will be on the lookout, as it were, for grammatical and spelling discrepancies so please pay special attention to those criteria. Are there any more queries?"

I glanced at Mr. Williger but thankfully he did not stab the air with his hand this time, so I said, "Class dismissed. I shall see you on Wednesday. Please attempt to be punctual this time."

Predictably, all the male members of the class dashed out of the room without so much as a polite goodbye. Only Ms. Bird remained for a moment following the departure of the others.

"I enjoyed your lecture, Professor Archer," she said.

"Very kind of you to say so, Ms. Bird."

"You must think me disingenuous, since I've complimented you and your abilities numerous times."

I looked at her. "Are you being disingenuous, Ms. Bird?"

"Not at all, Professor!" she said. "I have no ulterior motives. I never engage in flattery."

"Then I shall take you at your word."

She offered me a smile that was laden with warmth, or so I perceived it to be. "May I ask you a question, Professor?"

"By all means."

"How do you summon the enthusiasm to teach people who clearly don't wish to learn, such as these four young men?"

I was about to deliver a lofty discourse regarding the possibility that any mind, no matter how ostensibly vacant, can be stimulated by the power of words, but instead I merely said, "It's a living."

Five

Dean Fletcher was not scheduled to depart until mid-June, so Eliot and Sandra Altschuler took it upon themselves to bestow upon him a bon voyage party, which was to take place at their splendid Victorian home, an act that I interpreted as an attempt to further curry favor, as it were, with the man who had appointed Eliot to his temporary position. As I detested festive events, I was reluctant to attend but I concluded that the dean would certainly react unfavorably to my absence, so I elected to make an appearance, albeit a brief one.

I arrived at Eliot and Sandra's home ten minutes before the designated hour and thus found myself to be the first guest, the only advantage being that I was able to secure an excellent parking space in their circular driveway. The only ones present at this time were Eliot, Sandra, and a young woman clad in some sort of plaid Scottish outfit, no doubt a maid. All of them were involved in preparing the room with the usual festive party accoutrements. When the maid ushered me in, Eliot was astride a ladder, attempting to thumbtack a brightly colored sign that read Bon Voyage to the top of an arch that separated the parlor from the dining chamber, whilst Sandra stood a few feet away from him, directing his labor with the words, "Two inches to the left, a bit higher, no more to the right, Eliot, for God's sake," and so forth. The maid was occupied with the task of setting up edibles and potables on a long folding table that was covered by a paper tablecloth illustrated with the implements of golfing. As I had purchased a gift for the dean, I placed it at the end of the table.

When Sandra beheld my presence, she welcomed me with a warm embrace that lasted perhaps ten seconds longer than propriety would have dictated under these particular circumstances, one that involved enough frontal pressure for me to become more than aware of the considerable dimensions of her bosom as it pushed into my upper torso. Upon my entry into the parlor, Eliot caught sight of me and nearly fell off his ladder as a result of the distraction. "Hello there, Archer!" he said with some enthusiasm. "Happy to see that you're early. Can you give me a hand up here? I can't seem to center the damn thing to Sandra's liking. We have a step stool you can use."

"Alas, I'm afraid I cannot be of any service, Eliot," I said.

"Why is that?"

"You see, I am quite terrified of heights."

Eliot glanced at the floor below. "Archer, it's three feet off the ground."

"Which happens to be two feet higher than I am able to climb without suffering a bout of extreme dizziness and disorientation," I replied. "Regurgitation is also a distinct possibility, albeit a somewhat remote one, yet I do not wish to soil your carpeting with the bile-laden contents of my abdomen."

"Are you serious?"

"Quite."

Sandra rescued me. "Leave the poor man alone, Eliot," she said, whereupon she turned her gaze upon me. "You can help me with the hors d'oeuvres in the kitchen, Archer," she said. "If you don't mind."

"That would be vastly preferable," I said.

At that, Sandra took my hand and escorted me into the kitchen where I listened attentively to her detailed instructions regarding the placement of the hors d'oeuvres upon the serving platters, and then commenced to perform my appointed duties, making a painstaking effort to insure that the deviled eggs and raw dipping vegetables were arranged in perfect symmetry. From time to time, Sandra would stand beside me to survey my labors and on each such occasion I felt her arm encircle my waist, although once, when she voiced approval at my exemplary ministrations, she patted my buttocks as well. I tried to recall the last time a woman had performed such intimate gestures on my physical person, but I could not summon forth the memory.

Half an hour following my arrival, the guests began to stream into the parlor. All of them were bearing gifts, which they deposited on the table beside mine. Jollity ensued. When Dean Fletcher arrived, the room exploded with applause. Although I was uncertain as to the purpose of this display, I joined in.

After the dean shook everybody's hand, including mine, I wandered aimlessly about the room, hoping in vain that someone would initiate a conversation with me. I am woefully lacking in the art of fabricating small talk, so to speak, for I find this sort of chitchat most tiresome. But I was soon rescued from this impasse for I noticed Constance stroll through the front door, which had been left open due, most likely, to the unseasonable balminess of the weather. I was delighted to see her, for her presence meant that I would have at least one companion with whom to engage in colloquy that would rank above the usual mindless party chatter. I had not seen Constance for the last five days.

After a warm embrace, I followed her across the room to the table where she deposited her gift on what had become a mountain of considerable height. I watched as she offered her greetings to the Altschulers and bestowed a kiss upon Dean Fletcher's cheek, whereupon she returned to my station, extracted a beer from a cooler, expertly pried it open, and lifted it to her lips.

"I have not seen you of late," I said. "Where, if I may ask, have you been?"

"My favorite aunt had a stroke," she said.

"Please allow me to express my sincere condolences at your news," I said. "Poor woman."

"Thank you, Ishmael. I flew to Minneapolis to visit her. Got back last night. Luckily my class doesn't begin until next week."

"Alas, mine has already commenced."

"How goes it?" she asked.

"It is too premature to tell but I am not optimistic. Except for one, my students are thoroughly disinterested."

Constance nodded and delicately used a tortilla chip to scoop some guacamole from a large bowl. After consuming it, she glanced

41

at the gifts that were piled upon the table. "What did you get him?" she asked.

"Who?"

"Dean Fletcher, of course," she said. "What sort of gift?"

"I purchased an item known as a blender."

She gave me a confused look. "How do you know he doesn't already own a blender? Most people do."

This had not occurred to me. "I confess that I do not know if he is already in possession of a blender. I did not ask him, as a query of that sort would surely have spoiled the surprise element."

"Seems somewhat inappropriate to me since it's a bon voyage party and I strongly doubt he will have much use for a blender in Scotland."

"One never knows. He may need to blend something whilst in Scotland."

"Like what?"

"I do not know," I said. "But let us please cease discussing this controversy regarding kitchen appliances. What, pray tell, did you purchase?"

"A compact toiletry organizer," she said. "Very handy, very small. Won't take up much room in his suitcase."

"Admittedly a far better choice than a blender."

Constance and I then repaired to an unoccupied couch in a corner of the parlor. Deafening dance music now emanated from two small speakers. I noticed then that Constance's eyes were studying Dean Fletcher.

"Is Dean Fletcher married or otherwise involved with a woman?" she asked.

"I do not believe so. If he is attached to a female, he has never made mention of it to me."

"Do you think him handsome?"

I cleaned my glasses before attempting to examine the dean's features from afar.

"I am no expert on the subject of male magnetism, Constance,"

I said, "but he is certainly not in the same league as Quasimodo or Mary Shelley's monster, of that I am certain."

"Thanks. That's very helpful."

"You are welcome," I said. "Why pray tell do you ask?"

She shrugged. "No particular reason."

But apparently there *was* a reason because, after excusing herself, Constance rose and casually walked in the direction of the dean who now stood alone at the table, pouring himself a libation. I watched as Constance sidled up beside him and studied the deviled eggs that I had recently arrayed on a tray in perfect rows, and which I now noted were not perfectly symmetrical anymore as people had eaten some, thereby destroying my efforts. Such gall!

The dean turned to her, offered his hand and a moment later, they joined the others who were gyrating on the dance floor. Constance was something of a frenzied dancer and uninhibitedly thrust her arms in the air and wiggled her buttocks in a suggestive manner while the dean shuffled his feet attempting unsuccessfully to capture the rhythm of the music. Every now and again they leaned close to each other to converse and I observed Constance laugh heartily at nearly everything Bob uttered.

Carrying a gin and tonic with a wedge of lime, Sandra collapsed beside me on the couch, pulled off her high heels with a grunt and placed her feet atop the glass coffee table. As feet go, they were quite attractive, devoid of unsightly veins, corns, or bunions, although her flesh did bear the imprint of her shoe straps. Her toenails were painted a festive red.

"These fucking shoes are killing me," she said.

"Yet you appear to be quite healthy," I said.

She ignored my reply. "Having a good time, Archer?"

"It's a splendid festivity," I said in a monotone. As she was the hostess, I thought it wise to evade her question because I was not having a pleasant time at all. I was, in fact, thoroughly consumed by boredom.

"Neither am I," she said, placing a hand on my thigh, a mere three inches from the location of my genitalia. I felt a stir in that region, a sense not dissimilar to the one I had experienced when she had embraced me upon my arrival. "To be honest, I only agreed to throw this lousy bash because Eliot insisted. Who gives a shit if Dean Fletcher is going to Scotland to play golf? Do you?"

"Not in the least," I said. "In actuality, I—"

"Hey!" she said. "How about I show you the house? It's really quite charming. Come on, I'll give you the grand tour."

I cleared my throat and gazed at my timepiece. "Very kind, but to be perfectly honest, Sandra, I was just about to remove my buttocks from the couch and depart the premises, so perhaps we can perform this adventure at—"

But Sandra disregarded my unimaginative attempt to delay said guided expedition. "It sort of reminds me of the house in *The House of Seven Gables*," she said, "except there aren't any gables, whatever a fucking gable is."

"In point of fact, a gable is a canopy-like structure positioned over a window or a door, usually a window, I believe, although my knowledge of architectural embellishments is minimal," I said.

But she was not listening. After downing the remainder of her drink, she stood unsteadily on her bare feet, grabbed my hand, and attempted to pull me out of my seat. I gave in to her tug and rose. Ushering me across the dance floor, she led me directly toward the stairway and I followed her upstairs, although I was more than a little concerned that the other guests, and more importantly Eliot, might find this scenario somewhat questionable. There was no escape as Sandra had gripped my hand quite tightly and I did not wish to offend her by struggling to free myself. We walked down a long carpeted hallway and entered a room. As soon as we were inside, she closed the door.

"This, as you may have guessed, is the master bedroom," she said. "The place where all the magic usually doesn't take place."

I surveyed the room in a polite manner and made an ambiguous remark regarding the décor, a subject that held no interest for me.

"The bed is amazingly comfortable," she said. "Would you care to try it, Archer? It has one of those amazing mattresses that conform to your body. Memory foam, I think they call it."

"No, but thank you for the invitation," I said. "If I do as you suggest, I may fall into a slumber as the party has dulled my senses, no offense."

"None taken," she said. "I agree."

Sandra set her gluteus maximus on the edge of the bed and began to sniffle. This display soon turned into a bout of full-blown weeping, and she placed her hands over her eyes as if ashamed to be seen in her state of distress. "I'm so unhappy, Archer," she said. "May I cry on your shoulder?"

As this would either require her to stand up or for me to sit beside her, and as she did not stand up, I reluctantly sank onto the bed, hoping that the deluge emanating from her lachrymal ducts would not significantly dampen my garments. But the next words out of her mouth contained nothing pertaining to her happiness or lack thereof. "Is it warm in here?" she asked. She seemed to have recovered from her teary episode with stunning alacrity.

"Not especially," I said. "Perhaps a bit humid though."

"Well, I'm sweating," she said. Gazing at her, I perceived no evidence of perspiration on her brow. At that, she commenced to unbutton her blouse.

I was suddenly fearful regarding her intentions. "Perhaps I could open a window," I said.

"They're all stuck."

"Air conditioner?"

"We don't have one."

"If I may inquire, how do you provide adequate ventilation?"

"Is that important to you, Archer?"

"Not really."

Although I found Sandra Altschuler highly attractive and as I had not partaken of any sexual gymnastics for quite a long time, I was tempted to aid her in the dismantling of her blouse but I resisted the temptation. I did not savor the idea of being caught engaging in carnal relations with Eliot's wife, in Eliot's marital bed, in Eliot's house with a roomful of guests below that included Dean Fletcher and Constance. But how would I decline without hurting her feelings?

"Incidentally," I said. "It so happens that I am still in possession of the hat you so graciously lent me during the recent blizzard in April."

"I don't think I'll be needing it right now, Archer," she said. She hooked her index finger at me. "Come closer."

Fortunately, I was saved from any further entanglement by Eliot's voice that seemed to originate from the foot of the stairs. "Sandra, darling!" he shouted. "Where in blazes are you? Bob's going to open his gifts now. Please come down! You mustn't miss this."

With a groan, Sandra hurriedly re-buttoned her blouse, then stood up and walked toward the door. Before pulling it open, she sighed audibly and pronounced the word, "Fuck."

Although I did not wish to be present at the opening of the gifts, I counted to ten and followed her out.

Six

The following Wednesday morning, I was relieved to discover that all five of my students had deposited their assignments in my mail slot, although it was immediately apparent, though not in the least surprising, that save for Ms. Bird, none had submitted more than one short paragraph, which indicated to me that my male students had not ventured beyond the minimum requirement.

As I sat at my desk, I unfolded each of the pages, stacked them into a neat pile and leaned back in my chair to face the music, so to speak. Because I fully expected Ms. Bird's work to be infinitely superior to the rest, I decided to save hers for last—a sort of dessert following a dreadful meal—and placed it on the other side of my desk. And so, with a red pencil clutched between my fingers, I began my tedious chore, hoping to be pleasantly surprised. But it was not long before I comprehended why the seniors had failed their creative writing courses the first time around.

MY FAVORITE FOODS
By Adam Walker

My favorite food is Cheetos. They are very testy and I can eet a hole giant size bag of them while I watch a baseball game or a realtie show on my 45 inch flat screen TV, which also has a very cool sound system. I bought it at Radio Shuck last year and I think I got a pretty good deal. I enjoy beer too and spicey Gwacamolee with chips. Also the burgers at the College Cafateria are delicious with hot sauce. I don't like onions tho. They make my breathe stink and my girlfriend will not kiss me.

The End.

My Mom and Dad
By Terry Williger

I was born in Phoenix, which is located in the state, of Arizona, USA. My mother, is taller than my father is but she is a nice person anyway and I love her. My father took me to the horse races in town once when I was just a little kid? He bet five bucks on a brown horse name of Pokey and lost. Then he gave me two dollars that I bet on a horse called Sundance. I won two dollars and thirty-six cents. After that, we bought a couple of hot dogs and went home.

The Yellow Ferrari
By Tom Riverdale

Professor Archery teaches my creative writing class I think he is a great guy. I hope I will learn a lot about how to write things from him. If I get a C, I will graduate from college and get a good job in a factory or maybe be a lawyer, who makes a good salary. One day I'd like to have a yellow Ferrari because they are babe magnets but if I can't get a yellow one I'll take a red one.

Mr. Jones
By Brandon Weathers

Mr. Jones, of the Manor Farm, had locked the hen-houses for the night, but was too drunk to remember to shut the pop-holes. With the ring of light from his lantern dancing from side to side, he lurched across the yard, kicked off his boots at the back door, drew himself a last glass of beer from the barrel in the scullery, and made his way up to bed, where Mrs. Jones was already snoring.

After perusing these first four travesties, I was overtaken by the desire to bang my head on my desk, an exercise that I performed four times, once for each of the papers I had thus far read. How, I wondered, had these young men even managed to pass their other courses? Did History 101 or Biology 202 not require a modicum of ability in the use of the English language? How would they survive in the world with such a staggering paucity of basic writing skills?

With a weary sigh, I corrected the numerous misspellings in Mr. Walker's delightful saga about his love of junk food, although it was a passion I shared, and his pride regarding his oversized television set. I then penned a few suggestions in the margins, all of which I assumed he would ignore.

Following that herculean effort, I corrected Mr. Williger's grammatical errors, of which there were but a few, and pointed out that his mother's tallness did not preclude her from being, as he put it, "nice." I was pleased to note that there had been no misspellings. Bravo, Mr. Williger!

Mr. Riverdale's effort, although an obvious attempt to curry my favor, caused me to guffaw. I found it most interesting that he would attempt to influence me and then proceed to spell my last name incorrectly. In the margin I wrote the words, "Nice try, Mr. Riverdale."

Mr. Weathers' paper was an excellent piece of writing but I could not in good conscience give him anything above a failing grade because his submission was a verbatim copy of the opening paragraph of Mr. George Orwell's novel, *Animal Farm*. He had not even bothered to change the names. I marked a bold F at the top of the page and wrote the words "PLAGIARISM!" and "Unacceptable" in large letters over his written words.

Praying for a relief from the drudgery, I began to read Ms. Bird's composition.

THE ODYSSEY OF MY FIRST DATE
By Abigail Bird

The year was nineteen eighty-four. His name was Ulysses. For our first meeting, he had chosen a clean well-lighted place on the waterfront, far from the madding crowd, on Tobacco Road in a suburb called Wuthering Heights. Admittedly, I had great expectations. It was a beautiful day—the wind in the willows, fragrant leaves of grass—and I was overcome by a remembrance of things past because it reminded me of my life in Winesburg, Ohio. It was such a clear day I felt that I could see from here to eternity.

I saw him walk past the fountainhead and over the bridge of San Luis Rey where he almost bumped into the man with the tin drum. He was whistling the Song of Solomon when he entered. We said hello and he told me that he wasn't that hungry because he'd eaten cakes and ale at the Hotel New Hampshire.

He'd brought me a single flower, but I didn't know the name of the rose. I saw birds and watched one fly over the cuckoo's nest. Nearby I noticed a rabbit run.

We talked about a lot of things—about the importance of being earnest, of time and the river, of mice and men, of sons and lovers, of pride and prejudice, and about his sister Carrie. We decided to meet again the next day and have breakfast at Tiffany's followed by a naked lunch on the beach at the home-sick restaurant.

If all went well, he said, we would lie down in darkness and experience the joy of sex. The next day, he booked a room with a view.

Utterly delightful! A masterpiece by comparison!

Thoroughly captivated by her considerable authorial talents and humorous wordplay, as well as her superior imagination and inge-nuity, not to mention the spelling and grammatical perfection, I penciled in an enormous A-plus at the top of the page in block letters but then realized that I was not allowed to give her an actual grade for, as I mentioned previously, she was auditing the class. So I erased the A-plus and instead wrote the words, "Clever and humorous!" at the top of the page. In my fervor, I was tempted to add two more exclamation points but I have always found that particular redundancy to be both puerile and unprofessional.

This, I thought, was a most exceptional woman!

＆

Having completed my corrections several hours before the commencement of my second class, I decided to indulge in a bite of breakfast at the school cafeteria, perhaps a Belgian waffle swimming in an ocean of maple syrup and lathered with butter, accompanied by four strips of over-grilled bacon. As I strode toward the entrance, I noticed Ms. Bird standing quite alone beneath an oak tree attempting to ignite a cigarette with a lighter that appeared unable to produce a flame. So excited was I by her admirable submission, I could barely wait to inform her of my opinion so I strolled toward her and, upon arriving at her location, extracted a lighter from my pocket.

"Professor Archer!" she said. "What a pleasant surprise!"

"Allow me, Ms. Bird," I said. Gallantly, I held the torch beneath the unlit end of her cigarette. Before leaning in toward it, she swept her long auburn hair out of her face, no doubt a sensible precaution intended to keep me from accidentally setting her comely locks on fire.

"Thank you, Professor," she said.

"My pleasure."

"That was so...I don't know...charmingly nineteenth century," she said as she released a plume of toxic smoke from her mouth. Her face brightened with a delightful grin. "So very...refreshing."

"What is?"

"The way you said 'allow me' before you lit my cigarette for me."

"A damsel in distress and all that," I said.

She narrowed her eyes. "I don't mean to nitpick, Professor, but I'm not certain that this actually qualifies as distress in the classic sense. I would think that a damsel in distress would involve a more distressful distress."

"Such as what?"

"Well," she said, "for example, true distress might be if I had been tied to some railroad tracks by a villain and you rescued me from a horrible, gruesome death."

"Why would someone attach you to railroad tracks?" I said. "In point of fact there exists no railroad here in our fair town, thus making the existence of tracks unnecessary. Said absence of tracks would likely pose a problem for the feasibility of railroad travel for the very word implies the existence of rails. One would need to travel to Orangeville to find railroad tracks."

"I'm just citing a hypothetical example of what I take to be distress."

I ruminated. "To be truthful, Ms. Bird, I disagree regarding these so-called degrees of distress. Perhaps igniting your cigarette would not qualify but it seems to me that involuntary attachment to railroad tracks would be too severe and somewhat absurd, not to mention unlikely."

She swatted an insect that had landed on the tip of her nose. "Maybe you're right, Professor," she said.

At once, I felt that I may have been too harsh in my refutation of her theory regarding the severity of distress and did not wish to appear argumentative. "Nevertheless, perhaps we shall compromise and refer to your inability to set aflame your unlit cigarette as difficulty rather than distress. Is that more appropriate?"

"Yes," she replied. "But you were still quite gallant in relieving me of this difficulty."

"Thank you," I said. "I am occasionally given to gallantry if the opportunity presents itself."

She exhaled a stream of smoke out the side of her mouth so as to avoid blowing it in my face, although due to the breeze, I was soon engulfed in it. "Do you smoke cigarettes, Professor?" she asked.

"Why do you ask?"

"You carry a cigarette lighter in your trousers."

"Ah. No, I do not indulge in the smoking of cigarettes," I said, "but I do on rare occasions enjoy a pipe, although I find that the maintenance of said instrument tends to outweigh the pleasure derived from its use, what with all the accumulated saliva. The torch

I carry in my trousers is also quite convenient for igniting my stove."

Ms. Bird held up her cigarette and regarded it with a mixture of guilt and dismay. "It's an awful habit, I know, but I'm not a heavy smoker," she said. "I enjoy only three cigarettes per day. They seem to relax me and also give me an odd sense of clarity. I don't think I'm addicted."

"I would agree that such a minor indulgence would most likely not be considered addiction," I told her. "I do not wish to be too inquisitive but do you partake of cannabis and similar mind-altering substances?"

"Never!"

"Alcoholic beverages?"

"No more than the occasional glass of wine," she said. "And you?"

"I do not engage in the inhalation of any substance with the exception of oxygen. Nor do I care much for spirits although when proffered wine, I have been known to sample a sip or two for I have discovered that after two glasses of the grape, I become quite inebriated. You see, I have very little tolerance for alcohol."

I gazed at her. Clad in an oddly patterned shirt, a pair of khaki Bermuda shorts, white running shoes, and pea green socks, with her hair falling freely about her shoulders, she was even lovelier than she had been in class. There was some manner of indescribable warmth about her, a rare aura of kindness, if you will, that drew me to her.

At the same time, she appeared to be taking my measure, finally withdrawing her striking light blue eyes after a moment to stamp out her cigarette. "Do you always wear bow ties, Professor?" she asked.

"Yes," I said. "Ever since I was six years of age."

"That's a trifle eccentric for a six-year-old child."

"Perhaps."

"Although I do appreciate eccentricity," she said, "a bow tie is a defining choice of attire, one that lends its wearer an air of gravity. I am not being critical. Quite the contrary."

"I did not take it as such."

She appeared mollified. "May I ask why?"

"Why what?"

"Why, if I may ask, do you wear bow ties?"

"I have found in the past that I have a tendency to inadvertently dip the more customary neckties into bodies of liquid such as soup or sink water. This is less likely to happen when one sports a bow tie."

"True enough," she said. "Yet it's a little crooked." At that, she reached out to straighten it, an act that I found most pleasing for it seemed an intimate gesture of sorts. "It becomes you. You look quite handsome with a bow tie, Professor. Most men don't but you do."

"Why, thank you, Ms. Bird," I said with a slight tilt of my head. I was, of course, delighted that she found my appearance agreeable and a curious sensation of warmth, that I suspected was a blush, spread across my visage. "You are very kind to say so."

"I hope I was not again being too forward, Professor."

"Not at all, Ms. Bird. I enjoy complimentary words as do others."

Throughout our conversation, I had been bursting with the temptation to congratulate her on the inspired composition she had submitted to my class, but instead I opted to surprise her later when we convened in the conference room. I confess I was a bit surprised that she had not inquired about it. Perhaps she thought it inappropriate to do so in the present environment.

She glanced at her watch. "Oh my goodness!" she said. She appeared somewhat alarmed. "I'm fifteen minutes late for work!"

"Oh? Where might that be?" I asked.

"At the college library."

"So you are a librarian!" I said. "A noble profession indeed!"

"I'm just a part-time volunteer."

"And your profession, if I may be so bold as to ask?"

"It's not really a profession but I also work weekends as a lowly server at Phil's Rib and Steak Emporium in town. Have you eaten there, Professor?"

"I have not."

"Just as well. It's a dreadful place, but the gratuities are quite substantial."

"Has this always been your line of work?"

"No," she said. "I have a master's degree in English from New York University. I'm taking the summer off, escaping the hurly burly of urban life. I haven't as of yet decided whether I want to teach or write. Perhaps your tutelage in our writing forum will help me make that decision. But now, if you will accept my apologies, I must run, Professor. I'll see you later in class."

"I look forward to it."

"So do I!" she said.

"Adieu, Ms. Bird. Godspeed."

Disappointed that we would not be able to continue our engrossing discourse, I watched her scurry off, with some adorable clumsiness for she nearly ran into a bush. Across the lush wide lawn of the quadrangle she jogged, her long hair blowing in the breeze.

While Messrs. Williger, Walker, Weathers, and Riverdale scowled during my lengthy critique of their homework, Ms. Bird did not utter a single word, fearing perhaps that her superior effort and my complimentary words at the commencement of the class might cause resentment from the others. I utilized a fair amount of time lecturing Mr. Weathers on the inadvisability of plagiarism, pointing out that I had a vast knowledge of literature and would no doubt be able to discover heinous crimes of this nature. I also made it clear that anyone caught resorting to similar malfeasance would receive a failing grade and that I much preferred inept writing to copying the work of others. He admitted his culpability with appropriate humility, offering no excuse, and promised me that he would never indulge in this corruption again. Having adequately berated Mr. Weathers, I moved along to Mr. Riverdale, informing him that flattering me would not result in a superior grade, and that he had misspelled my surname. Mr. Williger received my congratulations regarding his spelling prowess and I suggested that Mr. Walker utilize the spell check feature of his computer.

Previously, after handing out copies of Ms. Bird's composition to the others and explaining to them why it demonstrated such an exceptional level of competency, I had been appalled to learn that none of them understood her references to the novels contained in the body of the work. Thus, I was compelled to explain it to them. Moreover, I fully expected each of them to display some form of verbal or facial disdain toward Ms. Bird but to my surprise, they treated her with graciousness. Perhaps they found her too humble in her attitude or too attractive to merit their contempt.

Near the end of class, I explained their next assignment, which consisted of writing a description of a character, a process that would require them to employ adjectives in order to bring that fictional person to life.

The incorrigible Mr. Williger thrust his hand skyward. "How long does it have to be?" he asked once again.

I was tempted to sigh meaningfully, as Mr. Williger's obsession with length revealed his lack of interest in actual writing, but I restrained myself.

"Two or three hundred words," I said in a monotone. Mr. Williger seemed to be stifling a groan but I ignored it and continued. "Try to be creative, choose your words with care and precision. This assignment will be due next Wednesday as I have decided to cancel class for Friday and the following Monday and thereby allow you to enjoy the Memorial Day weekend."

Predictably, upon hearing this happy news, the four young men burst forth with subdued hoots and Mr. Weathers punched his fist at some imaginary object in the air and said, "Yes!"

"Are there any further questions?" I asked.

They all shook their heads as I had expected.

"Then you may go now."

Again, they all dashed out of the room. Ms. Bird, however, remained in her seat once the others had shuffled out. After she had expressed her gratitude at the adulatory words with which I had described her composition, she said, "So how was your breakfast, Professor?"

"Splendid," I said. "The cafeteria concocts a delicious Belgian waffle. Do you have a liking for Belgian waffles?"

"Not really."

"Bacon?"

"I adore bacon!"

"Crispy?"

"Oh yes. As crispy as possible."

"Then we have much in common in the area of bacon."

"We do!"

She removed her glasses and wiped them carefully with a small, square microfiber cleansing cloth. Her eyes squinted as she performed this operation.

I glanced at my timepiece. "Hark, it is almost time for luncheon." I said. "I sense pangs of hunger, for my breakfast was not sufficient to satisfy my appetite."

"Coincidentally, I'm famished as well," she said. "I suppose I'll go to the cafeteria. They do serve a decent hamburger."

"I agree," I said. "In point of fact, my plan is to consume one. As it happens my destination for the afternoon's repast is also the cafeteria."

"May I ask, do you usually eat alone, Professor?"

"Occasionally I am joined by one of my colleagues at the breakfast hour, most frequently Professor Antoinette Moreau who teaches French and possesses a love of Belgian waffles as she herself is Belgian, although I do not mean to infer that hailing from Belgium requires a citizen of that country to love Belgian waffles. She is a rather stout woman and I have observed her ingest as many as five in one serving. But to answer your query, yes, most of the time I dine by myself."

"As do I," she said. Then, with a sigh, she added, "I don't really have any friends. I haven't lived here very long."

I began to pack up my materials. "Alas, I have only a few myself," I said. "They are Professor Potter, who is ill; Mr. Felix Eugenides, who happens to be my landlord; Madame Moreau; and a professor of anthropology by the name of Constance Oswald, whom I recently met. It seems that my closest friends are those that exist only in literature—Silas Marner, Bathsheba Everdene, Pierre Bezuhov, David Copperfield, to name but a few."

"Those are some of my best friends as well!" she said.

"A lively and entertaining cast of characters."

"So true." She watched as I closed my briefcase. "I was just thinking, Professor, since we're both going to the same place, at the same time, to have the same lunch, I suppose it would be sensible for us to accompany each other and eat at the same table. I hope I'm not once again being too forward, Professor."

Delighted by her suggestion, I said, "No, not at all, Ms. Bird."

She knitted her brow. "On second thought, maybe it would be inappropriate," she said.

"Oh?" I attempted to hide my disappointment. "In what way, pray tell?"

"I worry that this co-dining plan might be a violation of the student-teacher code, assuming that one exists."

"Hmm. I would doubt it," I said. "After all, it is only an innocent lunch."

"Are you sure you won't get into trouble?"

Again, I considered the issue. "It is true that you are my student, Ms. Bird, but you are not officially registered at the college and as a result will receive no grade from me, so indulging in a meal together would probably not qualify as a contravention of the rules as no favoritism is involved. We could always claim it was a conference if such an alibi would ever be required."

"True," she said. As she positioned her thick glasses back on her nose I noticed that she was not wearing a wedding ring. "But what will happen if you get into serious trouble and be reprimanded or lose your job? I would not want that on my conscience."

"I am willing to risk whatever fate awaits me," I said. "Shall we throw caution to the wind, Ms. Bird, and commit this potentially criminal venture?"

"Lead the way, oh captain, my captain," she said.

Seven

After Dean Fletcher had departed for Scotland and most of the faculty had vacated the premises, a delightfully peaceful ambiance reigned on campus, affording one the opportunity to wander about almost anywhere without being besieged by the usual hordes of students and teachers.

As someone who does not particularly enjoy social intercourse, I did not find this new state of affairs lonely in the least. Now, there were no lines at the cafeteria; the library and faculty lounge were usually unpopulated; most of the frat houses were closed; and, with the exception of the thirty or so gloomy summer school students, the campus was not the usual hotbed of hormone-induced under-graduate mayhem. I could walk along its stoned paths without the fear of being hit in the head by a Frisbee or a football.

Moreover, as my schedule consisted of a mere three short classes per week, there would be ample time during which I would be able to read and partake of relaxation. Perhaps I would even venture to New York City for a weekend and visit Woodlawn Cemetery in the Bronx where Herman Melville is interred. A pilgrimage to his burial place might well result in a lasting connection to the man who inspired my parents to name me Ishmael. This was an *homage* I had hoped to perform since I was a child.

But I digress.

Eliot was busy attending to his new duties as acting dean, thus he rarely made an appearance in public. I saw little of Sandra, who spent most of her days sunning herself on a chaise beside her forty-foot pool, a pastime that she invited me to participate in more than once and to which I declined, citing the tendency of my pasty white skin to easily acquire a sunburn. The only person I missed was Constance, who had been summoned back to Minneapolis on the Friday prior to the Memorial Day weekend—her poor aunt had taken a turn for the worse.

But my days were brightened by thoughts of the thoroughly beguiling Ms. Bird, with whom I had developed something beyond a mere rapport, or so I believed. Let us just say that she intrigued me, for she was a breath of fresh air, as it were, a welcome climatic change to my otherwise dreary, overcast life, if you'll pardon the meteorological analogy. I found her to be warm-hearted and possessed of a delightful sweetness that touched me. As an added element, she shared my profound interest in literature as well as bacon.

Of course, I did not act upon these agreeable sensations nor did I even hint at them. Having been callously rebuffed by my wicked spouse as well as the two aforementioned women, I felt the necessity to first determine conclusively whether or not Ms. Bird had a similarly positive attitude toward me. Most likely, she did not, for we had only known each other for a short period of time. Be that as it may, I strongly desired to see her again in a place other than the classroom, but asking her to accompany me on a formal assignation would, I concluded, be perilous. I certainly did not want to make a pathetic fool of myself by forcing my extracurricular presence upon her. Perchance she did not wish to involve herself in a rather clichéd affiliation with a professor. Or maybe she still harbored misgivings that such an association might be of some professional danger to me, despite my assurances that it would not. But as a youngish male of the species, I possessed a natural desire for friendship that perhaps held the promise of emotional and possibly physical intimacy.

But how would I determine whether Ms. Bird shared the infatuation I secretly held for her? Thus far I had not received any obvious indicators from her, at least none that I was able to decipher, although I admittedly possess a distinct tendency to be utterly oblivious to such subtle gestures. Yet she had recently voiced the opinion that I was handsome which I found encouraging, although her praise regarding the comeliness of my visage was insufficient evidence.

Having not seen her for several days, a state of affairs that was entirely my fault as I had stupidly canceled two sessions of my class, I decided to venture to Phil's Rib and Steak Emporium in the hope that she would be working that particular night. My strategy was to make her believe that my presence at her place of employment was nothing more than a coincidence. Thus, one evening, I appeared at said establishment and was ushered to a table by a hostess.

Edging my body into the booth, I surreptitiously glanced around the room, but alas I did not espy Ms. Bird on the premises. I contemplated departing but I was greatly in need of nourishment and I did fancy beef products of numerous varieties, thus I remained seated. Whilst my olfactory nerves experienced the pleasant aroma of barbecued meat, a young server of sizeable proportions materialized before me.

"Hi!" she said. Her tone was annoyingly cheerful. "I'm Leslie!" Why she felt the urge to exclaim this information, I did not know.

"Greetings to you, Leslie," I said. "I am known as Ishmael, but most people call me Archer."

"That's nice."

She then placed before me a paper placemat that was emblazoned with a badly drawn picture of a dancing steak, after which she performed the same action with a grease-stained menu, a set of flatware, several napkins, and a plastic container of water.

"Are we ready to order a beverage or would we like a little more time?" she asked.

This seemed somewhat premature as I had just received the menu and had not yet had an opportunity to inspect its pages. "The latter," I said. "I require a bit more time to decide."

"Take as long as you want, honey," she said.

While carefully examining the flatware and plastic water container for stains, I caught sight of Ms. Bird emerging from a hallway. I watched covertly as she ambled to the kitchen and then, a few moments later, departed said area with a tray stacked with foodstuffs, which she then carried unsteadily toward a table. She did not see me at first and I pretended that I did not see her either, but during her journey to this neighboring table she abruptly stopped which almost caused her to drop her tray.

"Professor Archer!" she said. "How nice to see you."

I commented that it was indeed a pleasure to behold her as well and marveled at the coincidental nature of our meeting. Her hair was stacked upon her head, held together by hairpins, though a few tendrils had loosened and fell about her neck. She wore an apron over her ensemble and sported black shoes that appeared to be of an orthopedic type. I presumed that she wore this footwear for the purpose of relieving her feet from the pain of lengthy periods of standing upright.

"What are you doing here?" she asked.

"I had planned to partake of a meal."

"I suspected as much, as this is a restaurant," she said. "But I didn't take you for the type of person who liked steak and ribs."

"*Au contraire*, I do indeed," I said. "Also my physician informed me…um…yesterday that my hemoglobin level was not up to its desirable level and suggested that I ingest large quantities of red meat, lest I become anemic. This appears to be the only restaurant in town that specializes in such delicacies."

"There are a number of burger establishments on East Main Street," she said. "A Burger King and a MacDonald's if I'm not mistaken."

"I am aware," I said. "But one never knows what sort of noxious debris is contained in the hamburger meat that is customarily offered at such fast food establishments."

"True."

"I have read several articles regarding the sort of animal refuse, including fecal matter, contained in these hamburgers."

"I've heard that too," she said. "Disgusting."

She then abruptly turned her head to sneeze and, after this nasal outburst had subsided, reached for the napkin holder on my table, accidentally knocking over the saltshaker in the process. She righted the shaker, swept the salt from the table and blew her nose quite loudly into the napkin. Then she sneezed again, and I mouthed the word, *"Gesundheit."*

"Thank you, Professor."

"Are you ill, Ms. Bird?"

"No," she said, "although I do suffer from allergies at this time of year. Ragweed and such."

"A pity."

"Sometimes I get a bad rash in the oddest places but mostly I just sneeze."

"How unpleasant."

"Runny nose too and some phlegm as well."

"My sympathies."

For some unknown reason, she was gazing at my neck. "I see you're wearing a bow tie again, Professor."

"I believe we had this conversation several days ago," I said. "I am beginning to think that you do not care for them."

"Not at all." I noted that her tone lacked conviction.

"The bow tie has quite an illustrious and fascinating history," I said. "Would you care to hear about it?"

"Perhaps at another time."

"Of course."

"What I meant to say before was that a tie of any sort is appropriate on campus, but I believe it's somewhat formal for Phil's Rib and Steak Emporium. Nobody here is dressed quite so formally."

I surveyed the room and perceived that she was correct. The other patrons sported T-shirts and blue jeans.

"You might consider removing it and opening your collar. I don't mean to be critical of your attire. I'm just concerned with your comfort."

"I will consider your advice," I said.

"If you plan to order ribs, I would also suggest that you roll up your sleeves as a precaution."

"Excellent point," I said. "Yet this would still expose the front of my shirt. Does this establishment perchance provide protective accoutrements known as bibs?"

"I'm afraid not."

"A woeful oversight," I said. "Bibs are most practical accessories."

"I completely agree."

I smiled. This was yet another subject upon which we agreed—the practicality of bibs!

At that, I noticed a nearby gentleman with a party of four waving his hand at Ms. Bird. In a tone of voice that was decidedly ill-disposed, he called, "Yo, miss, we're kinda starving over here, hello!"

"I'll be there in a second," Ms. Bird said. Then to me, in a low voice, she said, "I must go and attend to him before the poor man and his family die of starvation. May I join you when I'm on my break?"

"That would be splendid," I said, whereupon she smiled warmly and hastened to the booth that contained the starving man and his family. Oh joy, oh joy! She wished to spend her hiatus in my company!

While she was gone, tending to her duties, I removed my bow tie and opened the top button of my shirt, thus making my sartorial appearance more appropriate to my surroundings.

Ten minutes later, as I was chomping on an onion ring that tasted as if it had been fried in motor oil, she slid into my booth. Though she did not utter a word regarding the alteration of my image, she did glance at my neck and smile in an approving way. "I'm afraid to ask, but how do you like the food, Professor?"

"I can literally feel my cholesterol level rising toward the ionosphere with every bite, although the owner, who I assume is named Phil, should perhaps provide his clientele with hacksaws with which to cut the meat."

Ms. Bird laughed. "You're not the first one to point that out, although I imagine a chain saw might be more efficient."

I chuckled. Such a charming sense of humor she had! "Indeed."

"Although I'm happy to see you, Professor, I believe I mentioned several days ago that the food in this place is barely edible."

As I did not wish to reveal my true purpose in appearing on the premises, I merely said, "So you did."

"Yet here you are."

"As I am a devoted carnivore, I had a profound craving for a thick steak," I said. "I did not know it would be an arduous *carving* of a thick steak."

She erupted with a chortle.

And so we chatted for the duration of her break. Our conversation evolved into a spirited, albeit short discussion of *The Mill on the Floss* by Miss Mary Ann Evans (known by the pseudonym, George Eliot), specifically the complex relationship between Mollie Tulliver and her brother Tom. I found Ms. Bird's thoughts on the matter most perceptive. As we spoke, I was so enchanted by her eyes, her hair, her lips, her dimple, her chin, her forehead, her ears, her neck, and her shapely figure that I had to remind myself to occasionally look away, lest she think that I was engaged in ogling which, in actuality, I was. After a time, we spoke of other subjects of a nonliterary nature.

"Tell me, Professor," she said. "Do you have any exciting plans for the long Memorial Day weekend?"

"Not as of yet," I replied. "I was planning on relaxing with a good book or two, perhaps perform a few errands that I have been putting off for weeks."

"I may just stay home and read too. Or maybe I'll read in the park if the weather permits."

At that, Ms. Bird looked at her watch and I feared that she would soon leave the table and continue her work delivering oversized portions of meat to the restaurant's clientele.

But she did not rise. "I think there's an arts and crafts festival in town tomorrow," she said. "I've seen a few signs posted around town. I'm sure the artwork will be appalling, but I imagine there will be other amusements, maybe food and music."

"I too have encountered a great many placards of this nature plastered to telephone polls and in the windows of shops around the town," I said.

"There's so little to do in this town."

"Quite true."

"In truth, I had no plans to go to this event but I might get bored without some diversion," she said. "And I don't want to go alone."

A moment of silence ensued. As I did not know how to fill this break in the conversation, I sipped at my water. When I looked at her, she appeared to be staring at me with an expression that seemed somewhat impatient.

"Maybe I'll attend the art fair after all, dreadful as it will most likely be," she said finally. After another lull in the conversation, she added, "Would you, by any small chance…care to join me?"

My reply to this query did not require much thought on my part. "That would be excellent!" I told her.

"Although…"

"Although what?"

"Although once again I fear this may be a violation of college ethics, specifically the dictum regarding students consorting with teachers, if such a dictum actually exists."

"Pish tosh," I said. "As I have stated before, please do not worry yourself, Ms. Bird. If by some miniscule chance we are observed in each other's company, we shall simply claim that we encountered each other at the fair by coincidence. In truth, I do not really care and am willing to risk it."

"All right then." With that, she strolled back toward the kitchen, turning once to give me a wave and a goofy scowl, which I took to indicate that she did not savor the prospect of returning to her duties and would perhaps have much preferred to remain with me. Or was I imagining this? A moment later, after I had left the restaurant and was attempting to locate my car in the crowded lot, I noticed that the rhythm of my steps had become more than a little sprightly.

As good fortune would have it, Ms. Bird and I spent much of the Memorial Day weekend together, an unpredictably elongated date that commenced at the art fair and concluded at her front doorway two nights later. We had decided to take separate cars to the fair and when we noted each other's presence at the appointed meeting place, I was pleased to note that she had arrived at the exact time that we had decided upon. As per her previous advice, I did not sport my bow tie as I wished to please her sartorially. Her ensemble included a long summer dress, thick leather sandals, a floppy straw hat that sat asymmetrically on her head, and a pair of clip-on sunglasses over her regular spectacles. She looked so utterly stunning that I reacted with a gasp.

"Are you all right, Professor?" she asked. "You seem to be gasping."

"It is nothing," I said. I struggled momentarily to fabricate a credible explanation. "You see, I parked my vehicle a fair distance from our agreed-upon meeting place and was therefore compelled to jog in order to appear before you at the precisely scheduled time."

She closed one eye. "Do you often jog?" she said.

"At least once or twice a year but only in situations such as this to avoid tardiness. And you?"

"Yes, I try to exercise twice a week, though I'm afraid I'm not especially adept at it, because I occasionally find myself tripping over my own feet which are somewhat large."

I gazed down at her feet. Her assessment of their dimensions was accurate. "Alas, I own no clothing appropriate for jogging and I do not enjoy perspiration," said I.

"Neither do I, although I've read that perspiration is a good way to cleanse the skin," she said. "And I find that jogging accomplishes this and is also a worthwhile method for keeping the body fit as is the practice of proper eating habits and the occasional colon cleanse."

"And you are certainly the very picture of fitness." I regretted my words immediately for I feared that she would misinterpret them as a lewd observation regarding the shapeliness of her anatomy.

She blushed slightly. "Why, thank you, Professor. What a lovely compliment!"

As it happened, our prior assessment of the quality of the art had been correct as most of it consisted primarily of primitive render-ings of the town's waterfall, created with every medium imaginable including dyed gravel and colored chicken feathers. In most of these, the Falls had been enlarged to resemble the far grander one situated at Niagara. The food was the predictable mélange of home cookery but the crafts were of some interest, and at one of these booths Ms. Bird stopped to admire a set of inexpensive feather earrings, which the vendor assured her were of Algonquin provenance, though I strongly doubted that he was being entirely truthful. Nevertheless, she wished to purchase them, but after an interminable search through the debris of her enormous overstuffed purse, she was unable to locate her wallet so rather than wait for hours, I drew mine out of my trousers and bought said earrings for her. When I handed them to her, she thanked me profusely and promised to reimburse me for the cost at a later date.

"That will not be necessary, Ms. Bird," I told her.

"I insist."

"And I insist not. Consider it a gift."

"Are you sure?"

"Quite sure."

"How very sweet of you, Professor," she said. "Thank you!"

"My pleasure."

A few minutes later, feeling the urge to empty the contents of my bladder, I excused myself and followed some primitively hand-let-tered signs scrawled on erratically cut pieces of wood that led me to a phone booth-sized structure known as a Porto-Potty, which had been propped upon an elevated wooden stage in a shaded, well-hid-den section of the parking lot. As I was about to enter the reeking enclosure, I espied Sandra's convertible with the top up. Oddly, I had not seen her at the fair but I soon understood why. As a result of my altitude I was afforded a view of her head bobbing up and down, indicating quite clearly that she was in the process of performing fellatio on the gentleman who occupied the passenger seat. When he turned his head slightly, I immediately recognized him as one of the young lads who attended my writing class, none other than the talentless, length-obsessed Mr. Williger. Utterly fascinated, I watched them for a moment and then retreated into the revolting confines of the Porto-Potty, the toilet of which contained a floating piece of fecal matter the size of a bratwurst.

When I emerged from said moveable commode five minutes later, Sandra's car was gone. I must confess that I was astounded by her audacity in performing a sexual act with a man other than her husband in broad daylight in a parking lot, although she had shown the good sense to park in a secluded area.

When I found Ms. Bird in the crowd, she was seated on a bench licking a scoop of strawberry ice cream that was perched precariously on a waffle cone. Several dollops of it had dripped onto her garment and I quickly produced a handkerchief from my pocket and wiped them off.

"Thank you, Professor," she said. "Such a sweet gesture." Then, to my surprise, she offered me a long, penetrating look that seemed to bespeak such great warmth that I was forced to look away. Or perhaps I misinterpreted it.

"It was...um... nothing," I said.

Ms. Bird sighed wistfully. "You have once again rescued a damsel in distress although, as we once concluded, something as negligible as drips of ice cream do not really qualify as distress."

"Per our previous discussion of its definition, I would guess it does not," I said. "Perhaps just a minor attempt at gallantry meant to rescue a woman from inadvertently besmirching her attire."

"Nevertheless, you're quite chivalrous."

"Thank you. I was concerned that your dress would be stained, although in my experience, stains derived from dairy products can be easily dispatched."

"Do you have much experience with laundry?"

"I am loath to admit that I do," I said. "I wash my own clothing at a nearby laundromat as my landlord refuses to repair the laundry appliances located in the basement."

"An impressive talent," she said.

"And a handy one should I ever decide to abandon teaching and become a housekeeper, although that is not likely to occur."

Ms. Bird laughed. "It's always good to have a contingency plan," she said, continuing our amusing banter.

"Indeed."

"Would you care for a taste of my ice cream? It's homemade, or so I was told. It's probably not but it tastes great. Strawberry. My favorite."

"I find that strawberry fails to excite my taste buds," I said. "I'm afraid I am a devoted chocolate man, although I do occasionally have a fondness for vanilla if it is accompanied by a product known as Hershey's chocolate sauce."

We bid adieu in the parking lot, where I escorted her to her automobile. Once again, she dug through her purse but was unable to locate her car keys. Frustrated, she dumped the contents of said receptacle on the hood of said vehicle. These included three books that appeared to have come from the library—*Heart of Darkness* by Mr. Joseph Conrad, *The Wapshot Chronicles* by Mr. John Cheever, and *Seize the Day* by Mr. Saul Bellow.

"You will enjoy those," I said. "Excellent choices."

"I've read *Heart of Darkness* already," she said. "It was a long time ago. But I feel I didn't fully understand some of it so I've decided to read it again. It can be a little dense in parts."

"True. I had some difficulty with that identical dilemma when I first read it as a lad of seven."

"Seven! My God! Such a precocious little boy you must have been!"

"In all modesty, that is quite true—I was somewhat advanced, but alas, far from a genius. My young intellect did not comprehend mathematics or chemistry, nor was I proficient in music. I do, however, seem to have an analytical mind. Perhaps a trifle too analytical at times."

"Do you play a musical instrument, Professor?"

"At the behest of my parents, I made an attempt at learning the violin but after two excruciating years of private lessons, I concluded that a continuation of said instruction would be pointless as my fingers lacked the proper coordination. My father plays the violin quite adeptly, but I did not inherit his talent which disappointed him greatly as he wished to engage me in duets."

"I studied the tuba with a similar result," she said.

I reflected upon this. "An interesting choice. But the tuba is quite a heavy instrument, is it not?"

"It is," she said, "and I am ashamed to admit that I dropped it on my foot more than a few times."

"Perhaps a flute would have been a wiser choice."

She smiled and finally located her keys. I did not want her to depart just yet as I wished to see her again the next day. But I found myself stymied, for I had no idea as to what our next activity should be and it would be incumbent upon me to suggest something specific. But what would that be? I was at a loss.

Of course, I was also concerned that she would interpret such a suggestion as unwanted boldness on my part and thus reject my overtures so I said nothing. After all, we had already completed one outing and I was unsure as to whether she wanted to see that much of me.

"The weather is supposed to be glorious tomorrow," she said.

"Is it?"

"That's the prediction," she said. "It would be a shame to waste such a day indoors. How would you suggest I resolve that problem?"

"By being outdoors."

"Excellent suggestion. Do you plan to spend the day outdoors, Professor?"

"I have no specific plans, but perhaps I shall take a book and peruse it outdoors," I said.

"Then we'll be doing the same thing outdoors."

"It most certainly does appear that way," I said. "Perhaps..."

"Perhaps what?"

"Well, I was going to say…"

"Yes?"

"Perhaps the …um…weather report will prove to be wrong."

She gave forth with a deep exhalation. "I doubt it," she said. "But if that is not the case, and the climate is as expected, maybe we could find a place and read outdoors in each other's company."

"That would be most excellent!" I said. "But where specifically?"

She assured me that she would think of something interesting with which to occupy ourselves. Before we departed, she shook my hand and once again thanked me for the earrings, which now dangled from her earlobes.

"Good bye, Professor. Thank you again for the earrings. I had a wonderful time."

"As did I." It was then that I decided to say something audacious. "Perhaps we should address each other with our given names from this point on, Ms. Bird, for I feel we have progressed to a stage of friendship that surpasses the formal greeting."

"Good idea," she said. "I was hoping to suggest that myself."

I could barely mask my joy.

"However," she said, acquiring a more serious look, "I think we should probably revert to our surnames when we're in class or in any other situation that would require more formality."

"Yes, of course. Excellent point."

She was reflective. "But would you mind if I called you Archer instead of Ishmael? Please don't be offended. It's not that I don't like your given name but it would make me feel as if I'm addressing a character from Melville."

I understood this, for many others had expressed some discomfort with pronouncing my first name. "Not at all," I said.

"Well, good bye then, Archer."

"Good bye, Abigail."

I watched as she drove off, her car meandering dangerously through the lot and nearly colliding with a trash receptacle. After she had departed, I was forced to circle the parking lot on foot three times in search of my vehicle, for I was not able to remember where I had parked it, an embarrassing and frustrating predicament that frequently afflicted me. Of course, on this particular day, my confusion may have resulted from the fact that my mind was consumed with thoughts of Abigail. Eventually, I located it. Once safely inside my vehicle, I put on a compact disk of Mozart's *Requiem Mass* and sang along until I arrived home.

Abigail had packed a basket of comestibles that consisted of ham and cheese sandwiches, a variety of raw fruits, lemonade, yogurt, and chocolate cupcakes for she had suggested in the morning via cell phone that we indulge in a picnic near the Falls. I was agreeable, although in truth I did not care for consuming food on the grass, as there would doubtless be ants and other forms of intrusive wildlife that would take considerable interest in invading our chosen area in search of nourishment. Yet, to please her, I feigned enthusiasm and followed her along a circuitous path that led us through all manner of trees and brush until we came upon a grassy glade that she had visited before, and spread our victuals out on a blanket that she had provided.

Abigail surveyed the area. "Isn't this an absolutely beautiful spot, Archer?"

"Quite a scenic locale," I said. "A veritable Garden of Eden."

"Though absent of serpents."

I chuckled. "Happy to hear it."

"Aren't you glad we came?"

"Ecstatic."

In order to appear appropriately attired for our adventure, I had chosen an ensemble that included a light blue button-down shirt, a pair of khaki Bermuda shorts, black knee socks, dark brown dress shoes and a Panama hat to protect my face from the solar rays. To be prudent, I had smeared a layer of white zinc oxide on my nose and below my eyes, a precautionary rendering that resembled Native American war paint.

I did not wear a bow tie or, for that matter, a tie of any sort.

Abigail seemed pleased by my appearance, though she made no mention of it.

Once we had settled upon the blanket, we consumed our assorted foods. Abigail, who wore a pair of purple sweat pants, a frilly, short-sleeved blouse, and yellow running shoes, removed said attire, under which she sported a modest black one-piece bathing suit. She then took from her purse a giant tube of sunscreen, which she squeezed with too much force, causing a blob of the white goo to explode from its container and land on her thigh. After ineptly slathering her quite fetching body with sunscreen, she lit a cigarette, lay back on the blanket, and basked in the blinding sunlight as I sat nearby stealing glances at her anatomy while chomping on a cupcake and chattering on about *Wuthering Heights* and the contrary elements of Heathcliff's character. Perhaps I should have removed my shirt, applied some sunscreen onto my own physique, taken up the space beside her on the blanket, and let my fingers meander toward hers, but I was uncertain as to whether she would find such a gesture intrusive. What if she interpreted such a meeting of hands as an unwelcome act of intimacy? Did she consider our relationship to be a formal one between a professor and his student? Were we merely friends? Or did she desire a deeper affiliation? I did not know. After all, not long ago, she had glumly informed me that she possessed no friends. Perhaps I merely filled that vacancy.

No, such a bold physical advance would not do—I would require verbal permission of some sort. At first I did not know how to approach this delicate subject, but finally I said, "Abigail, I must tell you how delighted I am that we have become friends."

"So am I, Archer!" she said. "I truly enjoy your company. It's so pleasing to have finally found a friend in this dreary town."

This was not the reply I had hoped for, but I said, "Yes."

"And we have so much in common! A love for literature, punctuality, a passion for crispy bacon…"

"And we agree on the practicality of bibs."

"Yes. Bibs as well."

I waited for her to embellish beyond bibs but she did not, so I made another bold attempt at verbal seduction. "But all that aside, I believe we have come to a certain stage, at least I have, at which we—"

But suddenly, she sat up. "That reminds me," she said. "I have an announcement!"

"Oh?"

She smiled broadly. "I've decided to write a short story!"

This, too, was not the direction I had anticipated. Perhaps she had perceived that I was planning to express a greater interest in her and had therefore deliberately interrupted me rather than face an awkward query. Although discouraged by this, I said, "A short story! That is marvelous, Abigail! Do you as yet have an idea?"

She scrunched up her lips. "Well, not exactly. I may have spoken too soon."

"Well, I am certain you will think of something," I said. "From what I have gathered thus far, you have an excellent imagination."

"Thank you, Archer."

"You are most welcome."

She paused. I noticed that there was a streak of sunscreen on the left lens of her glasses. "May I ask you for a favor, Archer?"

"Certainly," I said. "I am at your service."

"When I finish it, or should I say *if* I finish it, I would love to have you read it and offer me your comments."

"I would be more than happy to."

"Maybe you could be my mentor if you have the time."

Thrilled by this notion, I said, "Most agreeable!"

"You must be honest in your critique though, Archer." She waved her index finger at me. "Totally ruthless. I'm afraid you may dislike it and claim otherwise to spare my feelings because you are most kind and sensitive to the feelings of others, but I must know whether I have any talent for fiction or if I'm just deluding myself."

"I promise you, I shall be brutally honest," I said. This was a lie for I knew I would certainly not be cruel if said attempt was not to my liking. "Tell me, do you suppose it will be a humorous tale?"

"Yes. That's my intention," she said, "although I hope there will be some meaning behind it."

"Well, I look forward to reading it, Abigail."

"Great." At that, she leaned toward me and, for a moment, I thought she was going to reward me with a kiss, but she merely grabbed her purse, which resided near my legs. A second or two of rummaging passed before she pulled out two hardcover books.

"Abigail, as I was trying to say before, I—"

But she interrupted me again. "Would you sign these for me?"

She held up both of my novels. I was astounded. "Certainly," I said. "I am honored. No one has ever asked me to do that before." I searched my pockets. "Do you by chance have a pen, Abigail?"

"Let me look."

Once again, after a fruitless search, she upended the purse over the edge of the blanket. Why, I wondered idly, do women carry purses if they are never able to locate the items they require? Alas, there was no writing utensil to be found.

"Well, maybe you can take them home, sign them, and bring them to class. You may inscribe them to me as well if you wish. I would like that very much."

"That would be my pleasure," I said.

"Wonderful! Thank you so much, Archer!"

"You are most welcome."

After we exchanged a smile, Abigail did something that I found to be a trifle odd. She abruptly rose to her feet and took several deep inhalations. Then, she launched into an impromptu display of gymnastics that included a series of deep knee bends, followed by a sequence of an exercise known as jumping jacks. When she ceased this performance, she was perspiring and a trifle breathless.

I handed her a cloth napkin and she wiped her face with it. "Abigail, pray tell, what inspired this sudden activity?"

She shrugged. "I suppose I just had a burst of energy. That happens sometimes after I've been lying about after a meal."

"I see."

I noticed then that she was gazing at the waterfall. "Are you athletic, Archer?"

"Beyond an insignificant talent for the game of croquet, I'm afraid I am not," I said. "And sadly, I am not much good at croquet either, having only engaged in it on one occasion. I do ride a bicycle but I feel that I am somewhat inept at that as well."

"Yes, I've seen you riding it," she said with a charming laugh. "In my opinion you would be well served to purchase a bicycle that isn't quite so wobbly and misshapen."

"I most heartily agree. Perhaps one day I shall."

"You might even purchase a Vespa for more rapid transport."

"I doubt whether I would survive a motorized vehicle of that nature, but I shall give it some thought."

Abigail dropped the cloth napkin on the blanket and then strode toward the stream that trickled beneath the waterfall, whereupon she proceeded to splash handfuls of water on various parts of her anatomy. This was indeed a most pleasant sight to behold for she resembled Botticelli's beauteous creature as portrayed in the artist's magnificent painting, *The Birth of Venus*. I could hardly take my eyes off her.

"Maybe I'll climb those rocks," she said, pointing to a wall of squarish boulders that began at the foot of the waterfall and ended at the top.

"Is that wise?" I asked. "Such an endeavor appears quite perilous to me. I fear for your safety."

"I appreciate your concern, Archer, but I've done it before several times without incident following my occasional morning jog. As you can see, it's no more than a staircase of rocks. I assure you, this is not very challenging. I believe you'll be impressed with my agility."

"You do not need to impress me with your physical agility, Abigail," I said. "You have already impressed me with the agility of your mind."

"What a sweet thing to say!" she responded with a warm smile.

"You're a perfect gentleman, Archer!"

I had hoped that my remark would cause her to abandon this climbing endeavor but apparently she seemed determined to engage in it, for she then sat down to put on her running shoes. After an exhalation, she strode toward the rocks. I watched with some anxiety as she easily clambered up the first rock and then proceeded to stride effortlessly to the second and the third. She stopped for a moment to catch her breath and to observe the view, and then continued upward. Within five minutes, she had reached the summit.

"My, what a breathtaking vista!" she shouted down to me. "Are you sure you don't want to join me up here, Archer? It's really very easy."

"Quite sure, but thank you for the invitation."

After a few more minutes of enjoying the vista, she climbed down, carefully watching her feet. Soon she was at my side again. A wave of relief coursed through me.

"Well done, Abigail. Brava!"

"Why, thank you, Archer," she said. "Why did you not join me?"

"I am afraid I suffer from vertigo," I said. "I first realized this when I was but a lad of thirteen. You see, my Uncle Alphonse, who was the only athlete in my family, had a fondness for the sport of skiing and he entreated me to join him on a trip to Hunter Mountain. I found myself paralyzed with fear as I sat in the chairlift. From that day on, I have eschewed heights beyond twelve inches."

"My goodness! Twelve inches!" She shook her head in disbelief. "I attempted skiing once myself and spent most of the time on my rear end in the snow. It was quite a spectacle as you can well imagine."

She then removed her footwear, adjusted the blanket and continued to bathe in the sunlight. As I had nothing to do, I pulled a book from my satchel.

"What are you reading?" Abigail inquired.

"I thought Dostoevsky would be appropriate for such a glorious day," I said. "I assume you have read *Crime and Punishment.*"

"Of course. It's one of my favorites."

"I suspected as much," I said. "I am of the opinion that—"

I stopped abruptly in the midst of my sentence for Abigail was once again overtaken by the need to sneeze repeatedly. After the third sneeze, I produced a cloth handkerchief from my pocket and handed it to her, whereupon she blew her nose in it until the cloth appeared to be saturated.

"Are you all right?" I said when the sneezing finally ceased.

"Quite all right," she said. "Thank you. But if you don't mind, I'll take the handkerchief home and wash it myself as it contains some mucus."

"As you wish."

"I'll iron it as well."

"You are most clairvoyant, Abigail," I said. "It is true that I do prefer my handkerchiefs pressed, although not starched for I fear that the introduction of a toxic chemical might have the effect of irritating the nasal passages."

"I totally agree."

More common ground, I thought. Starch.

At four o'clock, when the weather grew too hot to continue sunbathing, we decided to pack up our picnic basket and blanket, but before we departed for our hike through the meandering trail that would return us to the road, Abigail commenced to rummage through her purse again, for what I did not know. After five minutes of this hopeless endeavor she gave out with a weary sigh and concluded her fruitless search.

"Archer, would you mind taking a photograph of me?" she asked. "It appears that I've left my cell phone at home."

This elicited a smile from me for I suspected that she wished for me to have a photograph of her as a keepsake. "For what purpose if I may ask?"

"I've been promising my father that I would send him a picture," she said. "It will be his birthday soon and we haven't seen each other for quite some time."

"Oh," I said. "And your mother?"

Abigail's delightful merriment was contagious and I soon found myself enjoying this sport. Nodding in the direction of a young woman who was engaged in window-shopping, I said, "Lydia Bennet."

"Not at all," Abigail said. "That's definitely Jane Eyre." Then her eyes sparkled. "Amory Blaine. Over there by the car."

"Do you think so? To me he resembles Inspector Javert."

This of course was absurd and Abigail punched me lightly in the arm. "Not at all," she said. "You're kidding right?"

"Yes," I said. "The man who just passed by—Atticus Finch."

"You're not serious. That's the spitting image of Dorian Gray!"

I gazed around at the populace and pointed at a stout, jolly man. "And who is that?" I asked.

She squinted. "That's obviously Mr. Wilkins Micawber."

"Hmm. I do not think so."

"Maybe you need a new pair of glasses, Archer," she said. This was a new twist—I had not known that Abigail was so…feisty. But it was not displeasing as I suspected that she was merely being playful.

I removed my spectacles and cleaned them with a napkin. "No," I said. I placed them back on my nose, whereupon I looked at the fellow again. "Definitely not Micawber. Perhaps it is *you* who needs new glasses."

"These *are* new glasses. Without them I'm quite blind."

"Then we shall have to agree to disagree."

"All right," she said. Then with a wicked smile, she added, "But you are quite mistaken."

It was just past seven o'clock when we departed the restaurant, but we continued our game as I drove her home. When we arrived at her abode, I carried the picnic baggage and accompanied her to the door. We stood there for an awkward moment and I wondered whether she was expecting me to deliver a goodnight kiss upon her lips, but I was paralyzed and did nothing. A moment passed. Perhaps, I hoped, she would ask me to accompany her inside for a glass of lemonade or something of that ilk, but she did not, a gesture or lack thereof that I interpreted as a sign that she did not expect further involvement. Had I offended her during our argument regarding the fictional identities of the passersby? Could she be that sensitive? After all, it was just a game. In any case, I handed her the picnic basket and blanket and we shook hands. She did not search for her key, which would have taken her a good hour, but instead just opened the door. I found this odd, although crime was nearly nonexistent in Highland Falls so perhaps she felt safe enough to keep it unlocked. Or perhaps she had lost her key. Momentarily, she disappeared behind said unlocked door and I returned to my car. Once inside, I sat there banging the steering wheel with the heel of my palms until I felt them begin to bruise. Then I motored off into the night.

Eight

At first, I thought I would simply scrawl my name on the title page of each book but upon further reflection, I suspected that a mere signature would be dreadfully impersonal and might disappoint Abigail. I recalled then that she had said that an inscription would especially please her. The words, *To Abigail, Best Regards, Ishmael Archer*, were too impersonal and would not do at all. But what sort of sentiment should I concoct? Due to the abysmal failure of both novels, I had never been invited to sign or inscribe a book, so I was temporarily in a quandary.

I struggled with this question for at least two hours, considering more than a few potential inscriptions and scribbling them on pieces of paper before committing them to the title page of the first book. Should I merely write the words, *Love Ishmael Archer?* Was that too audacious? Perhaps just, *Your devoted friend, Archer?* Was that too ambiguous? Or simply, *Your excellent friend, Archer?* Or maybe, *Your Obedient Servant, Archer?* No, even for me, that was too archaic.

Hells bells!

It then occurred to me of a sudden that it would be most imaginative, and perchance quite pleasing to her if I formulated an amusing sentence or phrase to precede the signature. How marvelous it would be to observe her giggling joyously at the cleverness of my words! Yes, this would certainly add to her enjoyment as well as to mine! Excitedly, I penned a few possibilities. To wit:

Many thanks for being among the handful that have read this book!
Write what you know, but keep some of it for your next book.
The pen is mightier than the sword, but perhaps not in actual combat.

No, no, no. None of this twaddle would do. Thoroughly discouraged, I crumpled the page and angrily hurled it in the direction of my trash receptacle, missing it by at least a foot. Desperate in my search for inspiration, I located a stale Butterfinger chocolate bar in a kitchen drawer and eagerly consumed it. Miraculously, the sugar contained therein jolted my imagination and I wrote these words:

To Abigail—Books are food for the soul and should be consumed with relish. Affectionately, Archer.

Perfect!

After I carefully copied these words on the title page of the first book, utilizing a neat but somewhat loopy cursive, I was immediately plagued by another impasse. Should I duplicate that exact sentiment in the second book, formulate another inscription, or would it be preferable to simply sign my name? After all, I reasoned, what purpose would there be for redundancy? Yet, it would be a clever touch to add something of an equally humorous nature. After much deliberation, I came upon the perfect words:

To Abigail—My most talented and punctual student with whom I share an enduring affection for literature, bacon, and bibs. With affection, Archer.

As I wrote these words on the title page, taking care not to smudge them or in any other way obscure them, I found myself chuckling a bit at my own ingenuity and hoped that Abigail would be similarly amused and perhaps even touched by my words.

On the Tuesday following the Memorial Day weekend Constance reappeared on campus, having returned from another journey to visit her ill aunt. As my next class would not convene again until Wednesday, I had virtually nothing to take up my time save for an enchanting visitation to my neighborhood laundromat, followed by several hours of equally delightful starching and ironing at my apartment. So that afternoon I retired to the faculty lounge, where I read a seemingly endless and somewhat obtuse short story that had been published in a recent issue of *The New Yorker*, although I found it difficult to concentrate as my mind was cluttered by thoughts of Abigail and my frustration at not having been more courageous at the close of our weekend activities.

In the midst of my gloom, Constance strolled into the room and sat in the chair beside me. We exchanged pleasantries and I inquired about the status of her aunt's health. Apparently, the prognosis was quite encouraging, although Constance feared that it might soon become necessary to find a suitable assisted living establishment for the poor woman.

"I have some interesting news," I said, after expressing my sympathies.

"Do tell."

I paused. "I have made the acquaintance of a delightful young member of the fair sex, and I believe I have been struck by Cupid's arrow, as they say. It began as nothing more than a friendship but it has miraculously achieved, at least for me, significantly more depth within a short period of time."

Constance narrowed her eyes at me in a manner that implied confusion. "Ishmael, you told me weeks ago that you had no interest in women due to your unfortunate marriage and your previous and subsequent rejections. Has this state of affairs changed in such a short time?"

"I do believe so," I said. "Besides, I expressed that gloomy proclamation several months ago. A person can undergo changes in outlook."

"I suppose that's true, but it seems a bit sudden. If I may ask, who is this lucky young woman?"

Although the decibel level of her voice was louder than acceptable in the lounge, no one but the two of us inhabited the chamber so there was no need for me to shush her, yet out of habit I spoke in a low voice although I was virtually brimming with excitement.

"She is a student of mine," I said. "Very bright, very talented, an exceptional young lady in every respect and quite fetching as well. In fact, I happen to have several photographs of her. Would you care to see them?"

"Okay."

I located my cell phone and found the photos of Abigail that I had taken at the glade. I gazed adoringly at them for a moment and then handed the phone to Constance who took quite a long time inspecting them.

"Quite lovely," she said as she studied the pictures. "Very... soulful. Something warm and endearing about her eyes."

"Yes. She is even more breathtakingly beautiful in person."

"Well, I can certainly see why you're so taken with her," Constance added as she handed the phone back to me.

"I am quite smitten," I said.

"Well, I look forward to meeting this young lady who has succeeded in repairing the damage to your heart, Ishmael. She must be quite an amazing woman."

"Indeed she is," I said.

It was shortly thereafter that I received some distressing news.

I had encountered Abigail on the quadrangle one cloudy afternoon as she sat on a bench, consuming a Cobb salad. The intermittent shafts of sun lit up her hair in a most appealing way. I was delighted to see her and inquired as to whether I might join her on said bench. As she was most agreeable, I settled myself beside her.

"You look most lovely today, Abigail," I said.

"Thank you, Archer. I believe my sunbathing at the glade has produced a most pleasing tan."

"Indeed it has. Unfortunately, my anatomy remains quite pale."

"As mine will be in a few days once the coloration has faded."

A moment of silence prevailed, during which I was momentarily lost in contemplation. I thought this chance encounter might be a propitious time in which to give voice to my feelings for her. But once again the opportunity did not present itself. I had just formed some words in my brain when Abigail suddenly looked at her timepiece and rose to her feet.

"I wish I could stay longer and converse with you, Archer, but I'm afraid I have a bus to catch in an hour, and I must hurry home and make myself ready, as I may spend the night. Or I may simply take the night bus home so that I may be present at our class tomorrow afternoon. I'm not sure yet."

Foiled again, I thought. "Where are you off to, Abigail?" I asked.

"Syracuse."

"Why are you not driving?"

"Have you not heard the forecast?" she said. "Torrential rains have been predicted. I do not like to drive in such weather."

"Nor do I," I said. "The bus is a very sensible alternative."

"Yes, and it allows me the comfort to read."

I looked skyward and perceived a few darkish clouds. "And what, if I may be so bold as to ask, takes you to that fair city of magic and light?"

"Well…" she said. "An old college friend of mine is having a publishing party and I've been asked to attend. At first I declined, but he was adamant so I changed my mind."

This came as a bombshell. I was thoroughly taken aback. "He?" I asked, attempting to mask my surprise and shock.

"Yes. Perhaps you have heard of him—his name is William Octavian Butler."

"I have not," I said. "Whyever do you believe that I might have heard of this gentleman?"

"He's an author. His first novel was recently released. It has received the most marvelous reviews. Do you not read the *New York Times Book Review* section?"

"Religiously," I said. "But it might have escaped my attention."

"It was the lead review," she said. "On the cover."

I was struck speechless. Was this fellow perhaps a former paramour of hers? I wondered. For what reason would she be staying overnight, if that was what indeed she planned to do? Would he seduce her? Would she submit to such overtures? All manner of ghastly scenarios invaded my mind.

As she was in a hurry, I did not wish to further pry into this matter—perhaps at a later date I could couch my curiosity in a casual manner. Nervously, Abigail glanced at her watch again. "I'm so sorry, but I must be off, Archer," she said. "I hope to see you tomorrow, if I am back, which I hope to be. I would hate to miss your class. Goodbye for now."

In a weak voice I bid her farewell and watched with dismay as she scurried down the flagstone path.

Benumbed, I remained on the bench, once again overtaken by a profound sense of dread—the mere fact that she found this assignation in Syracuse more important than attending my class threw me into an abyss of despair. I was lost in thought and did not realize that I had been sitting there for half an hour until I gazed at my timepiece. Then, in a flash of enlightenment, I knew what I must do, so I arose from the bench and sprinted to my car.

As I sped toward town, my Subaru began to shudder and shake in a most worrisome way. I was so fearful that my crippled heap of metal would succumb to its automotive illness before I was able to complete my journey that I pulled into the nearest petrol station, the work place of my mechanic, Mr. Jack Nuckles. Glancing at the dashboard clock, I was reassured that I would have time to catch Abigail before the bus departed.

With the car quaking ominously, I parked in front of the service garage and was soon greeted by said Mr. Nuckles, a fellow of questionable honesty who resembled a ponytailed, tattooed version of John Steinbeck at the approximate age of forty. He was wiping his hands on a rag as he approached me and studied my car, which looked as if it was about to explode due to the recent appearance of a cloud of noxious steam that emanated from beneath the hood.

"Hmm," he said. "This doesn't look good, Professor."

"I gathered that, Mr. Nuckles," I told him. "I was of the opinion that you had repaired all the defective parts several months ago."

"I did."

"Are you now trying to inform me that the new parts you installed, which I might remind you, came with a warranty, have now become dysfunctional?"

Some of the steam that escaped from the hood floated in our direction and Mr. Nuckles waved his hand to scatter it about. "This looks like a whole different problem, Professor," he said.

"Oh?"

He snickered in a way that sounded ominous. Then he opened the hood carefully, using his rag to protect his hand from the heat. "Hmm," he said once again as he leaned his body forward to inspect the circuitry.

"Looks like it's finally headed for the junk yard, Professor. I'll give you two hundred bucks for it. Parts must be worth about that."

"But I am in something of a hurry, you see," I said. "I must get to the bus station in twenty minutes in order to bid bon voyage to a particular friend of mine who is about to depart. Surely there must be something you can do."

"Can't help you, Professor," he said. "It's dead as a door lock."

"Door nail."

"What?"

"Never mind." I sighed. "Is there a vehicle I can borrow for a few hours?"

"Nope."

I glanced at my watch and was alarmed to see that it was already 4:10. "It is imperative that I get to town posthaste," I said. "I must take a taxi."

"There's only one cab in town and it ain't available right now."

"And how may I ask do you know this?"

Mr. Nuckles hooked his thumb toward the area directly behind him. "Because it's sitting on top of the lift right there in the garage."

A quick look confirmed that the taxi was indeed hoisted above ground in the manner he had described.

"Tough luck, Professor." He then wiped his brow with his rag, an exercise that removed the perspiration but left a streak of grease on his forehead.

"Perhaps you could give me a ride," I said. "I will pay you."

"Wife's got the car today. Grocery shopping at Costco." He then looked down the road. "Probably take you about a half hour to run there. Twenty if you sprint."

I groaned in frustration. "I suppose that will be my only option," I said, whereupon I handed him the key. "In the meantime, see what you can do."

Mr. Nuckles then glanced toward the heavens. "Better get a move on, Professor. It looks like it's gonna rain in about five minutes."

I followed his gaze skyward and saw that his forecast was likely correct as a fleet of dark, foreboding cumulonimbus clouds had gathered overhead. The prospect of appearing soaked to the skin in front of Abigail was unsavory, but I bade Mr. Nuckles goodbye and began to trot toward the gas tanks.

As good fortune would have it, I saw Eliot Altschuler's truck pull in beside a gas pump just before I made it to the highway. Eliot removed himself from the vehicle and walked around toward the tank.

"Eliot!" I shouted.

He stopped and turned his head. "Archer," he said. "What are you doing here? Don't you have a class?"

"No, it's tomorrow," I said. "I desperately need to get into town, Eliot. It's an emergency. Can you perhaps give me a ride? I would be eternally grateful."

"Sure. Just let me fill my tank. Shouldn't take but a few minutes. I'm just topping off, which is an unnecessary precaution I often take."

I breathed a sigh of relief. "You know, Eliot, this will be the second occasion on which you have been my roadside savior. I sincerely thank you for your courtesy. I hope to return the favor one day."

"No need," he said. "I'm happy to help."

Several minutes later, I was seated in Eliot's truck as he drove toward the town at a speed that was ten points below the speed limit. I contemplated asking him to increase his velocity but decided not to. Even at forty-five miles an hour, I would doubtless arrive at the Greyhound station on time.

"I haven't seen you lately, Archer." Eliot fumbled with the radio dial. "Where have you been?"

"Here and there," I said. "I believe it is *you* who have seldom emerged from your…or rather Dean Fletcher's office."

"Yes, I suppose I have been something of a phantom lately," he said. "There is so much work to be done. And those damned orchids."

Before I could offer commentary on Dean Fletcher's curious obsession with plant life, a flash of lightning lit up the darkening sky and was predictably followed seconds later by an ear-shattering bolt of thunder.

"I've been meaning to talk to you about something, Archer," Eliot said.

"And what would that be?"

He paused and switched on his windshield wipers although there was barely a drizzle. "It appears that you have been seen more than a few times in the company of a student of yours, a Ms. Abigail Bird."

My first reaction was to cough.

He looked at me. "Quite an attractive young lady, if I do say so. I believe she is enrolled in your writing class."

Trying to sound casually dismissive, I said, "She has demonstrated some bonafide talent for writing. I have merely taken it upon myself to mentor her."

Now the rain was beginning to fall more forcefully and Eliot increased the metronomic speed of his wipers.

"I assume you are aware, Archer, that there are rules regarding the fraternization between male teachers and their female students."

"I am aware of that, Eliot, but strictly speaking, does this edict include local folk who are merely auditing the class?"

"I don't know but my instincts tell me that a sexual liaison between even unregistered students and teachers might be frowned upon."

I feigned a bout of boisterous laughter. "Sexual liaison!" I said. "That's absurd! I assure you, Eliot, this sort of salacious activity has not taken place between Ms. Bird and myself."

But Eliot did not respond immediately. "Well, my advice to you would be to tread with caution during the mentoring of Ms. Bird."

"You may trust me, there is no need to tread with caution."

Eliot stopped at a traffic light, for we had finally reached the top of Main Street. It was now pouring. Then he turned to me and asked, "Now where was it you wanted to go, Archer?"

"The Greyhound bus station on Elm Street."

"Are you embarking on a trip?"

"No," I said. "I am merely seeing someone off. Bidding them bon voyage, as it were. Perhaps you could drive a trifle faster."

"In this downpour? I can barely see through the windshield as it is and I do not want to wreck my truck."

By the time Eliot and I arrived in the center of town, enormous puddles had formed in depressed areas of the streets and drivers were compelled to proceed at a snail's pace in order to avoid hydroplaning. Several vehicles had stalled, thus making it nearly impossible to proceed. The time of Abigail's departure was fast approaching, so when Eliot braked for a stop sign, I opened the door and leaped out of the truck.

"Where in blazes are you going, Archer?"

"I'll arrive there faster if I run. It's a mere two blocks."

"You'll get soaked to the skin."

I did not wish to lose precious time by engaging in a conversation about my impending state of wetness, so I quickly thanked Eliot and began to run.

I was, as Eliot had predicted, drenched by the time I progressed to the corner, my shoes squishing with every footfall. Half a minute later, I reached the station and stopped on the sidewalk across the street, gasping for air and mournfully watching as Abigail's bus took leave of the depot. As I stood there in a veritable waterfall of rain, I immediately became aware of the foolhardiness of this entire enterprise. My crazed race to the bus station had been meant as a subtle gesture to demonstrate my fondness for her and thus give her reason to abstain from a romantic entanglement with this Butler fellow, but even if I had succeeded would she have perceived it as such? What if Abigail, upon seeing me before her, drenched and breathless, had interpreted my appearance there as bizarre? After all, she was merely going to Syracuse for a short period of time and not traveling to far off parts of the world for three months. Romantic gesture indeed! What sort of insanity had overcome me? Yes, I realized, I had been on a fool's errand.

Accompanied by a deafening soundtrack of thunder, I trudged to my apartment, barely aware that my clothing had stuck to my skin. The only impediment was trying to navigate because my glasses were fogged up and dotted with drops of water but somehow I managed to arrive home without walking into any trees or slipping on the dangerously slick sidewalks. I was, however, splashed upon by several passing cars but it made little difference as I was already quite saturated.

My landlord, Mr. Felix S. Eugenides, was standing precariously at the top of a ladder busily removing clumps of leaves from the gutters when I arrived at my palatial dwelling. Wisely, he was wearing a yellow rubberized hat and matching rain parka and pants, the sort of garb sported by—dare I say it?—seamen during rainstorms. He did not espy me, nor did I say anything to make my presence known to him. I was simply too desolate to engage in conversation with Felix, who I knew would question my foolhardy decision to stroll in this monsoon without a raincoat or umbrella. Then, he would most likely offer me a glass of ouzo or a plate of *dolmades*.

But apparently he had spotted me. "Hello there, Professor Archer. Could you help me out up here?" he shouted. "I got another ladder in the garage."

I cupped my hands around my mouth in imitation of a bullhorn. "I would be happy to, Felix, but as you know I suffer from vertigo."

"Oh yeah, I remember."

"We shall talk again soon, Felix," I said.

"Looking forward to it, Professor."

Inside my apartment, I dashed to the bathroom, so as not to create puddles on the parlor floor, removed my sopping garments, folded them neatly, and placed them in the bathtub. I then applied a towel to my rain-soaked anatomy and, once I had achieved an acceptable degree of dryness, stepped into a pair of flannel pajamas. Thus outfitted, I located a box of stale Oreo cookies in my pantry, poured myself a cherry Coke in which to dunk said cookies, repaired to my parlor and dropped into my armchair to sulk.

Eventually, curiosity got the better of me and drove me to my laptop computer, whereupon I entered the name "William O. Butler" into a space provided by my search engine. Several people of that identical name appeared on my screen—one, an award-winning podiatrist from Biloxi; another, a deceased Las Vegas lion tamer that had succumbed to the angry jowls of a lion inadequately tamed; the last was our esteemed author. Admittedly, I felt a slight jolt of glee at the fact that his name had not appeared first and did, in fact, follow those of a podiatrist and an inept lion tamer. Of course, this most likely would not have occurred had I included his middle name.

I noted that Abigail's paramour resembled Ernest Hemingway in hair and beard style, although Butler was of considerably greater girth. He hailed from South Carolina and possessed a master's degree in creative writing from Harvard.

The young author's novel was entitled *Stones in the Wind*, a concept I did not comprehend, for any wind that could lift a stone would have to be of tornado strength. Was it perhaps a novel about meteorological phenomena or geology? Or both? The reviews, however, were indeed exceptional. The *New York Times* called it a "brilliant debut." *Publishers Weekly* gave it a starred review. Other publications of note also gushed with similar praise, anointing Mr. Butler a young novelist with great promise. Not wishing to perform any more research, I switched off my computer.

After further rumination concerning the nature of Abigail's involvement with this fellow, I made myself a cup of cocoa, promptly burned my tongue as I drank it, and retired for the evening, eventually falling into a fitful sleep.

&

To my considerable relief, Abigail was present in class the following day, although she was twenty-three seconds late. When the church bell had struck three o'clock, I had grown quite agitated at the prospect that she would not attend at all. Although she arrived well before the others, her lack of precise punctuality did not bode well. Yet I was overjoyed to see her. I did, however, notice that she yawned three times before she took her seat and twice thereafter, which caused me to conclude that she had arrived home at a late hour. Her eyes were a trifle reddish and her hair slightly disheveled, though neither of these minor conditions in any way lessened the quality of her beauty. Just gazing upon her had the effect of reinvigorating my affection for her.

"I'm so sorry I'm late, Professor," she said breathlessly as she took her usual seat beside me.

"No apology necessary. Your past record of punctuality allows me to excuse this one occasion of tardiness."

"I thank you for your magnanimity, but it's inexcusable."

Dismissing her statement with a wave of my hand, I said, "Nobody is perfect, Ms. Bird. But you appear to be somewhat fatigued or perhaps under the weather." (I had addressed her as "Ms. Bird" as per our agreement to use formal appellations during classes.)

"Yes, I'm a bit tired, Professor," she said. "You see, I missed the first bus back to Highland Falls last night."

"Ah, I see. Perhaps the torrential rain delayed you," I said. "I assume there was precipitation in Syracuse?"

"Oh yes! It was like the flood that plagued Noah, although I don't believe Noah actually existed."

"Nor do I."

"In my opinion, the Bible is nothing more than a fairy tale."

"I am in complete agreement on that point."

"Why the heck would the Creator, if such a phenomenon exists, choose a five-hundred-year-old man with no carpentry skills to build a ship the size of an aircraft carrier?"

To this I added, "And, who cleansed said ship of what must have been a constant deluge of fecal matter?"

"Good point," she said. "But I must say, the Bible is quite an amusing work of fiction."

"With which I also agree," I said. "Except perhaps for all the abomination business which seems a trifle barbaric, not to mention repetitive."

"True."

"Are you by chance an atheist, Ms. Bird?"

"Yes, I am," she said. "And you, Professor?"

"Good Lord, yes!"

Abigail laughed. "Ha! Very funny, Professor!"

"Thank you," I said. "Occasionally, I am given to engaging in humor, particularly dreadful puns, although mostly by accident."

There followed a quiet moment. I was delighted to learn that we shared religious beliefs or, as it were, nonbeliefs, but I was more intent upon diverting the conversation to her activities of the previous night.

"I suspect it was an excellent party," I ventured cautiously.

"Oh yes," she said with some excitement. "There were many interesting people from the world of publishing present—authors, editors, agents, and such. I believe you would have enjoyed it."

I hesitated. "And your friend, Mr. Butler? Was he pleased?"

"Oh yes!"

"So I imagine it was a pleasant reunion for you both," I said. "Are you and Mr. Butler close friends? I do not wish to pry."

"He was at one time my boyfriend."

"I...uh...see." Though I had suspected as much, the words of truth emanating from her lips horrified me. "Forgive me as I do not mean to intrude into your personal life." I noticed then that I was holding my breath.

"You and I are good friends, Professor, so I don't consider it an intrusion," she said. "So yes, it's quite true that we were involved romantically at one time, but my present relationship with the gentleman is strictly platonic."

"Ah," I said, exhaling. "You do not have to divulge any more information if you do not wish to, Ms. Bird. It is none of my business. I fear I am being too forward in asking you these questions."

Abigail shrugged. "Not at all, Professor. It's simply part of my past and you're most welcome to hear it. There's nothing secretive about it. But I don't want to bore you."

"You could never bore me, Ms. Bird," I said. "I have a sympathetic ear, so to speak. You may divulge further if it pleases you."

She was silent for several seconds, perhaps gathering her thoughts. "Well, the fact is, William ended our romantic relationship several years ago. You might say he broke my heart. I was quite devastated as you can well imagine. The experience made me quite wary of further involvement with men."

This gave me pause. Was Abigail's wariness regarding romantic entanglements the reason behind her reluctance to express her feelings for me, assuming those feelings actually existed? If so, this would be a difficult barrier for me to overcome since I suffered from the identical problem.

"I suspect you admire him for his authorial talent," said I.

"Yes. In fact, I think you would like him, Professor. I believe the two of you would get along famously as you are both writers. So much to discuss!"

I wanted to say "doubtful," but I restrained myself. "Well, if he ever visits our fair burg, I—"

"He might!" she said. "I'm trying to persuade him to come to Highland Falls and give a reading at the local library."

Had I, at that moment, been masticating a piece of Juicy Fruit, my favorite chewing gum, I would doubtless have either swallowed it or accidentally spat it upon the table. Why, I wondered, would a novelist "of great promise" wish to visit a library as insignificant as the one located in our fair town for the purpose of reading an excerpt of

that their attendance record was perfect. All four of them were over-joyed that they would now be allowed to graduate, and on their way out of the room, each shook me by the hand and thanked me. Mr. Williger did so with great fervor and mentioned that his father would have assassinated him had he not graduated, though I assumed this to be an exaggeration.

"You saved my ass, Professor," he said. "Thank you."

"Happy to be of service, Mr. Williger."

"Ya know, for a prof, you're pretty cool," he said, and then he took my hand again and shook it warmly.

Abigail remained for a moment or two in the classroom on the final day of our gathering. "Have you commenced writing your short story?" I asked her.

"I have made an outline, Professor, and I hope to commence the writing of the actual story shortly."

And then, much to my sorrow, she vacated the premises.

Although Eliot assured me that it was unnecessary to dress formally for my temporary position, I ignored his advice and sported a light summer blazer, my usual bow tie, dress shoes, and matching formal summer slacks on my first day as temporary dean. It seemed to me that a college dean, whether temporary or not, should be prop-erly attired so as to project an air of dignity. I did not know what to take along to the office other than a bag lunch, my favorite pen, and my laptop. The day before, I had borrowed a copy of Mr. William Octavian Butler's acclaimed novel from the Highland Falls' library, so I brought that as well, albeit reluctantly. These items I placed in my old leather briefcase, the one given to me by my parents for my sixth birthday, along with a copy of the Oxford English Dictionary.

Eliot and I met in front of Dean Fletcher's office door and he handed me the keys.

"A word of advice, Archer—do *not* forget to water the goddamn orchids," he said. "Probably the biggest responsibility of the job. An insanely thorough list of instructions for their care and nurturing is lying on the desk."

"The orchids will be attended to with great attention," I said.

"Oh, another thing," he said. "Make sure you do everything yourself. Ms. Goldfine is efficient but not terribly reliable."

"I shall tread with caution."

Shaking my hand, he said, "Well, good luck then, Archer."

"Many thanks, Eliot."

He patted me on the back and walked off. Before entering Dean Fletcher's sanctum, I noted that the ancient Anastasia Goldfine was standing over a file cabinet, holding a piece of paper two inches from her eyes. I bid her a good day and she acknowledged my presence with a somewhat condescending smirk.

Unfortunately, I was not sure exactly what it was I was supposed to do as temporary dean, but there was a stack of file folders on the desk so I proceeded to examine them. After a cursory inspection, it appeared that they consisted of memos from members of the English Department, résumés of the students that would be entering Longfellow as freshmen in several months, and personnel files sent down from Human Relations. After I had carefully perused them all, Ms. Goldfine shuffled into the office and removed them from the desk.

"Pardon me, Ms. Goldfine, but what are you doing?" I said.

Her face configured into an expression of confusion. "I'm filing them, of course."

"Filing them where?"

"Oy. Where else?" she said. "In the filing cabinet."

"Yes, I am aware that files are frequently placed in filing cabinets, but should I not first review them?"

"Why?"

"Is that not *my* job?"

She snorted. "What, if I may ask, were you planning to do with them?"

"I really do not know," I said. "Compose replies to the memos?"

With a wave of her bony hand, she said, "Not to worry, Professor, I usually write the memo replies." She pulled one off the top and held it close her eyes. "Take this one, for instance. Professor Moss is complaining about his office air conditioner again."

"And how will you answer said memo?"

"Professor Moss is a *putz*," she said. "Do you know what the word 'putz' means?"

"I believe I do, Ms. Goldfine," I said. "It is a Yiddish term that refers to a useless personage who engages in unproductive activity. It also refers to the male sexual appendage, I believe."

"Close enough," she said. "Professor Moss sends a memo about his air conditioner once a week in the summer. The maintenance guy says there's nothing wrong with it. Professor Moss just doesn't know how to adjust it."

"I see." I recalled Eliot's advice about the danger of entrusting Ms. Goldfine with executive duties and narrowed my eyes. I did not wish to insult her by insisting on dealing with the paperwork myself.

She seemed to have read my mind regarding the needlessness of me performing any actual work. "That Eliot fellow was a very nice man but he didn't trust me," she said. "He wanted to do everything himself. He's also a *schmo*. You don't look like a *schmo* to me. Just relax, eat your lunch, water those *cockamamie* flowers, read a book, take a nice little nap, play Solitaire on the computer, do whatever you want. It's only the summer session, not much to do. I'll take care of everything."

At that, she shuffled out. I did not know how to proceed. Should I ignore Eliot's advice and let Ms. Goldfine perform all my duties or not? After a moment of thought, I decided that I would give her a chance to prove her aptitude. If there were complaints, I would gently inform her that I would take the reins, so to speak.

This left me with nothing to do. After idly leafing through Dean Fletcher's exhaustive four-page list of watering and fertilizing instructions, I rose and inspected the orchids, bidding Esther good day, and then returned to my desk. As it was too early for lunch, I put my feet up and extracted the local library's only copy of Mr. William Octavian Butler's novel from my briefcase.

And so, I occupied Dean Fletcher's dreary office day after day, allowing Ms. Goldfine to perform all my responsibilities, save for the care of the orchids, which appeared to be the only task that she would allow me to fulfill, as she did not wish to. Contrary to Eliot's warning, I found her to be admirably qualified. My only exposure to actual paper involved applying my signature to certain documents, although she offered to forge it on my behalf. Thus far, there had been no complaints, except for the incessant memos from the somewhat technically challenged Professor Moss.

Within two days, I had finished William Octavian Butler's novel and, much to my annoyance, had found it to be most compelling and more than worthy of the complimentary reviews it had received. It was abundantly clear that the man was truly gifted, albeit a trifle wordy with his descriptions, as if he were trying too hard to display his literary agility. The characters sprang to life, the action proceeded at a perfect pace, and his style of writing was both original and highly amusing. More importantly, the book explored its subject with great profundity.

To say that I was envious would be an understatement, for the quality of my own work in the art of fiction was amateurish in comparison to his, yet I was objective enough to set aside jealousy and applaud his achievement, even if it exposed my own literary shortcomings. Although Abigail had assured me that she was not interested in Mr. Butler, I continued to worry that she would take a more romantic interest in him. After all, fiction was her passion and I feared that Mr. Butler's work would, for her, eventually translate into the passion of romance. It did not help that my own efforts as a novelist were sorely lacking, which was more than apparent given her critique of my work. While I was no expert in affairs of the heart, I had learned from certain novels that love was not entirely dependent upon achievement but rather a matter of seemingly inexplicable factors. Could this be true?

Unfortunately, I had not seen Abigail for the past ten days and wondered whether I had offended her in some way. But one morning, to my considerable relief, she entered my office whilst I was in the process of applying my signature to some documents, the subjects of which I did not entirely understand. Ms. Goldfine had merely dropped them on my desk, with the words, "Sign these." At least I appeared to be busy when Abigail strode into the room, and I was glad she had not caught me in the midst of a nap, a habit I had developed following my afternoon repast.

"I have some excellent news!" she said.

A bolt of acid shot through my stomach. "Oh yes?"

She frowned. "I'm not disturbing you am I, Professor? I simply couldn't wait to tell you!"

"Not at all. Do tell me what has caused you to be so overcome with joy."

She clapped her hands. "I've completed my short story!"

My apprehension instantly vanished and I realized that I, too, was grinning. Perhaps her writing had been the reason behind her lack of attention toward me.

"That is indeed excellent news!" I said.

"I've so enjoyed the writing process, Professor!" Her eyes sparkled with happiness. "I've been a hermit, writing during the early morning hours and then staying up all night for the last week to complete it. I have not been able to tear myself away!"

"But now you are satisfied with it?"

"I believe I am," she said. "And I can't wait for you to read it!"

"I look forward to it."

"I hope I'm not being too forward, but I was hoping that we could meet several times in order for you to help me improve it. That is, if you have the time. I know how busy you have been lately."

As she finished speaking, something auspicious occurred to me: perhaps she thought that a series of mentoring sessions would afford her the opportunity to see me more frequently. Yes, I thought jubilantly, that might have been the reason all along!

"I do not think it forward at all," I said. "I'm certain that I can find the time. Perhaps we can convene in the evenings after your duties at Phil's Rib and Steak Emporium. I am available most evenings."

"Perfect!"

"Splendid," I said. "Do you perhaps have the pages with you? It might be helpful if I was able to peruse the manuscript prior to our meeting."

"I have yet to print it out in manuscript format, which I would prefer. I will do so tonight. You may read it when we meet."

"That will do nicely. When do you wish to begin?"

"Are you busy tomorrow evening?" she asked.

I was encouraged by her wish to commence without delay. "I believe I have no plans."

"Then Friday it is!"

"Shall we say about eight o'clock at my apartment?" I said.

"Okay. It should be ready by then. Before I print it, I just need to double check for grammatical or spelling errors."

"Your grammar, as displayed in your homework, has always been quite exemplary," I said. "Impressively so, I might add."

"Why thank you, Professor. I try very hard to achieve perfection in everything I write."

"As do I."

Although I had possessed no ulterior motive when I suggested my domicile as our meeting place, it occurred to me a moment later that this would be the ideal location. I would make some wine available to her and hope that its consumption would lead to a confession. Seduction was not my objective, for I am not the type of fellow to take advantage of a woman. Perhaps I would indulge in a glass or two myself and thereby find the courage to elucidate the depth of affection I felt for her. Yes, this would be the perfect occasion!

She thanked me again quite profusely, bid me farewell, and exited the office, only to reappear five seconds later.

"Oh, I almost forgot," she said. "I have some more news."

"And what might that be?"

"William Octavian Butler, the novelist I spoke of, will be coming to Highland Falls on Saturday afternoon to read passages from his book at the town library! Isn't that exciting?"

In a decidedly flat tone, I said, "Yes, that is indeed most electrifying."

"The librarian, Miss Tuttle, was absolutely beside herself when I told her of it. She believes it will draw quite a crowd."

I attempted a facial expression that I hoped resembled a smile. "If I may ask, where will he be staying?"

She pondered the query. "That hasn't been arranged yet," she said. "The Motel 6 is certainly not appropriate for a man of his stature so I suppose—"

"He may stay at my apartment," I said. "It is no palace but I have two bedrooms and sufficient towels."

Abigail broke into a smile. "Really?"

"Of course."

"It seems like an imposition."

"I'm happy to oblige."

"That's so generous of you, Professor," she said.

"Then it is done!" I said. "If I may ask, how long will he be staying in our fair town?"

"The reading will be on Saturday afternoon, just after he arrives, and I believe he said he would depart later that day, for he has another event to attend. I can't thank you enough."

I tilted my head in a bow. "I live to fill your days with joy."

Perhaps she thought this a witticism, for she laughed softly. It had not been intended as such. "I will leave you to your labors now, Professor," she said, and before I was able to inform her that my duties required very little in the way of actual labor, she had vanished.

Ten

Several hours prior to Abigail's scheduled appearance at my apartment on Friday evening, I visited the supermarket and purchased a bottle of affordable Pinot, a scented candle, and an array of hors d'oeuvres that I hoped she would enjoy—a triangle of Brie, a box of crackers, a jar of Greek olives, an onion dip, miniature carrots, cornichons, and a giant bag of Cheetos. As I was about to pay for these items, it occurred to me that I did not possess a single wineglass, so rather than subject her to ingesting wine via a plastic cup or chipped tumbler, I scurried off to the wine section and found a package of four, which were on sale for $4.95. I also realized that I lacked a corkscrew and chose one of those as well.

Just then, I felt a hand tickle the back of my neck. "Hello, Ishmael," Constance said as I turned.

"Heigh-ho, Constance!" I said, quite delighted to see her.

We then embraced, as was our custom. A shopping basket, laden with an assortment of victuals, was parked on the floor beside her. I then noted that she was surveying the contents of my cart with great curiosity.

"If I were to guess, it would seem that you're having a party, Ishmael."

"I would not call it a party per se as there is but one bottle," I said. "Tonight I will be commencing a mentoring session with the young woman I spoke about when last we encountered each other. You might remember her?"

"Of course," she said. "Abigail Bird."

"Quite correct."

Constance smiled. "I've been meaning to tell you, I met the young woman just this morning."

Stunned by this bizarre news, my visage registered confusion and

110

I concluded that she was playing a trick on me. "Surely you jest, Constance."

"Nope. I'm completely serious."

"And how, may I inquire, did this encounter come about?"

"Well," Constance said, "it was quite by accident, of course. We happened to be standing in line together at the bank. I found myself staring at her. She looked familiar and at first I thought she was one of my students."

"Continue."

"We struck up a conversation and I suddenly realized that she was your Abigail," Constance said. "I recalled the photograph you'd shown me."

"How utterly amazing!"

"Not really," Constance said. "It's a small town."

"True."

"She's quite charming, as you told me, although a bit shy," Constance said. "Yet, I must say, we got along famously."

"What did you speak of?"

"The annoying existence of long lines at banks and random chit chat of a similar nature."

"Did you happen to mention that you knew me?"

"Of course not. That would have been a little odd, don't you think?"

"Yes, I suppose it would have been a trifle suspect."

"But when she confessed that she barely had any friends in town, I suggested that we meet for coffee one day."

"When?"

"We haven't decided that yet," she said. "We exchanged phone numbers. I will call her next week."

"Well," I said, "this is certainly a most interesting turn of events!"

"Yes."

I glanced at my watch. "I do not wish to be rude, Constance, but I am afraid I must depart. The hour of my consultation with Ms. Bird approaches and there is much to be done."

"I won't keep you," she said. "Good luck."

"Many thanks, Constance. We shall see one another anon."

Moments later, on my way out of the supermarket, I passed through an area of the store that displayed bouquets and potted floral arrangements. On an impulse, I stopped to inspect several of these horticultural items and, after a moment of contemplation, decided that presenting Abigail with a bouquet of roses would be an excellent way in which to begin the evening's proceedings as they symbolized romantic intentions. Thus, I purchased one dozen red roses and asked the attendant to wrap them in colorful tissue paper. As I watched this procedure, I silently applauded my ingenuity.

Upon returning to my apartment with my sack of groceries, wineglasses, and flowers, I began the process of making the place presentable. I removed the debris from my coffee table and vacuumed the floor, although the receptacle bag of said vacuum device, purchased at the thrift store, bore a minute puncture and thus nearly exhaled as much dust as it inhaled. I then commenced to spray the glass with a remarkable product known as Windex that the prior resident had left behind, flung my bathroom towels into a hamper, replaced them with fresh ones, and straightened up the kitchen.

Following this, I brought a table and chairs into the parlor and set them in a dark corner. After placing a tablecloth on said table, I decided to put the candle in the middle of it, although I possessed no candelabra or any other means of displaying the taper. Should I glue or tape it in an upright position to the table or place it in a drinking glass?

In the end, I decided to forego the candle. After all, I had no idea why I required such an item for there was sufficient illumination to be had from the overhead lights.

Then it occurred to me that a more potentially romantic arrangement for our discussion of her story would be for us to sit side by side on the couch rather than at a table, so I moved everything back to the kitchen. The top of the coffee table would suffice as a surface on which to place materials. Finally, I filled my kitchen sink with two inches of water, into which I placed only the stems of the roses, as I did not possess a vase.

At six forty-five, I shed myself of my clothing and stepped into the shower. At seven o'clock I exited said shower, applied a generous lathering of deodorant, combed my hair, glanced critically at the mirror's image of my physiognomy, and made a journey to my closet. After surveying my choices, I decided on a striped, button-down shirt, a pair of beige pants, and brown loafers.

At seven-thirty, I reentered the kitchen and arranged the hors d'oeuvres on a large plate, which I brought into the parlor and placed in the center of the coffee table beside the bottle of Pinot, two of my recently purchased wineglasses, and the corkscrew. For a moment, I was indecisive about exactly where to position the throw pillows but eventually I placed each one at the corners of the sofa. The correct placement of throw pillows has always been a challenge for me.

Once I had completed my preparations, I placed myself on a chair by one of the front windows and awaited Abigail's arrival. I knew from experience that she would appear at precisely eight o'clock. At seven fifty-five, I peered between the slats of my ancient Venetian blinds and waited, hoping to espy her car when she parked it at the curb.

☙

But Abigail did not arrive at eight o'clock. Nor did she appear at one minute after eight or eight-fifteen or eight-thirty. At first, I thought that I had mistaken the date, but after consulting my calendar, I determined that I had not. Perhaps she had been unpredictably detained and had attempted unsuccessfully to telephone me. Reception in certain areas of Highland Falls was frequently inadequate, especially in some of the more remote locations, so I postulated that she might have experienced a vehicle breakdown in such an area. At precisely eight-thirty-five, having recently charged my cell phone, I called her but received no answer other than an invitation in her lovely lilting voice to leave a voicemail, which I did. I knew however that, like me, she often failed to charge hers. Two hours passed with no communication from her.

Could she have forgotten about our appointment? This was unlike her, but people occasionally suffer from lapses of memory, as have I on more than one occasion. Moreover, she had been anticipating our session with considerable eagerness and had never missed a writing class or any other assignation.

By eleven o'clock, my displeasure at her tardiness soon developed into disappointment at her absence and was then transformed into anxiety over her well-being. Not knowing what else to do, I called Constance who had apparently been asleep when her phone chimed, for her voice was muffled and hoarse as if interrupted from slumber.

"Who the hell is this?" she asked.

"It is Ishmael Archer," I said. "And there is no need for vile language."

"For God's sake, Ishmael," she said. I could not help but perceive a distinct note of displeasure in her tone. "I was sound asleep."

"So I gather from the irate tone of your voice."

"I hope this is an emergency."

"I believe it is," I said. "You see, Abigail was supposed to arrive at my apartment for our mentoring session at precisely eight o'clock and she has yet to make an appearance."

"*That's* why you called? Jesus Christ, Ishmael. Maybe she just forgot."

"Doubtful, for Abigail is a most responsible and punctual woman. And please do not invoke the name of the Christian savior when addressing me."

"I'm sure she has a good excuse," she said. "May I go back to sleep now please?"

I ignored her request. "I am quite worried that something sinister has befallen her."

"Sinister? In Highland Falls? I doubt it. But why are you calling *me?*"

"Because I do not know who else to call or what I should do," I said. "Perhaps it would be wise to notify the local constabulary."

"I think they usually require forty-eight hours before acting on the information. Do it tomorrow if she hasn't shown up."

"But perhaps she has suffered a burglary or a mugging," I said. "There are a thousand possibilities. The mind boggles, so to speak. In any case, it is my considered opinion that we should perhaps repair to her apartment at once and see for ourselves."

"*We?*"

"Are you not an aficionado of Mr. Sherlock Holmes and his friend Mr. Watson as you once informed me?"

"Yes, but as a reader not as an aspiring detective," she said. "Besides, I am not breaking into her apartment."

"No need. Abigail does not lock her front door."

"How do you know?"

"I once observed it."

"I'm going back to sleep," Constance said. "Goodnight, Ishmael."

"I shall pick you up posthaste and we shall hie via my vehicle to her dwelling," I said.

"Absolutely not. I—"

Twenty minutes later, after a cursory search of Abigail's apartment, yours truly, Sherlock Holmes, and his trusty sidekick Watson, in the guise of Constance Oswald, did not find her. More worrisome was the fact that Abigail's car was not parked in her driveway.

Although Constance wished to return to her bed following our inspection of Abigail's abode, I beseeched her to accompany me to the police station to report Abigail's disappearance. At first she refused but after much groveling, I managed to persuade her, although she was decidedly ill-tempered on our drive to the head-quarters of the local police.

When we arrived, Sheriff Walter Grimsby's feet were propped upon his cluttered desk and his attention was directed to a television set that was attached to a corner wall. He was watching a police show. His fingers were orange, and crumbs of an identical color had created an asymmetrical pattern on the part of his light brown shirt that covered his sizeable abdomen. The explanation for this was a half empty bag of Cheese Puffs that lay between his legs. He was munching on one of these flavorsome snacks when we approached his desk. I have always been a devotee of cheese snacks so I felt an immediate rapport with him.

Sheriff Grimsby then inquired as to the purpose of our visit and I informed him that Abigail was missing. Years ago, he had stopped me on Route 11 for driving at night with an unlit taillight but I doubted that he recognized me.

Sheriff Grimsby did not move from his position. "How old is she?" he said. "Is she a kid?"

"She's twenty-four."

"Okay," the sheriff said. "That's good. I'm glad it's not a kid. And how long has she been missing?"

"We do not know for certain," I said. "I last encountered her at approximately two o'clock yesterday afternoon in my office on the campus of Longfellow College, where I presently am employed as a professor of English literature and acting dean. We had then scheduled an appointment to meet again this evening at eight o'clock, but she did not appear."

"Professor of literature, huh? Read any Grisham?"

"I'm afraid not."

"I highly recommend him."

"I shall look into it."

"You won't regret it."

Constance sighed and then yawned. This was clearly not an occasion for a discussion of popular literature.

Sheriff Grimsby asked, "Are either of you next of kin?"

Constance looked at me questioningly. I wondered whether this information would in some way be a requirement in his pursuit of the case. Grimsby looked impatiently at both of us.

"Well?" he said. "This isn't a trick question."

116

"I am...her uncle," I said with a stammer. "And this is her... mother."

Constance gave me a look that displayed extreme disapproval.

The sheriff then scratched his head, which had but a few strands of wispy hair pointlessly arranged to cover a wide terrain of baldness. "Technically, we don't usually look for missing persons for forty-eight hours. You probably know that from watching cop shows on TV. But I got nothing better to do right now so I can take down the info."

He then proceeded to ask us a number of predictable questions. I produced the photos I had taken of Abigail and followed this with information concerning the make, color, and approximate age of her automobile.

"Is there a husband, ex-husband, or boyfriend?" he asked. After I said no to all of those queries, neglecting to mention William Octavian Butler, he asked whether Abigail had committed any crimes, consumed alcohol heavily, or utilized illegal drugs.

"Certainly not," I said.

"I'm not accusing her," Grimsby said. "I just gotta ask. Regulations."

Following ten minutes of further interrogation, Sheriff Grimsby informed us that he would alert the highway patrol and instruct them to be on the lookout for Abigail's car. Then he asked us for our addresses and telephone numbers and promised to contact us should there be any result. We bid him adieu.

Five minutes later, as we walked through the parking lot, Constance said, "Dammit, Ishmael, I can't believe you told him I'm her mother! What possessed you?"

"My apologies. I'm afraid it just spilled out of me, so to speak. I gave it no forethought."

Constance gazed at me and gave forth a sound that bore a close resemblance to a growl.

❧

When I maneuvered my vehicle into my driveway after taking Constance home, I noticed a somewhat portly gentleman whom I could not identify, sitting on the front stoop of the building, smoking a cigarette. Though it was dark, I was able to discern that a duffel bag, packed full like a sausage, lay beside him and that a fedora graced his skull. Fearing that he might be a burglar or some other species of interloper waiting for entry to the building, I quietly opened the trunk of my rental car and extracted a tire iron, although I knew I would not use it for I am not a man given to violence. It was merely a scare tactic. When he saw me approaching with this makeshift weapon, he casually flicked his cigarette butt into the street, missing my head by about ten inches.

With some jocularity, he asked, "Are you planning to use that thing as a weapon? Or do you have a car inside the house that needs a tire removal?"

The Southern accent first hinted at his identity, which was confirmed when I drew close enough to observe his facial features.

"Mr. Butler?" I asked.

"Bill," he said. "Or William. Up to you."

"I am—"

"Ishmael Archer."

"A pleasure," I said, extending my hand.

"Likewise."

I was now confused. "Today is Friday."

"I know."

"I believe you were not scheduled to arrive in Highland Falls until tomorrow, which is Saturday."

"Yes," he said. "Saturday does usually follow Friday."

"Indeed it does, although not on the Mayan calendar."

"I decided to come today so I could spend a little more time with Abby," he said. "I called her this morning and left a voicemail and a text."

"I see." I realized then with some dismay that his earlier arrival would have coincided with my mentoring session with Abigail and would have thus spoiled my plans had they been fulfilled. "How odd that she did not inform me of this new development."

"Last minute decision," he said. "Somebody didn't show up for the flight. I got lucky." He then rose and grabbed the handle of his duffel. "Listen, do you mind if we go upstairs? I really have to take a piss."

"Certainly," I said. "How terribly rude of me."

At that, I unlocked the front door and he followed me up the stairs to my apartment. When I pointed in the direction of the bathroom, he made a beeline for it. As he did not bother to close the bathroom door, I was able to hear the familiar sound of a stream of urine making contact with the toilet water, followed by the sound of a rising zipper and then the flush. To my disgust, he did not wash his hands but merely returned to the parlor. There was a certain swagger about him that I found somewhat annoying.

After he flopped onto my couch, he asked, "Where the hell is Abby? I texted her when I got to Syracuse. Said I was arriving this evening but she never texted back. I waited at the airport for two hours. She never showed up. Lucky for me, I caught a ride with a young couple from Highland Falls who took pity on me. Nice people except for their screaming baby."

"Abigail seems to have gone missing I'm afraid," I said. "I just returned from the police station. It is quite worrisome."

He sat straight up. "Jesus! For how long?"

"I am not certain," I said. "Since this afternoon I would guess."

"Oh." His countenance registered relief. "That's not too long. You scared the shit out of me for a minute there, Ishmael."

"Most people just call me Archer," I said.

"Archer it is." Then, perhaps noting the grim expression on my face, he asked, "Why are you so worried about her?"

"We had an assignation of some significance at eight o'clock this evening. She did not appear for that either and she is impeccably punctual. Moreover, she has not responded to any of my voicemails or texts either."

He narrowed his eyes at me in a manner that implied suspicion. "What sort of assignation?"

"It just so happens that I am mentoring her," I said. "At her request of course."

"Hmm. You're *mentoring* her, are you?" he said. "Uh-huh. I see."

I got the distinct impression from his tone that he had interpreted the word *mentoring* as having an implication far less innocent than its actual definition.

"By the way," I said. "I very much enjoyed your novel. It is indeed quite an impressive achievement. Congratulations on the reviews."

"Thanks." He then yawned expansively. "Listen, I'm kind of beat, Archer. Haven't slept in a couple of days. I've had so many interviews and events to attend. You mind pointing the way to your guest room? Maybe we can discuss all this tomorrow."

We both stood up simultaneously. "Right this way," I said. I led him down the hallway. "Make yourself comfortable. There are clean sheets and towels. Help yourself to anything that resides in the kitchen."

"Got it." He stepped into the room, surveying it. "Thanks, Archer. I appreciate the hospitality. Good night and pleasant dreams."

"To you as well," I said. Before I could utter another word, he yawned again, this time even more expansively, and closed the door. Shortly thereafter, I retired, but I did not sleep a wink. I was too worried about Abigail.

෪

The following morning, I was aroused by loud clattering sounds emanating from the kitchen, so I removed my sleeping mask, rose, and threw on a bathrobe to investigate. William Octavian Butler, who was clad in a pair of faded shorts, flip-flops, and a wrinkled T-shirt that barely covered his belly, had brewed a pot of coffee and was presently opening and closing cabinets.

"Good morning to you, Archer," he said. His hair was an asymmetrical tangle. "Where the hell do you keep the coffee mugs, in a wall safe?"

"Third cabinet beside the dishwasher which, incidentally, does not function."

He then located a mug and poured some java, whereupon he meandered toward the refrigerator, yanked open the door, found a carton of milk, and poured some into the black liquid.

"Got any sugar?"

"Yes." I opened a drawer and pulled out several packages, which I placed on the counter beside the milk. He tore one open and unloaded its contents into his coffee.

"I have orange juice if you're interested," I said.

"No, but a shot of whiskey in this coffee might hit the spot."

I raised an eyebrow. "You wish to consume whiskey at eight o'clock in the morning?" Was he emulating the hard-drinking tendencies of Hemingway or Fitzgerald? "I do not stock hard liquor," I said. "My apologies."

"No problem. I can live without it."

Armed with our coffees, we repaired to the parlor and sat down across from each other.

He lifted his mug to his lips. "Do you think they've found Abby?" he asked.

"Sadly, I do not believe so, for I assume they would have contacted either my friend or me."

"Mind if I smoke in here?"

He leaned forward to extract a package of Lucky Strike cigarettes from the back pocket of his shorts.

"To be honest, I would prefer you did not. It causes the furniture to absorb the noxious smell, but you may venture out to the fire escape if you wish."

I pointed to the window. Butler then strode across the room, opened the window and crawled through. While I watched him ignite his cigarette, the phone chimed.

"Dammit, Ishmael, the sheriff just called me," Constance said. Her tone was that of a person who wishes to strangle someone. "He woke me up."

"I am sorry, Constance," I said. "Clearly, it wasn't such a wise idea for me to prevaricate regarding your relationship to Abigail."

"No kidding."

"Well, I fear it is too late to disabuse him now. You must continue the charade. What precisely did he say?"

"They haven't found her yet. No sign of her car either."

"This is most upsetting," I said.

"They want us to meet them at Abigail's apartment in thirty minutes," she said. "As her...*ahem*...mother, they will of course expect me to attend. Can you get there by then?"

Having concluded our conversation, I rose to commence my customary ablutions in the bathroom, whereupon Butler climbed back into the room. "Any news?" he asked.

"I am to meet the police at Abigail's apartment in thirty minutes," I said. "Perhaps we can chat later."

"Okay." He then collapsed on the couch, but a second later, sat upright. "Hey, maybe I should come with you?"

"That will not be necessary. The sheriff requested that only I appear. I trust you will find something with which to occupy yourself while I am gone."

"Sure. I brought my laptop. Got some writing to do. By the way, where's the goddamn library? I'm supposed to give a reading there later. Abby talked me into it."

"Five blocks away," I said. Thereupon, I gave him precise directions, handed him a spare key to my domicile, and left the room.

Present at Abigail's apartment were Constance, Grimsby, and the latter's deputy, a young man of about thirty who happened to be the sheriff's progeny and was named Walter Grimsby Junior, although Grimsby referred to him simply as Junior, most likely to avoid confusion. Junior's cheeks sported sideburns commonly known as muttonchops, a peculiar name that would imply a British form of ovine-derived edible. His were somewhat asymmetrical.

The sheriff sat down with his notebook whilst Junior made a cursory search of the premises, an act that involved opening and

122

closing drawers, gazing behind doors, and inspecting the space beneath Abigail's bed.

"Have a seat, Professor," Grimsby said in an amiable tone. I kissed Constance on the cheek and sat beside her. "I just have a few questions. Shouldn't last long."

"Fire away, as they say," I said.

Grimsby opened his notebook. "I understand that Ms. Bird is a student of yours," he said.

"Correction, she *was*," I said. "But she is no longer. And in point of fact, she was merely auditing the class so she was not enrolled in the college."

"I see," he said. "So you were her teacher. And you're also her uncle."

"Yes," I said, stealing a furtive glance at Constance. "One can be both."

"Did you socialize?"

"Of course. On several occasions."

"And where did you go on these occasions?"

I sighed. What was the point of this insipid conversation? Did the man have some preposterous notion that *I* had assassinated Abigail?

"We partook of luncheon in the school cafeteria once; we attended a ghastly art fair in the town, and we engaged in a picnic near the waterfall."

This monologue caused him to furrow his eyebrows. "What do you mean by *ghastly* art fair?"

I had no idea how this particular query pertained to his investigation, but I replied nonetheless. "Well, the art was beyond horrendous," I said with a laugh. "All those infantile renderings of that ridiculous waterfall."

The sheriff gave me a hard look. "For your information, Professor, my daughter, Tilly, exhibited a bunch of her paintings of the Falls at the art fair."

I proffered a weak smile. "I'm sure hers were the exceptions. I did not see everything. Just a few examples."

Grimsby squinted at me. "Tell me about this picnic of yours."

"I do not see how any of this pertains," I said.

"Humor me."

"There is nothing much to tell. We hiked through a forest to a glade that she frequented. We consumed lunch, which consisted of some delicious sandwiches and other morsels that she had prepared. Would you care to hear the details of the menu?"

"Not particularly. Please continue."

"Following the ingestion of said repast, Abigail sunbathed while I offered her some interesting information pertaining to the relationships between several characters in *Wuthering Heights* by Ms. Emily Brontë. Have you perhaps read it, Sheriff Grimsby?"

"Maybe in high school, I don't remember." His voice sounded a trifle irritable. "Go on. What else happened at this glade near the Falls?"

I attempted to think back upon that day's activities. "Oh yes. Abigail performed some aerobic exercises—deep knee bends, jumping jacks, and so forth."

"And then?"

"And then she decided to climb a staircase of rocks beside the Falls. It appeared somewhat perilous to me so I attempted to dissuade her from undertaking this venture, but she would not hear of it, informing me that she had performed this vertical journey without incident many times before after her jogging expeditions and found it most enjoyable. In particular, she appreciated the glorious view it afforded of the valley."

Sheriff Grimsby was now staring at me for reasons that I did not comprehend. As Constance and I sat there, he proceeded to remove from his belt a communications contraption known as a walkie-talkie. Static erupted when he switched it on. When the noise abated, he spoke into it; to whom he spoke, I did not know.

&

Our search party consisted of Sheriff Grimsby, his son Junior, Constance, and yours truly. We did not see Abigail's car parked off the highway, which I interpreted as a bad omen but I speculated that Abigail might have jogged to the area as she often did and stationed her vehicle elsewhere.

Naturally, as I was the only one in the group who had made this journey through the forest on a prior occasion, I was chosen to lead the way. After a number of wrong turns, one of which took us back to the highway, I somehow managed to escort our little ensemble to the area in question. It was there that we immediately beheld a horrifying sight that caused Constance and me to gasp in unison—Abigail lay seemingly unconscious at the foot of the rock wall. A trickle of blood, now dried, had meandered down her forehead.

Struck by the fear that Abigail had succumbed, my first instinct was to run toward her but the sheriff physically restrained me.

"You two stay put until I've had a chance to look things over." His voice had a firm quality. "That's an order."

I struggled to get free. "We must go to her posthaste! Kindly step away, Sheriff! Time is of the essence! We must determine whether she is still alive!"

"I'll do that," he said. "I need to examine the scene first."

"Why?" I said. "Kindly let me go!"

"This could be a crime scene, Professor." At that, Grimsby turned his head toward his deputy. "Junior, get your ass over there and help me out for Christ's sake."

"A crime scene?" I said in a mocking tone. "Poppycock. Stuff and nonsense. It's quite obvious that she fell!"

Grimsby was growing impatient. "You can take a few steps closer but don't step into the surrounding area. There might be evidence. Now please, do what I say so I can see if she's alive."

Leaving Junior to guard us, Grimsby walked gingerly toward Abigail, squatted beside her, and placed two fingers on the side of her neck.

PART THREE

Eleven

Fortunately, the Highland Falls Medical Center was reputed to be the most distinguished medical facility in the county. Why a hospital of such lofty status was situated in a town of such insignificance was a mystery to me, although on this particular day, I was grateful for its proximity.

Constance and I had been transported there in the backseat of Grimsby's police car as it sped, sirens loudly wailing, behind the ambulance. Later, she and I placed our buttocks into uncomfortable molded plastic seats in the hospital's unpopulated waiting area as Abigail was wheeled into a room to undergo various tests.

"I have a class in two hours," Constance said.

"As they believe you to be her mother, I think it might appear suspicious if you were to depart," I said. "But I suppose I can, as they say, hold the fortress if you must be off."

"I'll stay for a while," she said. "My presence may calm you."

"Thank you, Constance. I am most appreciative. You are an excellent friend, and I shall not forget this act of kindness."

As neither Constance nor I had partaken of nourishment for many hours, I inserted several coins into a nearby vending machine and purchased some edibles and two paper cups of barely potable coffee, whereupon Sheriff Grimsby appeared before me.

"Mind if I ask you a few questions, Professor?" he said.

"Whatever for? Do you by chance consider me a suspect? I am her uncle."

"Standard procedure, Professor."

I sighed and allowed him, albeit reluctantly, to make his inquiries, which consisted primarily of questions regarding my whereabouts on

Friday. He prefaced his remarks by informing me that his forensics department had already postulated that the accident had occurred early Friday afternoon.

Grimsby seemed impatient. "Please begin."

"Well, I commenced the day in my apartment, where I awoke from my slumber at precisely seven-thirty, as is my custom. After removing my sleeping mask and attiring myself in a bathrobe, I entered my kitchen where I concocted a modest breakfast that consisted of a bowl of Kellogg's cornflakes—"

"Maybe not so much detail," Grimsby said. "Then what?"

"I motored to my office, or rather Dean Fletcher's office, at eight-thirty and remained there until five o'clock, after which I drove my vehicle to the grocery store. Following this adventure, I returned to my abode at six-thirty and proceeded to organize my apartment in anticipation of Abigail's arrival."

"Can any witnesses account for your whereabouts?"

"Yes," I said. "When I departed from my apartment that morning, my landlord, Mr. Felix Eugenides, bid me good morning. I stopped for gasoline at the Chevron station on Route 11. Then I proceeded to my office, as Ms. Anastasia Goldfine can verify."

"Go on."

"Must I?"

"Please."

After another dramatic exhalation, I continued. "Then, as I stated earlier, I motored to the supermarket where I conducted a brief conversation with Abigail's…um…mother as we spotted each other quite by happenstance. When I arrived home, I saw Mr. Eugenides and we greeted each other again. You know the rest, Sheriff. Constance and I proceeded to your office where we found you watching TV and consuming a snack food from a plastic bag."

I considered mentioning my initial encounter with William Octavian Butler on my doorstep Friday night but decided it would be irrelevant, as the accident had occurred during the day.

Evidently satisfied with my testimony, Grimsby closed his notebook and placed his pen in his shirt pocket. "Okay, you're good to go, Professor. Thanks for your time."

"Perhaps we can do this again sometime after you chance upon criminal activity in which I was not the culprit."

"I don't make up the rules, Professor."

But I had more pressing questions. "Have you heard anything from the doctors yet? Will she be all right? Is she conscious?"

"I haven't heard anything yet," he said. "I'm guessing it's just a minor concussion. I've seen that before."

"That would be a profound relief," I said.

Following Sheriff Grimsby's departure, I rejoined Constance. An hour passed. The longer we sat there, the more agitated I became. I was compelled to pace the room several times, partly out of anxiety and partly because the plastic chairs upon which we sat had a painful effect upon my buttocks.

Constance glanced at her timepiece from time to time. "I'm sorry but I have to go, Ishmael." At that, she rose to her feet.

"I know," I said. "This is not really your concern."

"Don't get me wrong, Ishmael—I am truly sorry about what happened to Abigail. And, as your close friend, I feel terrible that you must go through this. I will be here to offer you moral support."

"Most kind of you, Constance," I said. "Will you be able to return later?"

"I don't know. I'm a bit busy today. Two lectures and a student conference, but if I have time, yes."

A few moments after Constance had departed, a physician sporting a white lab coat materialized through the sliding doors and approached me. He was a gentleman of about forty, and I immediately noticed that his appearance was not unlike that of Edgar Allen Poe, although his expression did not feature the author's characteristic grimness, and he lacked a mustache. He introduced himself as Dr. Martin Van Buren and took a seat across from me.

"I thought her mother was here," he said.

"I'm afraid she was compelled to depart for a short time," I said. "You may inform me, as I am her uncle."

Thereupon, he explained that Abigail, apart from having sustained a fracture to her patella—or, in layperson's terminology, her kneecap—was presently in a coma due to a blood clot, the result of a traumatic brain injury. He assured me that there was no cause for alarm and that a simple operation, to be performed the following morning, would most likely relieve the pressure on her brain. Dr. Van Buren then told me that the procedure would require several hours, whereupon he bid me farewell and disappeared behind the sliding doors.

Half an hour later, I decided that I required some fresh air, so I departed the waiting lounge and paced in the parking lot for several minutes. When I returned I was surprised to find William Octavian Butler occupying my seat. He was tapping the keys of his laptop computer. I noted immediately that he wore a bow tie, one that was not dissimilar to the types I frequently sported, and a blazer made of a fabric known as seersucker, an ensemble that caused him to resemble an old-time Southern attorney. I was particularly struck by the bow tie. *Hmm.*

"I came as soon as I heard," he said.

"Greetings," I said in a monotone. "How did you hear about it?"

"I called the police station. How is she? What happened?"

I lowered myself into the chair beside his and offered him an abridged version of the day's activities, ending with the words, "Fortunately, the prognosis is good."

"My God, that's a relief," he said. "I'd like to be here when she wakes up, but regrettably I must catch a plane in two hours."

"If I may ask, how did you get here? It's five miles from my apartment."

"I stole a bike," he said. I found his tone of voice to be distressingly casual.

I was outraged. "You stole a bike! There are taxis. Well, one taxi anyway. You did not have to resort to criminality."

"I didn't want to wait for a cab. It was an emergency. I wanted to be here. Besides, where's your sense of adventure, man?"

"More than a few rungs below my sense of decency on the ladder of morality, if you'll pardon the poor analogy."

"Actually, it's not a bad analogy," he said with a low chuckle. But he must have noted that my face did not display amusement. "Don't worry, Archer, I plan to return it."

This was something of a relief but did not, in my mind, absolve him of his misconduct. I imagined the poor soul who owned the bicycle, possibly a student, reacting with shock at its absence. As we waited, William Octavian Butler gradually grew impatient. Finally, he stood up and grabbed his duffel.

"I must be off," he said. "I'll return as soon as I can. Please call me if there is any news."

I nodded.

"Archer, would you mind taking me to the bus station?"

"I am afraid I cannot. I was transported to the hospital by the police and my vehicle is currently stationed at my friend Constance's apartment."

"No problem. I'll call for the taxi." At that, he handed me my apartment keys, removed his cell phone from his pocket, and made the call.

At this juncture, I realized of a sudden that Abigail's true next of kin, namely her father, had not been alerted to his daughter's traumatic accident. In all the brouhaha, it had simply escaped my perception, but I felt it incumbent upon me to notify him as soon as possible. Unfortunately, I was unaware of either his first name or his whereabouts. No doubt this information was contained in Abigail's cell phone but this device was in the possession of the police department and considered to be evidence. Lest I arouse suspicion—after all, I was supposed to be Abigail's uncle—I concluded that it would not be prudent for me to ask Sheriff Grimsby if I might examine it.

That night, I drove to Abigail's dwelling and parked my vehicle several blocks away so as not to appear suspicious. As good fortune would have it, her apartment door remained unlocked, for the sheriff did not own a key, and I suspected the authorities were no longer interested in searching the place for clues as they had already done so. Stealthily, I entered and commenced to search for something that would yield the information I required.

Fifteen minutes passed before I discovered a bureau drawer that contained several birthday cards that had been addressed to Abigail, all of them in the same handwriting. One of these had been placed back into its envelope, and said enclosure yielded the information I had been searching for, namely the return address: "Dr. Balthazar J. Bird, St. Mary's Medical Center, Newburgh, NY."

After returning to my abode, I easily located St. Mary's phone number on my search engine and placed the call, informing the operator that it was of some urgency. I was then connected to a receptionist who stated that Dr. Bird was in the midst of performing a heart transplant, and that he would not be able to return my call for several hours.

It was not until nightfall that Dr. Bird rang. Predictably, he was quite beside himself when I informed him of his daughter's condition. He then asked me a great many questions, only some of which I was able to adequately answer, for my knowledge regarding her injury was limited.

"She is sleeping now," I said. "They plan to operate tomorrow."

As the distance between Syracuse and Newburgh was but three hours via automobile and one hour via aircraft, he promised that he would travel to our small town as soon as his schedule would allow him to depart. Apparently, he was required to perform several serious procedures early the following morning. As he wished to make an appearance at Abigail's bedside as soon as possible, he would attempt to find another doctor to substitute for him but warned me that such an endeavor might prove fruitless, as the surgical schedule was quite full of patients who required immediate surgery and the hospital only employed three heart surgeons. He then inquired regarding my precise relationship to Abigail. I simply told him I was a close friend.

"However, I must warn you of one slight dilemma, Dr. Bird," I said. "You see, the police and hospital officials required information regarding Abigail from next of kin. Thus, I felt compelled to prevaricate on this issue. The authorities currently believe that I am Abigail's uncle and that a female friend of mine named Constance is her mother."

I was relieved by his reply. "I thank you for doing that, Professor Archer," he said. "When I arrive, I'll be happy to verify that information if the local police and hospital officials should ask. I don't want you or this woman named Constance to get into any trouble. Thank you again for your help."

"My pleasure."

"I will see you tomorrow afternoon if I can get away."

Constance and I were present in Abigail's hospital room when a nurse ushered Dr. Bird in the following evening. Before acknowledging our presence, he dashed to Abigail's bedside, took her hand and kissed her cheek. When he turned to us, I saw that his eyes were filled with worry.

"Dr. Bird, I presume?" I said.

"How rude of me," he said. "You must be Professor Archer."

"I am indeed. And this is Constance Oswald, Abigail's fictitious mother. I believe I mentioned that."

We all shook hands. "I suppose that makes you my wife, Ms. Oswald, and you either my brother or brother-in-law, Professor Archer."

"Call me Ishmael," I said with a glance at Constance, who smirked.

"Constance," Constance said.

"Balthazar," he said. "And by the way, thank you both for taking such good care of my princess. She's all I have in the world."

"Of course," I said. "I only wish that I had been able to contact you earlier. It was irresponsible of me."

134

"Nonsense, Professor. I'm sure you were distracted by events. At least I am here now. Fortunately, I was able reschedule a minor surgery."

I smiled at him. He was a gentleman of medium height, perhaps in his late fifties, and possessed of a neatly groomed beard and mustache as well as a prominent chin, although his forest green blazer, yellow trousers, and ascot made him look as if he had just attended a Nantucket yacht club event. If one looked closely, one could detect a slight resemblance to Abigail in the structure of his face and the kindness in his eyes. He seemed an amiable fellow by disposition, and it occurred to me that had I been in need of cardiac surgery, I would find him trustworthy and most likely quite capable.

"Where will you be residing, Balthazar?" I asked him.

"I've booked a room at the Hilton in Syracuse and rented a car," he said. "I understand there is a motel in town but it has a one-star rating."

"That much?" I said, somewhat awestruck that a reviewer would summon that much magnanimity. I was tempted to ask the good doctor if he wished to reside temporarily at my apartment but thought better of it and refrained. After all, a man of Dr. Bird's stature and wealth would likely find my dreary abode, with its lumpy single bed and lack of laundry appliances, quite unsatisfactory. Moreover, I was not certain I could endure playing the role of host for an indefinite length of time.

Balthazar approached Abigail again. He glanced at the heart monitor, examined the contents of her IV bag, took her pulse, and then moved to the foot of the bed where her chart was located. After studying its pages for several moments, he placed it back in its slot.

"If you two don't mind, I think I'll see if I can find Dr. Van Buren," he said, heading for the door. "Time for a doctor-to-doctor consultation."

"By all means," I told him. "We will see you again shortly."

He nodded and slipped out the door.

Twelve

Four days later Balthazar was compelled to return to Newburgh. He was most distressed at having to leave his daughter's bedside, but I assured him that, should there be any new developments, I would alert him immediately.

Unfortunately, nothing of import changed regarding Abigail's condition. She remained in a coma following the completion of another minor surgical procedure during which Dr. Bird was present, and Dr. Van Buren was at a loss regarding the possible duration of said coma, although he postulated that it would probably not continue for more than a week or two in spite of her low score on the Glasgow Coma Scale. Sadly, this optimistic prognostication proved inaccurate. Abigail stirred from time to time, but she did not regain consciousness.

Of course, I was present at Abigail's bedside nearly every day, usually in the early evenings and on weekends. Constance, who was also concerned, joined me on several occasions, a gesture that greatly touched me. The vague prognoses offered by Abigail's neurologists had left me in a state of despair, tempered by the hope that one day she would magically awaken.

Dr. Bird made regular appearances at the hospital and on one such occasion, I questioned him regarding Abigail's condition and what developments might be expected. He was not a neurologist, of course, but he had studied the subject in medical school and had conferred with Dr. Van Buren a number of times.

"I'm afraid the prognosis is unpredictable, Professor," Balthazar said. "It's my understanding that people who suffer traumatic brain injuries that result in a comatose state, even with no verbal or optical responses, can wake up and act normally within a short period of time."

"And if that is not the case?"

He took a deep breath. "The most common consequence of brain injury is memory loss but it's usually manageable. Reminders of the past such as old photos, music, or common odors can often jog the memory back to normalcy. This is what Dr. Van Buren told me."

I braced myself. "Please continue."

"A second possibility is a form of delirium characterized by hallucinations. The patient hears voices or sees things that aren't there."

Dr. Bird seemed reluctant to continue, but perhaps he sensed that I was adamant. "One of the rarest outcomes is a type of paranoid delusion in which the patient believes that a loved one is an imposter."

Although the information he had imparted placed me in a state of profound anguish, I asked him to continue.

He paused. "Dr. Van Buren also described another reaction in which the patient believes that every person is the same person in disguise."

"This is most upsetting."

"Apparently, it, too, is extremely rare."

Once he had finished, I gave forth a sigh and said, "I suppose we must simply hope for the best." Balthazar responded with a somewhat forced smile and a pensive nod.

We were stationed in Abigail's room at the time of this dispiriting discussion, and for a moment both of us watched her as she slept. I glanced over at Balthazar and noticed the liquidity in his eyes. We both sat down.

"She was such a goofy little girl," Balthazar told me in a voice laden with sorrow. "Did she tell you she played the tuba?"

"Yes, she did."

"I'm afraid she wasn't very good at it. It sounded like a type of baritone flatulence most of the time."

"Hah!"

"She was in the marching band," he continued, his eyes brightening with a smile of reminiscence. "But her hat was always too big and it fell over her eyes." He laughed. "Half the time, she bumped into the person in front of her or just wandered out of the line-up."

I suppressed a laugh. The image was endearing.

"Smart as a whip too. Always beat me at checkers. Later chess."
He sighed as if visualizing his words. "At the age of twelve, she could
finish the *New York Times* crossword puzzle in an hour. In ink no less!"

"I was not aware of that."

"But then her mother died," Balthazar said. "Abigail was only
thirteen at the time."

"She informed me of this dreadful tragedy."

"After that..." he began with a gloomy shrug. "After that, she
became withdrawn, timid, and suspicious of peoples' motives. The
only things that seemed to give her joy were books. She abandoned
the tuba and spent half her time at the library. We're great pals,
though, Abigail and me."

"I sympathize with your grief, Balthazar, as I am experiencing it as
well," I said. "I am confident that our Abigail will soon awaken from
her slumber and that you shall enjoy the depth of your rapport with
your beloved daughter once again."

But Balthazar just nodded and glanced away at the heart monitor.

As I was able to delegate practically all of my work to the very
capable Ms. Anastasia Goldfine, I had sufficient free time to see
Abigail nearly every day. By then, Dr. Bird and I had become great
friends. When he was not present, I would sit beside Abigail's bed
and either quietly hold her hand or read to her, my words punctuated by the rhythmic beeps emanating from the heart monitor. By
the third week, I had gone through *The Great Gatsby* and the first
third of *Anna Karenina*, both of which I knew she had already read.
The reading proceeded slowly, for the attending nurses and doctors
frequently interrupted me.

On one such night, when I was alone with Abigail, I put the book
aside and gazed at her. In spite of everything, she looked beautiful
to me. I gripped her hand, stroked it, and leaned close enough to
whisper in her ear.

"Abigail," I said in a soft voice. "It's Archer. I must tell you something. I do not know if you can hear me but perhaps you can and maybe one day you will remember what I am about to say." I paused for a moment and placed several strands of her hair behind her ear. And then I told her how I felt about her. Sadly, I fervently wished that I had done so when she was conscious.

When visiting hours concluded, I reluctantly made brief appearances at the office specifically to water Dean Fletcher's orchids. Fortunately, the plants in question managed to prosper in spite of my lack of proficiency and experience.

One evening, as I was watering the damned plants, Eliot stuck his head in, as the door was ajar.

"How goes it, Archer?" he asked.

"Quite well," I said. "So much work to be done."

"Yet your desk appears to be devoid of paper."

"Quite correct. I have found that the one task that Ms. Goldfine performs with alacrity and skill is the filing of papers."

"Very true."

"But, as you so helpfully warned me, she is utterly hopeless at all other duties, so I perform these myself, tiresome as that often is."

"By the way, Archer, I heard about your student, Ms. Bird," Eliot said. He had solemnly lowered his voice. "Such a terrible tragedy."

"Indeed," I said. "How did you learn of it, if I may ask?"

"The local paper, of course," Eliot said. "This sort of thing is big news in Highland Falls. It said you led the police to the site of her accident."

As I did not wish to arouse suspicion regarding my relationship with Abigail, I fabricated a denial. "Balderdash," I said. "The newspaper must have misquoted the sheriff. The fact is, Ms. Bird had mentioned to me in passing that she frequently journeyed to that very spot to relax and sometimes to read. The police were able to deduce where it was, not I."

Eliot gave me a look of profound skepticism. "Is she making any progress?" he inquired.

"I think not," was my reply.

Eliot nodded. "You must come over for dinner sometime, Archer. I suspect you're existing on junk food or skipping meals entirely. You look very pale and undernourished."

His perception was quite correct. "That would be delightful," I said. "Thank you, Eliot."

"I'll ask Sandra about a date and time," he said in a kindly voice before departing. "In the meantime, get some rest, Archer. You look like hell."

One humid morning, I happened to espy Mr. Williger approaching me. At the time, I was making an effort to unlock my bicycle from the rack that stood a few feet from the building that housed the English Department. I attempted to ignore him, for I was in a hurry to hie to Abigail's bedside.

But he was jogging quite rapidly toward me. Arriving at my side, he said, "Hold on, Professor."

"Ah, Mr. Williger," I said in a tone that was more polite than authentic. "So nice to see you again."

"Hey, guess what? I got my diploma in the mail," he said. "My father was really impressed. He didn't think I could do it. Graduate, I mean. It's all thanks to you, Professor."

"Glad to be of service," I said. "But having received your diploma, why on earth are you still on campus? It is summer vacation."

"I decided to stick around. I have a girlfriend who lives in town."

I suspected that he might be referring to Sandra, although at forty she could hardly be considered a girl. Rather than continue the conversation, I concentrated on opening my bicycle lock, which was hopelessly intermeshed with the tire spokes of the bicycle beside it.

Mr. Williger squatted next to me. "Let me help you with that, Professor."

I welcomed his aid. To my amazement, he accomplished this task in a few seconds, which I found embarrassing as it indicated the depths of my ineptitude.

"That thing doesn't look too safe, Professor. Your tires need air and your handlebars and pedals look a little loose. A few spokes are bent too."

"Be that as it may, it manages to transport me to my various destinations often without incident, although I confess that I am somewhat maladroit at times."

"Tell you what," he said. "I owe you one, Professor. Bring it by the Delta House on College Lane and I'll find some tools and fix it for you."

"Truthfully? You would do such a thing for me?"

"I don't wanna see you hurt yourself, Professor."

I looked at him. He was a surprisingly affable young fellow. I regretted that I had misjudged him in class. "I shall do that, Mr. Williger. Most kind of you to offer and I appreciate your concern for my physical wellbeing."

"No sweat," Mr. Williger said. "In the meantime, try not to hurt yourself."

PART FOUR

Thirteen

As July concluded, my anguish deepened, for Abigail still displayed no signs of wakening from her deep slumber. I continued to read to her, hoping that the resonant passages of the great classics would somehow bring her to consciousness but thus far my efforts had been fruitless.

"I want you to know that I appreciate everything you're doing for my daughter, Ishmael," Balthazar said on one occasion.

"Think nothing of it, Balthazar."

He took a moment to consider his next statement. "I don't mean to pry, but I take it that your relationship with my Abigail exceeds mere friendship."

"It does indeed."

He patted me on the shoulder. "I'm happy that she found a man such as you," he said. "I hope both of you can continue your relationship one day."

"This is my hope as well."

"You certainly have my blessing."

As the days passed, I continued to whisper my declarations of affection in Abigail's ear but this exercise had thus far accomplished nothing that I was able to perceive, not so much as a blink or a twitch, although I still entertained the hope that she would recall my words upon awakening.

Since Dr. Van Buren had suggested that the introduction of certain sense stimuli might hasten an arousal, I endeavored to perform this strategy by playing Abigail's favorite music, such as the *Moonlight Sonata* and various Mozart concertos, but none of my musical selections achieved the desired effect. One day, I brought several strips of bacon to her hospital room and held them beneath her nose but this strategy also produced no result. I could think of little else to do but wait patiently. The days passed with no progress.

ॐ

The dressing that covered Abigail's surgical scar was removed a week later. Neither Balthazar nor I was present at this unveiling, although we saw the result the following morning. The jagged four-inch line of tiny stitches that appeared on a small shaved part of her cranium was ghastly to behold. My poor Abigail, I thought. The next day I purchased a baseball cap to cover the area. I found it difficult to look at this surgical evidence, not because I was squeamish but rather because it nearly made me weep. Yet, in spite of the shaved area and the stitches, my Abigail still looked exquisitely gorgeous to me.

Regrettably, I was at home, engaged in conversation with Felix and therefore not present at the hospital when Abigail at last regained consciousness. Constance, who had ventured to the hospital to recover a cell phone charger that she had accidentally left there the day before, called my cell phone to convey the thrilling news. At the time, Dr. Bird was not present.

"Her eyes just popped open, Ishmael!" Constance said. "It looked as if she had suddenly awakened in the middle of a nightmare."

I was exuberant. "I will depart for the hospital forthwith!"

"There's just one thing, Ishmael…"

"What?"

"When Abigail looked at me for the first time, she called me 'Dolly,' and she is still calling me by that name."

"Dolly?" I said. "Hmm. Perhaps she was referring to a childhood plaything, a doll, as it were. Perhaps a toy commonly known as Barbie."

"I don't think that's it," Constance said. "When I told her that I was a friend of yours, she didn't seem to recognize your name."

This was indeed odd. "I will be there momentarily!" I said.

As I raced to the hospital, I began to worry. Yes, it was a considerable relief that Abigail had finally awakened, but I was concerned about this Dolly business. Could she be suffering from one of the delusionary or hallucinatory syndromes that I had been cautioned about?

Twenty minutes later, when I entered Abigail's hospital room, she looked at me, smiled brightly, and said, "Why, my dear Count Vronsky! What brings you here at this early hour? I was under the impression that you were in the process of preparing your horse for the regimental race."

Constance shrugged in perplexity and summoned me closer. I quietly informed her that Count Vronsky was a character from Tolstoy's *Anna Karenina*. I also postulated that Abigail was most likely under the impression that Constance was Princess Darya Alexandrova Oblonsky, otherwise known as Dolly.

Constance looked at me blankly. "Did you read her the book?" she whispered. "*Anna Karenina?*"

"I confess that I read her the first third of it."

Abigail then cleared her throat and said, "Why are you silent on the matter, Count Vronsky? Is something amiss?"

I stood there silently for a moment as Abigail stared at me, no doubt expecting a response to her query. But what was I to do? Should I participate in this charade and take up the identity of Count Vronsky or attempt to persuade Abigail that I was in actuality, Ishmael Archer?

Involving myself in her fantasy seemed to be the most sensible strategy, as she appeared to be growing impatient.

Impulsively, I said to her, "I decided that I had to see you, my beloved Anna, before the race." This appeared to please her so I continued. "I find I simply cannot endure long periods of time without gazing upon your incomparable beauty and hearing your delightful voice. Just being by your side makes my heart beat with immense joy."

"As does mine," Abigail said. "But as you know, my dear Count, I am still conflicted about the wisdom of our romantic liaison."

"Of this I am aware, my dearest," I said. "I completely understand and feel great sympathy for your plight."

"And that is my only salvation. My heart overflows with deep and enduring passion for you."

Of course, the words we spoke were not identical to those in the novel but they conveyed the true passions that the characters felt for one another. My responses seemed to please her, so I said, "A deep passion that I too feel at the very core of my being."

Pensive, Abigail continued. "At times, I feel as ill as poor Kitty, though for different reasons."

"Ah, Kitty. My heart weeps for her," I said, fully cognizant that internal organs cannot shed tears. "Yet I confess that I treated her in a dastardly way and I shall always regret it but I did not love her."

But Kitty no longer concerned Abigail. "Tell me you love me, dear Count," she said. "I desire to hear those exact words emanate from your lips, for they uplift my spirits so."

I stared at her for a moment before replying. How I loved hearing my Abigail give voice to those words, although I realized they were actually spoken by Anna Karenina. Yet perhaps if I told Abigail-as-Anna that I loved her, Abigail-as-Abigail might one day recall my declaration. "I do indeed love you, Abigail," I said with a sincere tone. "With all my heart and soul and any other part of my anatomy that is able to feel love."

Constance looked at me and smiled. She knew that this was indeed true, that I truly loved Abigail, though I had never voiced this sentiment before, except during Abigail's long slumber.

But Abigail furrowed her brow. "Who is this *Abigail?*" she asked with some irritation. "What an odd name. Dolly called me by the same name earlier. I do not understand. I assure you, Vronsky, I am not this woman of whom you speak. Are you perhaps engaged with another woman?"

"No, no, no, of course not, dear Anna!" I quickly said in order to distract her from my error. "You are my sun and my moon."

"But not your stars? Do people not generally say 'sun, moon *and* stars'?"

"Yes, I suppose they do, Anna," I said. "It was thoughtless of me to omit this significant part of the galaxy. Astronomy has never been my forte. My sincere apologies."

"Accepted," she said. "But you have not answered my query, Vronsky."

"Which query would that be, my darling?"

"I wished to know why you used this foreign-sounding name, 'Abigail.'"

"An inaccuracy, for which I apologize. It is the name of my... um...prized steed. I have recently come from the stables."

"Such an odd name for a horse."

"Perhaps." As I did not wish to continue this equine banter, I returned to the issue that had preceded it. "But Anna, you have not replied to my words of affection."

"And so I shall, although I trust you already know what my response will be," she said.

"True, my darling, but I wish to hear the words from your beautiful lips."

"And so you shall," she said. "I love you as well, Count."

I studied Abigail. Apart from the fact that she was occupying a hospital bed in upstate New York, clad in a hospital gown and a baseball cap, she did bear some small resemblance to the Anna I had always visualized in the book, a woman whose kind heart and honesty were reflected in the depths of her bright flashing eyes and in the confidence of her bearing.

Abigail turned to Constance. "Tell me, Dolly," she said. "How did Stiva find Levin? I have heard that he visited the poor soul at his farm."

Constance looked at me quizzically. "Um..."

"I have heard that Stiva found him quite well," I said, rescuing Constance. "But as you know, Dolly and Stiva are not speaking to one another due to Stiva's indiscretion."

"Ah yes," Abigail said. "That awful young governess." She turned to Constance and continued, "You must forgive the poor man, Dolly. It was merely, as Vronsky says, an indiscretion, a diversion. It is *you* that he loves with all his heart. I am convinced of it."

"I am certain that, over time, Dolly will take him back to her bosom," I said. "Is that not correct, Dolly?"

As I surreptitiously nodded to her, Constance said, "Yes."

"Splendid!" Abigail said. "One must always think of the children."

At that, Constance cleared her throat meaningfully, and I suspected that she wished to engage in a private conversation with me before Abigail proceeded to travel any deeper into the Dolly and Stiva controversy.

I faced Abigail. "Will you pardon me for a moment, my dear Anna Arkadyevna Karenina? I have some urgent business to attend to. I shall return momentarily."

"As you wish, Count," she said. "Please hurry back to my side. The mazurka will begin soon and I would very much like to dance."

"Thank you, my dear Anna," I said with a bow. A mazurka? I wondered where she thought we were? A ball?

"Come to me and bid me farewell, Count," she said.

"But I shall not be gone for long."

"Be that as it may," she said, "I still wish for you to embrace me."

I hesitated. But after observing the profound expression of yearning in Abigail's eyes, I lay upon her bed and took her in my arms. How I had longed to do this! I lay beside her for more than a few moments.

"Will you not kiss me, Count? Do your lips not ache to touch mine?"

"Of course. Nothing would give me more pleasure."

Our lips met. It was a glorious moment for me, spoiled only by the realization that I was enjoying this with Anna Karenina and not Abigail Bird.

"That was sublime, my dear Count," she said. "You leave me quite breathless and..." Her voice trailed off and I noticed that she was blushing.

"And...?"

"Dare I say it? I feel a distinct...stirring in my loins."

Fearing that Abigail might then request a sexual encounter, I looked at Constance and motioned my head toward the door.

"You are leaving me as well, Dolly?" Abigail asked.

"Just for a moment, Abigail," she said. "I have to use the commode."

"Why do you insist on calling me by that name?" Her eyes flashed with anger. "One wishes to be called by one's proper name and not by the name of one of Vronsky's steeds."

"I'm terribly sorry…Anna," Constance said. "It will not happen again."

"We shall return in the blink of an eye, dearest Anna," I said.

"I await your return then, Count. Be quick about it!"

At that, we smiled at her and slowly exited the room. As soon as the door closed behind us, I said to Constance, "This is a most bizarre turn of events."

"Very perceptive analysis, Ishmael," she said.

"Well, at least she's not in a coma anymore." I gazed down the long corridor. "Where the devil is Dr. Van Buren?"

"I haven't seen him."

I grasped the doorknob. "I suppose we should return to her bedside. She may become agitated if we do not appear."

Constance pulled me away from the door. "Ishmael, I haven't read that book in years. I have no idea how to respond."

"I shall guide you."

I moved toward the door again, but Constance grabbed my elbow.

"Ishmael, I can't go back in there unless I know what the hell to say."

Sympathetic to Constance's dilemma, I commenced to offer her a hasty, abridged summation of the plot and characters of *Anna Karenina.*

"I must say, Constance, I am not entirely gratified that Abigail has chosen to visualize me as Count Vronsky. You see, Vronsky is a rather shallow fellow, albeit a charming, good-natured, and quite handsome scoundrel but—"

"It doesn't matter, Ishmael. This is hardly the time to complain about her casting choices."

"Of course. How utterly imbecilic of me."

"Maybe I should just leave," Constance said.

"No, please remain," I said. "Unless you have a class to attend to."

Constance consulted her timepiece. "Not for another hour."

"Excellent."

She took a deep breath. "Okay, let's go back in."

I nodded and pushed open the door. Both of us were greatly relieved to see that the tragic heroine of Tolstoy's great classic had drifted off into a peaceful sleep and heartened to perceive that there was a contented smile on her face.

When Constance departed for her class, I rushed off in search of Dr. Van Buren. Eventually, I located him as he emerged from a patient's room on the third floor, whereupon I informed him that Abigail had regained consciousness.

The good doctor was quite delighted, a reaction that gradually began to dissipate when he perceived the confusion in my eyes.

"Alas, there has been an unusual development," I said.

As I accompanied Dr. Van Buren to Abigail's room, I explained in some detail her bizarre transformation from Abigail Bird to Anna Karenina and her delusion that Constance and I were characters from Tolstoy's novel of the same name.

"Fascinating," he said.

"Indeed. Have you by chance read the novel, Dr. Van Buren?"

"In high school," he said. "Unfortunately, I barely remember it."

"I suspect that she will identify you as one of the book's characters when you appear in her room," I said.

"I'll wing it."

We took an elevator to the second floor and proceeded to walk down the hallway toward Abigail's room.

Dr. Van Buren asked me to remain in the corridor while he performed his examination. "I'll be out in a few minutes."

At that, he entered Abigail's room and roused her out of her slumber. I was able to watch them converse, as the door was slightly ajar.

Approximately five minutes later, Dr. Van Buren joined me in the hallway and closed the door. I studied him closely but the expression on his face did not appear to be one of concern. He took me aside.

"In all my years as a neurologist, I have never seen this sort of thing," he said. "It is certainly a type of delusion, one that we call dissociative fugue. The patient loses identity and prior memories. In Abigail's case she has substituted the identity of a fictional character. Very unusual."

"Is there anything you can do?"

"We'll wait and see for a while," he said. "She may snap out of this eventually. In the meantime, I would advise you to play along as best you can. Maybe something you say will cause her to return to reality."

"A simple task for me as I am well-versed in literature."

"I will mention this to a few physicians from New York," Dr. Van Buren said. "She's dozed off again so you might as well go home. Come back tomorrow morning and let's see what happens."

"Thank you, Doctor."

Although comforted somewhat by the doctor's words, I must confess that I was a trifle apprehensive. What if Abigail never snapped out of it? Would she spend the remainder of her life as Anna Karenina? Would I have to court her as Count Vronsky? Alas, the novel does not end well for poor Anna.

Naturally, I phoned Balthazar immediately and informed him that his daughter had awakened from her coma. He was jubilant until I apprised him of her unfathomable literary delusion. When he promised to travel to Highland Falls the next day, I suggested that he first obtain a copy of *Anna Karenina* and read it, although this proved unnecessary as he was already quite familiar with the book.

After making a brief appearance at the office, I conveyed myself home and consulted my copy of Tolstoy's novel. Perhaps there was a passage in the book that could be utilized to stimulate Abigail's memory. I was in the midst of skimming chapter twenty when there was a knock upon the door. I suspected that it was Felix, who occasionally visited me for reasons that pertained to the belatedness of a rent payment, but I was incorrect.

"Sheriff Grimsby!" I said as he stood in the doorway. "Have you heard the wonderful news? Abigail Bird regained consciousness!"

Grimsby frowned. "Jesus Christ," he said with irritation. "Why didn't anybody tell me? I'm the goddamn sheriff around here. I need to question her."

"I'm afraid that will not yield the desired results, Sheriff."

"How come?"

"It appears that she is under the delusion that she is a fictional character, specifically Anna Karenina."

"Who?"

"The heroine of the book by the same name by the great Russian novelist, Mr. Leo Tolstoy."

"Oh. Well, maybe she can tell me what happened anyway."

"Doubtful," I said. "Anna Karenina did not fall from a pile of rocks at the Highland Falls waterfall."

"I'm gonna have to try anyway."

I then realized that he was still standing in the doorway. "May I come in?" he asked and before I could apologize for my lapse in manners, he strode past me and set himself down on an easy chair.

"So what brings you here, Sheriff?" I asked.

Grimsby retrieved his notebook. "You left something out the day I interrogated you at the hospital. You didn't tell me about Butler."

I shrugged. "I assumed it would be irrelevant as he arrived on Friday evening and the incident involving Ms. Bird, according to your forensics, had occurred during daylight hours."

"How can you be sure he actually *arrived* in the evening?"

"Because that is when he appeared on my doorstep."

"That's not what I meant," he said. "Maybe he arrived during the day."

"I suppose that's possible."

Grimsby then rose to his feet. "Thanks for your time, Professor," he said. "I doubt Mr. Butler had anything to do with it but I gotta check."

"Have you contacted him?"

"Not yet. He's in Canada," he said. "By the way, what kind of weird name is Octavian anyway?"

"I believe Octavian or Octavius, as he was originally called, was a nephew of Julius Caesar. When Caesar was assassinated, Octavian became his successor and was known as Caesar Augustus. That is the sum total of my recollection."

"I should get to the hospital." I followed him to the front door and opened it. Before he stepped outside, Grimsby turned to me. "Soon as Butler gets back home, we'll have to bring him out here to question him in person. Standard procedure. I'm sure you'll be happy to see him again."

I did not reply.

Prepared to once again assume the identity of Count Vronsky, I conveyed myself to the hospital the next morning. Much to my surprise, Balthazar was waiting for me in the lounge area—apparently he had flown to Syracuse immediately following our conversation but had decided to wait for me before seeing her.

When we entered Abigail's room, we found her attempting to manipulate the remote control.

"Good morning, Anna," I said.

She frowned. "Anna? Have you had too much to drink? Who the devil is this 'Anna'?"

At last! My Abigail had returned! Hallelujah! I glanced at Balthazar, whose eyes had brightened.

"Oh, Abigail!" I said. "You're back! This is a most happy occasion!"

I was about to continue when Abigail's brow wrinkled. "Abigail?" she said. "First I am Anna, and now I am Abigail?" Then she pointed a finger at me and smiled. "I see! Is this some kind of new parlor game? I do simply adore parlor games."

Balthazar and I exchanged expressions of perplexity. If Abigail was neither Anna Karenina nor Abigail Bird, who indeed was she?

"This box on the wall is such a ridiculous contraption," Abigail said. She spoke with a distinct Southern accent. "It's like a moving picture in a tiny box and the actors are speaking. *Speaking!* My word! Such a stupid idea, isn't it? Where is Mary Pickford? Valentino? Fairbanks? I can't seem to find any decent music either. What must a person do to find Sophie Tucker and the divine Mr. Jolson on this infernal contraption? But I'm just a silly fool, aren't I, Gatsby?" This was followed by a girlish giggle.

It did not take me more than a second to understand what had occurred—Anna Karenina had evidently transformed herself into Daisy Buchanan overnight. I had no choice but to assume the character of Gatsby.

"Please, Daisy," I said to Abigail. "I insist that you call me Jay."

"Oh, I'm awfully, awfully sorry. I certainly am glad to see you again, Jay. We haven't met for many years. How long has it been?"

"Five years next November," I said, recalling the exact line from the book. "You were Daisy Fay back then, the most popular girl in Louisville."

"Such a long time ago. Eons! My goodness! I do remember how dapper you looked in your military uniform."

"And you were beautiful. You still are of course."

Abigail then noticed the presence of her father and said, "Hello, Nick! How lovely to see you!"

I hoped that Bathazar had read the book, a concern that evaporated when he said, "How are you, Daisy?"

"Utterly terrific!" she said. Her command of the Southern dialect was uncanny.

"You look a little peaked," Balthazar said.

Abigail gave forth another girlish giggle. "Oh, I confess, I tilted back a few cocktails last night. I do believe I've become something of a lush in my old age. Ha! How sad, don't you think, Nick?"

"I'm not exactly a teetotaler myself," Balthazar said.

Abigail turned to me. "I don't mean to be rude, but I desperately need a whiskey or some other species of alcohol."

"Nick has made us some tea," I said.

"Tea? *Tea!* Why would anyone but a reptile want tea on such an awfully hot day?" Abigail said with a laugh. She began to fan herself with her hand. "Although, I doubt reptiles drink tea. How silly I am!"

"It was I who invited you to tea, Daisy," I said. "Nick arranged it."

"How very sweet of you, Jay. But why so mysterious?"

"I wanted to surprise you, Daisy."

"Well, you certainly succeeded!"

I paused for a moment, attempting to recall the next stage of the chapter. "Have you seen my house?" I asked. "It's right next door. You can see it from the window."

Abigail followed my gaze. "Is it that huge place over there?"

"Yes, that's it! It looks well, doesn't it? See how the whole front of it catches the light."

"Why it's a… palace!"

"I suppose so," I said. "Much too big for one person to live in, of course, although I do seem to have several permanent houseguests."

"Heavens, what do you do for a living?"

"This and that."

I then told her about the rooms and all the interesting people who came to my, or rather Gatsby's, wild parties. These, I explained, included movie stars, financiers, musicians, and a variety of party girls.

"What a simply marvelous life you must lead!"

"Yet I find myself to be quite lonely," I said.

"Oh? Why is that?"

"You see, Daisy, I pine for a certain woman. A woman I met some time ago, a thoroughly delightful woman. I have never forgotten her. I wish that I'd been able to tell her how I felt about her but I could not."

"You loved this woman?" Abigail asked.

"I did," I said. "I do."

I decided to change the subject. "Did you know I can see your house from mine, Daisy? There's a green light at the end of the pier."

"What a coincidence! Why we're practically neighbors!"

"It's not a coincidence, Daisy," I said. "I bought my house so that it would be near to yours. I often stand on the balcony and look at your house."

"Why ever do you do that?"

"Because—"

At that, the door to the hospital room opened and a male orderly, clad in blue scrubs, entered and approached Abigail's bed. "Time to check your vitals," he said.

"Go away, Tom," Abigail said in a harsh voice. "Go off to your... wench."

"Huh?"

"Go away, Tom. You make me positively sick."

"My name's Charlie, not Tom, and I don't have a wench," said the orderly. "Actually, I'm gay."

"Why would I care about your state of mind? What is there to be gay about?"

The orderly frowned in confusion, wrapped a blood pressure sleeve around Abigail's arm and glanced at the monitor.

She must have misinterpreted the orderly's frown for she narrowed her eyes at him. "You're a pompous ass, Tom," she said.

"Huh?"

"I have no idea why I even married you!"

"You didn't."

"Don't be a fool, Tom!"

I noticed Balthazar tilting his head toward the door. "We'll see you later, Daisy," I said. "I have an appointment with a man called Wolfsheim, a business partner of sorts. Perhaps you can come to one of my parties some time."

"That would be divine," Abigail said. "And are you off too, Nick?"

"Just for a moment, Daisy," Balthazar said.

She pouted. "Must you *both* go?"

"I'm afraid so," I said. "We'll be back shortly. I promise."

Her face brightened. "All right, you may go then. Go, go, go. Fact is, I could use a nap. But at least bring me a bottle of whiskey when you return. Gin will do. Or rye."

"Your wish is our command," I said with a salute.

Grinning widely, Abigail shooed us out with a wave of her hand and we both exited the room.

The moment we stepped into the hallway, we beheld Dr. Van Buren striding toward us, accompanied by Constance. In a low voice, I whispered a reminder to Balthazar that the hospital authorities, including Abigail's physicians, were all under the impression that he and Constance were husband and wife.

"Looks like I'll be playing two roles today," Balthazar said with a trace of jocularity.

When they were in our midst, Balthazar addressed Constance. "Good morning, darling."

Momentarily flummoxed, Constance soon comprehended the ruse and gave her bogus husband a hug. "How is our Abigail today?" she asked.

I glanced at Balthazar. "She no longer thinks she is Anna Karenina," I said to Constance and Dr. Van Buren. "Today she believes herself to be Daisy Buchanan."

"Oh my," Constance said, placing her arm around Balthazar's waist. "How many books did you read to her, Ishmael?"

"Just the two. Fortunately, I did not read her *Metamorphosis* by Mr. Franz Kafka, for had I done so she might have taken on the identity of a cockroach, which would have been most bizarre, to say the least."

Balthazar turned to Dr. Van Buren. "May I speak to you, doctor?"

Van Buren looked at his watch. "I have fifteen minutes."

Once they were off, Constance and I repaired to the hospital cafeteria for some mediocre refreshment. After a moment, Constance said, "I just had an epiphany."

"Pray tell."

"There's a possible theme to all of this, Ishmael," she said.

"To all of what?"

"Abigail's delusions."

"And what might that be?"

"So far, the two literary heroines she has become believe you to be their lovers. As Anna, she immediately recognized you as Vronsky; you were Gatsby to her Daisy."

I confess this observation had not occurred to me. "And what is the significance of this?"

"Just a theory, mind you, but maybe she's trying to tell you something in her way, via a fictional character. Maybe she's subconsciously trying to tell you she's in love with you."

At first, I was skeptical, but the more I pondered Constance's hypothesis, the more I was heartened by the possibility that Abigail might indeed be trying to communicate her affection for me. "Interesting," I said. "If true, this would be most encouraging. Thank you for enlightening me."

"You're welcome."

Having voiced her theory, Constance appeared to have something else on her mind. A flicker of a smile passed across her visage. "You know, Ishmael, having Balthazar as my pretend husband makes me think of my ex."

"A subject of which you have spoken very little."

Constance offered up a shrug. "Hardly the most stellar period of my romantic career, such as it is, or was, but somewhat comical in retrospect."

"Perhaps you would care to elucidate the reasons behind your marital discord?"

Constance gave it careful thought. "I can do that in one sentence. Boy meets girl, girl falls in love with boy, girl marries boy, boy turns out to be an asshole, girl divorces him."

"Brevity, as they say, is the soul of wit."

"And what of your marriage?" Constance asked. "I believe you once promised to reveal the reasons behind your employment at this second-rate college. You said it was the fault of your former spouse."

"Yes, that is true. Yet I find it a trifle difficult to relive those toxic memories. But I shall try if you insist."

"I'm waiting with bated breath," Constance said. "Whatever the hell that means."

"In point of fact, the word 'bated' is a contraction of the word 'abated.' So the term 'bated breath' means a condition in which one nearly ceases breathing in anticipation of—"

"I'm not really that interested in the derivation of the phrase, Ishmael," she said. "Just tell me the story."

And so, after a deep breath, I commenced my soliloquy. I told Constance that I had made the acquaintance of Amanda Archer, née Blackstone after I had just completed my master's degree and was supporting myself as a teaching assistant while studying for my PhD.

"Amanda and I had first encountered each other as a result of a minor traffic mishap at a supermarket parking area. Later, she postulated that we were destined to meet as our respective vehicles were drawn together, as if by some magnetic cosmic force of destiny, or some such poppycock.

"I was prepared to claim that it had been her fault but when she stepped out of her vehicle, I was so taken by her breathtaking beauty that I blamed myself for the damage. We chatted briefly and I was able to determine that she was a woman of some education and a great deal of charm and kindness. I was immediately infatuated. We exchanged the usual papers and telephone numbers and then we parted.

"I confess that, at this time, I had not had much experience with the female of the species. Books were my mistresses, if you will. I am loath to admit it, but at the age of twenty-two I had not yet engaged in sexual relations with any representative of the fair sex. Much to my surprise, Amanda telephoned me several days later and, following a short discussion concerning insurance auditors, she invited me to attend a concert with her.

"We convened frequently thereafter and she relieved me of my virginity on our second encounter. Apart from pure lust, I felt a strong fondness for her that I believe was requited, for she showered me with physical attention. After a mere two months of dating, we tied the matrimonial knot, so to speak. Clearly, I should have gotten to know her better prior to our betrothal, but I am sorry to admit that I was hopelessly smitten.

"It soon became apparent that we had very little in common, save for an unflagging sexual attraction. She had lied to me about having received a bachelor's degree and demonstrated no interest in culture of any sort. She did not read the books I had recommended, and I soon learned that her preferred genre consisted of slightly pornographic romance novels, which stimulated her lust to such a degree that she constantly wished to engage in carnal relations. She told me on numerous occasions that she found me stuffy and that I was a dullard. Moreover, the kindness that she had once displayed toward me had gradually transformed itself into disdain and mockery.

"I soon realized that I felt no real love for Amanda Archer, née Blackstone. I had fooled myself into believing that I had. As a result, I began to withdraw from her. This was partly due to the fact that I was working furiously on my PhD thesis and I spent much of my time in the college library. When I finally completed a first draft, my thesis was no less than six hundred pages long, although it was not due for another three weeks.

"By this time, Amanda Archer, née Blackstone, had grown bitter about my inattentiveness. Not surprisingly, she blamed my thesis for this, claiming that I loved my work more than I loved her. We fought relentlessly and I soon realized that she was in possession of a stormy temper.

"Two days before my thesis was due, I printed a copy, enclosed it in a plastic folder, and placed it on my desk. On the day upon which I was scheduled to deliver it to my sponsor, I was surprised to find that both the manuscript and my computer were missing. After a brief search, I located both the manuscript and my computer in the bathtub, which was filled with hot water and bubble bath suds. The manuscript was black, having been burned to a crisp, and I soon determined that it was unsalvageable. The computer was in pieces that were scattered in the water like metallic water lilies.

"Predictably, the university did not believe my claim that my spouse had destroyed my thesis. As a result, I was dismissed from the PhD program. We were divorced two months later with the provision that I pay her alimony once every month for eight years, as I was the breadwinner. So endeth the reading."

"Wow," Constance said when I had completed my tragic monologue.

"I suppose I am partly to blame. I should have insisted on a longer engagement prior to marriage. When I reflect upon it, I conclude that I was simply starved for affection."

"Why do you suppose she wanted to marry you in the first place?" Constance said.

"I believe she thought that my pursuit of a doctorate meant that I was going to be a medical doctor and thus quite wealthy."

"In other words, she was a gold digger."

"I believe so. Had I known, I would have disabused her of her incorrect notion regarding doctorates prior to our marriage."

Constance gave me a look of perplexity and frowned. "But I thought you had a PhD. Don't you?"

"Yes. I received my PhD one year later."

"From what institution?"

"Irvin University."

"Do you mean Irvine? The one in Southern California?"

"No. Irvin." I then spelled it.

"I don't believe I've heard of that one," Constance said.

"That might perchance be because it is an internet university," I said sadly. "Four thousand dollars for a PhD."

"I see."

"It is an utterly worthless piece of paper but, amazingly, this so-called Irvin University was actually accredited," I said. As Constance put forth a look of sympathy, I felt an odd wave of emotion sweep over me. "I had once hoped to secure a position at Harvard or Yale or another prestigious university but, alas, only Longfellow would accept me."

Constance, doubtless perceiving the expression of utter desolation on my face, reached over the table and placed her hand over mine. "I'm so sorry, Ishmael."

"I sincerely thank you for your sympathy, but I am afraid I have only myself to blame for my poor judgment."

"You shouldn't blame yourself, Ishmael," she said. "You were young, innocent, and you acted on impulse. I would guess that testosterone probably played a role as well. You're hardly the only person who has ever made a poor choice. It happens all the time."

I merely shrugged and stared off into space.

Fourteen

It was with considerable apprehension that Balthazar and I motored to the hospital the following day to pay a call on Abigail. What fictional character, we wondered, would fill the delusionary void in her brain on this occasion? Would she remain Daisy Buchanan or revisit the life of Anna Karenina? Given the plethora of novels that she had consumed throughout the years, it was entirely possible that we would stride into her hospital chamber and be greeted by Hester Prynne, Becky Thatcher or even Tinkerbell. The mind virtually boggled at the possibilities.

When we entered her room, her head was propped up on her pillows and she was manipulating the remote control. As soon as she noticed us, Abigail smiled and placed it beside her on the bed.

It was I who first tested the conversational waters. "Good morning," I ventured, deliberately refraining from the use of a given name, lest she again react with annoyance.

She studied my face carefully, as if examining the geographical details of a globe. "And who might you be?" she asked. "Have we met?"

Who indeed was I? Vronsky or Gatsby? On an impulse, I said, "My name is Ishmael Archer and, yes, we have indeed met."

"And what exactly is the nature of our relationship?" she asked.

"We are particular friends."

"I see." After ruminating upon this information for a moment, she turned to Balthazar. "And who is this gentleman?"

Balthazar smiled. "I am your father, Abigail," he said.

"Abigail?" she said. "Is that my name?"

"It is," I said. "Abigail Bird."

She gave forth a giggle. "That's a rather absurd name, don't you think, Ishmael?"

"On the contrary. I think it suits you."

"May we sit down?" Balthazar asked.

"Of course," Abigail said. "How very rude of me. Forgive me."

Simultaneously we lowered our buttocks upon the two plastic chairs near her bed. Abigail looked at Balthazar. "Are you certain you are my father?" she said. "I don't recall ever seeing you prior to this occasion, but I admit that I am somewhat confused and have been since I awakened."

"Yet it is the truth," Balthazar said.

Abigail sighed. "I have so many, many questions. Where do I begin? I don't know where we are or why I am here or much of anything at all. Isn't that peculiar?"

I was about to launch into an exhaustive explanation regarding her whereabouts and other items of information regarding her circumstances when Dr. Van Buren stepped into the room and bid the three of us good day.

"Another gentleman caller!" Abigail said. "I feel quite popular this morning."

Van Buren glanced questioningly at Balthazar and me and from the look on his face, I gathered that he had not yet visited Abigail today and was thus unaware of this new development.

"I don't think we have met before either," she said to the doctor.

After a moment of hesitation, he said, "My name is Martin."

"Hello, Martin. I am pleased to make your acquaintance," she said. "I am Abigail Bird or so I am told. This is my particular friend Ishmael Archer, and my father."

"We have met," Dr. Van Buren said. "They are close friends of mine."

Abigail gave forth a delightful smile. "How nice."

At that, Dr. Van Buren said, "Would you please excuse us for a moment, Abigail? The three of us must attend to some important business."

"Please do come back," she said. "I have so enjoyed our conversation—it has been so very illuminating—and there is absolutely nothing of interest on the television."

"How very odd," Dr. Van Buren mused when the three of us stood in the corridor. "Two different literary delusions in a row, followed by what can best be described as amnesia, with no apparent memory of her temporary literary identities at all." He shook his head in wonderment. "Quite remarkable."

As we strode down the corridor, Balthazar and I offered the doctor a detailed recapitulation of every word that had transpired between Abigail and ourselves. He was particularly relieved to hear that we had not mentioned anything regarding her reasons for being in the hospital, informing us that any mention of her fall and subsequent coma could very possibly upset her. Moreover, the doctor explained that nothing could be done to resolve the amnesia but added that her memory could very well return on its own.

"In the meantime, to prevent any further literary delusions, we must be sure to keep Abigail away from books of a literary nature," Dr. Van Buren stated.

The following day, Abigail was moved to the psych ward. As Dr. Van Buren was not schooled in the science of psychiatry, he placed her in the hands of Dr. Olivia Partridge, a somewhat frazzled woman who possessed the annoying habit of pausing in the midst of sentences, as if the words that exited her mouth were separated by ellipses. Balthazar and I convened in Dr. Partridge's office, for we both had numerous queries regarding the continuation of Abigail's care.

"Here is the…good news," Dr. Partridge said. "Abigail's prior personality has not, and will not, change appreciably. Her past life will…simply be…a blank."

"But she just learned her name and who we are," I said.

Dr. Partridge formed a lopsided steeple with her fingers. "Yes, I am…aware," she said. "You both may…help by reacquainting her with…the superficial details of her current life such as her job, her residence and so forth. This will help her to function normally and be comfortable in her old surroundings."

"She seems quite eager to learn about these things," Balthazar said.

"I am glad to hear it," Dr. Partridge said. "Some sufferers…of amnesia are…resistant."

After a moment of hesitation, I asked, "And the bad news?"

"She will not be able to recall…past emotional attachments."

I frowned. "So if Abigail had an affection for, let us say, a certain individual from her previous life, she would no longer recall that emotion?"

"Correct," Dr. Partridge said. "Unfortunately, it's impossible… to go that deeply into her psyche. Emotional memory exists…at a much deeper level. However, she *will* be capable of…feeling *new* emotions."

Balthazar sighed. "Well, I suppose that's preferable to living her life as Anna Karenina or Daisy Buchanan. Don't you think so, Ishmael?"

I was disturbed by Dr. Partridge's professed inability to reawaken Abigail's past feelings, but I did not wish to undermine Balthazar's shaky optimism so I merely said, "Indeed."

"One more thing," Dr. Partridge said. "For her own good…I will attempt to instill in Abigail's mind…via hypnosis…a total lack of interest in…literature. I'm sure you…understand why that is essential."

Of course, this particular component of Dr. Partridge's strategy saddened me but I fully understood why it was necessary.

"So be it," I said.

⛥

Dr. Partridge's treatment, combined with the information provided to Abigail by Balthazar and me, proved remarkably successful and after a few weeks, Abigail was dismissed from the hospital and permitted to return to her apartment, which Balthazar and I had cleared of all works of fiction. I visited her at least four times a week to make certain she was faring well. Although I was deeply distressed by Abigail's loss of emotional memory, as well as her disinterest in literature, I attempted to remain confident that she would eventually regain her past identity and thus recall the details of our relationship. Of course, I found the present situation nearly unbearable for, having finally found a woman for whom I felt a profound affection, she had been taken away from me in a most unpredictable way.

Having witnessed the depth of my despair, Eliot invited me to his abode for dinner, as he had promised some time before. Apparently, he was no longer consumed by our competition over which of us would assume the duties of dean for he did not mention the subject. I found this sensitivity to be most admirable. He wished only to cheer me up, which would prove impossible, though I was grateful for his attempt. Even Sandra was sympathetic to my tragic plight.

As it was a warm evening, Eliot, Sandra, and I consumed our dinner outside on Eliot's terrace, which afforded us a breathtaking view of the valley and the mountains.

"So," Eliot said after I had explained Abigail's state, "what's the prognosis?"

"Nobody really knows," I said.

"Maybe she'll wake up one morning and her memory will just magically return to normal," Sandra said.

"That is always a possibility and one to be hoped for," said I.

"You're quite fond of her, aren't you, Archer?" Eliot said. "Feel free to decline from answering that if you find it inappropriate or too personal."

I paused, momentarily uncertain as to whether or not it would be prudent to divulge my true feelings for Abigail. "Truth be told, Eliot, I'm afraid my feelings for her have ventured far beyond mere fondness."

Sandra stared at me and said, "I don't mean to meddle, Ishmael, but have you fallen in love with this woman?"

"Sadly, I fell in love with the version of Abigail that existed prior to the accident. Yet, I have decided to begin the courtship anew."

"And she loved you?" Sandra asked.

"That I do not know. And I may never know, for at this time she possesses no memory of our past together."

Sandra reached over the table and took my hand. "I'm sure she'll fall in love with you again, Archer. You're a pretty lovable guy."

"Thank you."

"Even if she doesn't recall you from her past life, I imagine that she is the same person emotionally," Sandra said.

"We shall soon discover whether or not that is true," I said.

Later, Sandra excused herself, after informing us that she was drowsy from having consumed too much of the grape. Eliot walked inside and returned momentarily with another bottle of wine. We spoke of literature for a bit and then he rather abruptly changed the subject.

"Ever thought about writing another novel, Archer?"

"I'm sorry to say that I have given up the art of writing fiction."

"Why?"

"Simply put, I believe I lack the gift for it."

"I disagree," he said. "Your prior attempts were clearly imperfect but I enjoyed them."

"You're kind to lie," I said.

"No, I mean it. There was something there, believe me. Don't give up, Archer. You have talent."

Of a sudden, I was overcome by a wave of nostalgia, for I recalled how Abigail had spoken similar encouraging words to me at our very first encounter in the library conference room. It seemed such a long time ago.

"Perhaps I shall," I said, although I was relatively certain I would not undertake such an arduous chore ever again.

"Good man!" Eliot said. "If you think you need any editorial guidance or merely an educated opinion, I would be happy to offer my services."

"Very kind of you to offer."

I glanced at my watch and was astonished to learn that it was twenty minutes past midnight, well beyond my usual bedtime. The hours had passed so quickly! As I took my leave, Eliot embraced me warmly and inquired as to whether I was sober enough to drive. If I was not, he said he would gladly take me home. After thanking him for this kind gesture, I assured him that, in spite of my alcoholic intake, I was capable of driving and requested that he convey my deepest thanks to Sandra. Their kindness and generosity had uplifted me for the first time in many weeks.

As the fall term was scheduled to commence shortly, I made it my purpose to visit Abigail as frequently as possible. By this time she was comfortably situated in her apartment and walked about without the aid of a cane. She no longer took an interest in libraries or bookstores. Dr. Partridge had performed her task admirably. As Abigail's apartment was devoid of novels, she read nothing but newspapers and magazines, neither of which caused any delusionary relapses.

By this time, Balthazar and I had begun to think of Abigail as Abigail One and Abigail Two, the former being Abigail as she had been prior to her fall, and the latter as she was in her present state. The numerical designations to her name simply made it easier for those who knew her to make references regarding her two identities.

Sadly, she regarded me as no more than a new friend, or at least that was how it appeared to me. Occasionally, I would bring her flowers or boxes of chocolates, for which she expressed gratitude but did not interpret as romantic gestures. Yet I could not help but hope that one day she would lift herself on her tiptoes and kiss my cheek as she had done once before.

Most pleasingly, her eyes always glowed with delight at the very sight of me. "Hello, Archer!" she said on the occasion of my most recent visit. "How lovely to see you! You seemed a trifle gloomy when we last met."

"I am in excellent spirits today, Abigail, especially now that I am in your presence. Thank you very much for inquiring."

She flushed. "You're most welcome."

I handed her a box of chocolates that I had painstakingly wrapped.

"These are for you. They are called Godiva chocolates although I haven't the slightest notion why anyone would name such confections after a woman of British nobility who rode unclothed upon a horse."

"Thank you, Archer. You are so thoughtful." Abigail then proceeded to carefully remove the paper, whereupon she opened the box and extended it to me. "Would you care for one?"

"Perhaps I shall indulge my sweet tooth," I said, liberating three of these delectable items from their enclosures. It had become my habit to consume most of the chocolates I brought her. "Quite tasty!" I said.

After placing the box on a nearby table, I said, "And how are you getting along today, Abigail?"

"Just fine. I do so much enjoy seeing you," she said. "Except for my father you are my dearest friend. Actually, come to think of it, you are my one and only true friend and for that I am most grateful."

Thereupon, after a cursory glance at her half-empty bookshelf to check for literary trespassers, I sank into the cushions of her couch. "May I offer you a drink of some sort?" she asked politely.

"Do not trouble yourself. My thirst was recently quenched by a gargantuan container of Coca Cola."

Then she sat at the other end of the couch but only after accidentally banging her right shin on the coffee table. "Tell me," she said, massaging her leg. "How goes your job as acting dean?" I had recently informed her of this temporary appointment.

"In truth, I have delegated much of the work to my assistant, Ms. Anastasia Goldfine. You may recall that I mentioned her to you previously."

"Of course," she said. "And how are the orchids?"

"Thriving."

"Excellent! Perhaps you have a green thumb after all, Archer."

"I would attribute their well-being to good fortune."

"You're being too modest. I wouldn't be surprised if you have many hidden talents."

"Perhaps," I said. "Unfortunately, few have come out of hiding."

Abigail chuckled, but as her laugh faded, she looked into the distance and I could not help but notice a profound sadness in her eyes.

"Is something amiss, Abigail?" I asked her.

Turning her eyes to me, she said, "You'll think it's silly."

"Please tell me. I must know."

"Well…it's just that I get so awfully…bored," she said. "I spend most of my days alone just watching the television but, except for the occasional educational program, there's little of interest to me."

"Yes, I too can seldom endure that miserable contraption."

"Perhaps…" she began to say.

"Perhaps what?"

"I suspect that you're very busy, but maybe you'd be kind enough to escort me somewhere when time permits—a film, or dinner. Perhaps just a walk in the park."

As Dr. Partridge had not discouraged the viewing of films, it would not be problematical for me to accompany Abigail to the cinema. "I would be most delighted to do that, Abigail. I wish I had thought of it myself. Perhaps we can enjoy some diversion together this coming weekend. I will give some thought to what sort of entertainment is available in this wasteland."

Her eyes sparkled in a most adorable manner. "I would so enjoy that," she said. "Thank you, Archer. You are so thoughtful and kind."

"That is because I like you very much, Abigail. Very much indeed."

"And, as I hope you know, the feeling is mutual," she said.

As she looked at me, I searched her eyes for the slightest glimmer of recognition but, alas, I perceived none. Perhaps I hoped she would utter an observation that would indicate a recollection of our past association but this did not occur. Yet I did my utmost to remain optimistic. At least she liked me. This was an excellent start.

Abigail had been allowed to return to her job as a server at Phil's Rib and Steak Emporium and I had hoped that the aroma of barbecued red meat emanating from Phil's kitchen might stimulate a memory but that did not appear to be the case. To her carnivore-loving patrons and restaurant colleagues, she appeared perfectly normal. She simply did not remember any of them until they were reintroduced to her. I had forewarned them about her amnesia and they were most understanding.

On the Tuesday following the extended Labor Day weekend, Dean Fletcher returned to campus and informed Eliot and me that he had not yet chosen his successor, but that his choice would be imminent. In the meantime, he would occupy the position himself although he assured us that he would vacate the premises within a week. I personally returned his keys and followed him to his office to recover some of my belongings. The moment we stepped into the room, we were greeted by a horrific surprise that caused both of us to register extreme shock—the orchids were quite dead, their leaves black and wilted. When he beheld this unanticipated devastation, the dean gasped as if he had just witnessed an automobile accident and, after giving me a look of extreme displeasure bordering on fury, scurried toward them to inspect the extent of the damage.

"What the hell happened, Archer?" he said.

"I'm afraid I do not know," I said. "I watered them as per your detailed instructions and fed them precisely the correct amount of fertilizer."

"Obviously, you did something horribly wrong."

"Inconceivable," I said. "I dutifully tended to them yesterday afternoon and they were quite alive and prospering. It seems impossible for one to believe that they would simply perish overnight."

"Well, evidently they have!"

"In my humble opinion, a gradual decline in their well-being, such as a browning and a slight wilting of the leaves would have most likely preceded total annihilation. Do you not agree?"

"You were responsible for their care. I trusted you, Archer. This is a catastrophe of considerable dimension. A virtual abomination!"

I thought at that moment that the dean was perhaps inflating the parameters of the tragedy that stood before us. The word "abomination" seemed somewhat of an overstatement and one that was customarily used to describe events of a far graver nature. However, fearing a further outburst of anger, I did not call his attention to this.

"Please leave now, Archer. I would like to mourn in private."

"Yes, of course," I said and hurried out of the room.

Directly following this disquieting encounter, I stormed down the hallway and barged into Eliot's office where I found him at his computer.

"Ah, Archer," he said. "To what do I owe this——?"

"You did it, didn't you?" I said in a voice filled with rage, which was unlike me, as I seldom lose my temper.

"Did what?"

"Poisoned Dean Fletcher's orchids, of course!"

Eliot's visage registered a look of confusion. "I beg your pardon?"

"Bob's orchids are quite deceased. As they were in tip-top condition yesterday, my conclusion is that you viciously destroyed them in order to sabotage my chances of becoming dean."

Eliot raised his eyebrows. "I did no such thing!"

I did not believe him. "Who else would have a motive to undertake such a ruthless act? Clearly, you sneaked into his office last night and watered them with some poisonous concoction. There exists no other logical conclusion."

"Still, I tell you I am innocent."

I gave him a look of profound skepticism. "You were until recently in possession of the keys."

"I gave them to you a long time ago!"

"You could easily have made copies."

"I swear on the grave of my mother that I did not do this," he said.

"I thought you recently informed me that your mother is still alive."

"Technically she is, but she's very ill and will probably succumb in a short period of time, the poor lady."

"Oh. Well, I am sorry for your imminent loss and subsequent grief, and please accept my condolences in advance, but as she still breathes, you can not swear on her grave as she does not yet reside underground."

Eliot stood up. "Archer, please believe me when I tell you that I did not commit this heinous crime. I would never resort to such underhanded shenanigans, I promise you."

"But you desire the position, do you not?"

"Yes, but if I am to be selected, I want it to be for my proficiency alone, not because of some childish act of subterfuge. I hope you know me well enough by now to see that I am not that sort of vile person."

His statement gave me pause. I thought about how kind Eliot had been to me in the recent past. It was indeed difficult to believe that he would resort to such abhorrent and infantile behavior. I looked into his eyes and saw no trace of guilt in his expression.

"Perhaps I am mistaken then," I said. "If so, please accept my apologies, Eliot. I may have jumped to an incorrect conclusion. You have indeed shown me great kindness in the past weeks."

"That's because I have grown to like and admire you, Archer."

"As do I you."

"I'm glad to hear that."

"Then who might the vile culprit be?" I asked.

Eliot looked me in the eye. "I haven't the slightest idea."

Although I was troubled by the mysterious orchid catastrophe and curious as to the identity of the perpetrator, I pursued no further investigation into the matter. At this stage, I no longer held out much hope of succeeding Dean Fletcher. The promotion to a loftier position, in spite of the added remuneration, was of no great concern to me, for Abigail remained my foremost focus. As I had promised her, we attended the cinema together. Unfortunately, there was but one theater in our town and therefore the choice was limited to a rather insipid love story. Although I enjoyed the soundtrack—Dvořák's

Slavonic Dance Number 2 in E Minor, which I had struggled in vain to play on the violin as a child—I found the film to be somewhat maudlin. But I noticed halfway through, when the lovers parted, that Abigail was sniffling. Thinking that this nasal congestion might have been an outbreak of allergies, I glanced at her and noticed a lone tear meander down the crease of her nose. As a consoling gesture, I attempted to place my hand over hers but her hand was not available at that moment as it was in the process of moving popcorn from a bag to her mouth.

We followed this outing with several strolls though the town's many parks, and suffered through a dreadful one-act play at the Methodist Church. Sometimes, we would simply sit on a bench and converse, and I soon came to the realization that, as Dr. Partridge had predicted, Abigail Two was essentially the same delightful creature that she had been as Abigail One.

Then one day, I was visited by an ingenious idea. In the hope of stimulating her dormant memory, I decided to escort her to a place we had visited together during the weeks preceding her fateful accident.

Although there would be no art fair in Highland Falls until the following summer, I managed to find a notice in the redundantly named *Highland Falls Tribune Bugle Gazette* that advertised a similar event to be held in the neighboring town of Orangeville. Abigail appeared quite excited about the prospect of attending said event and when she asked me to suggest suitable apparel, I surveyed her armoire and suggested the same ensemble she had sported at the Highland Falls affair. Clad in the identical clothing I had myself donned previously, we drove to Orangeville on a sunny Saturday afternoon.

We wandered from one exhibit to another, trading humorous critiques of the amateurish art as we had done before. Many of these appeared to be the very same waterfall paintings we had encountered at the Highland Falls art fair many months before. I wondered idly whether any of them were the handiwork of Sheriff Grimsby's daughter, Tilly.

After completing our tour of this museum of horrors, I led Abigail to the area of the fair where crafts were displayed. I watched her carefully as she roamed from one table to the next, examining ceramic bowls, silver jewelry, wood-crafted salad bowls and the like. Then, as luck would have it, I happened to spot a pair of feathered earrings not dissimilar to the ones I had bought her at the Highland Falls art fair.

"These are quite charming," I said, pointing to the aforementioned trinkets. "Do you not think so, Abigail?"

She arrived at my side and took them in her hands. "They're lovely!" she said. Having observed this exchange, the vendor then stood up from his stool and indicated a mirror that was suspended nearby. Quietly, Abigail gazed into the glass and raised the earrings to a position in front of her earlobes, and I saw her expression light up with a most satisfied smile.

"You're right, Archer," she said. "They are quite fetching. I think…I will take them!" At that, she began to rifle through her purse.

"Allow me to purchase them for you," I said.

"That's all right. My wallet is in here somewhere."

"I insist."

"But Archer, I mustn't let you spend all your money on gifts for me."

Gazing at the price tag, I said, "I strongly doubt that the expenditure of eight dollars and ninety-five cents will reduce me to abject poverty. I wish to make them a gift, a memory, if you will, of our pleasant day."

Later, as we made our path to the parking lot, I recalled that Abigail had consumed a strawberry ice cream cone on the day we visited the Highland Falls art fair so I set about to find a vendor who offered such comestibles but there were no such vendors present. Little matter. If she could not recall the previous purchase of the earrings, there was little doubt that an ice cream cone would make a significant difference.

But when I brought her home that night, she did something that astonished me. Before she had opened her front door, she suddenly stood on her tiptoes and gave me a peck on the cheek. I was taken aback. This seemingly spontaneous gesture excited me greatly and I wondered whether Abigail Two was gradually turning back into Abigail One.

❧

"I'm sorry, Professor, but I...do not believe so," Dr. Partridge said after I had reported Abigail's kiss of the previous night.

Thrilled by the possibility that this encouraging sign indicated a moment of recollection, I had excitedly phoned the doctor. Now I was deflated by her reaction. "But she had performed just such an act of affection when she was Abigail One, albeit in a different location," I said.

I could hear her sigh as she probably sensed my disappointment. "As you know...Abigail Two is still a woman with...normal emotional reactions. It was merely her way of...expressing her appreciation."

"I'm afraid I do not understand," I said.

"Let's say she had a dog...and the dog did something that she found...pleasing. Her reaction would probably be...to pet the dog. It would not mean that...she had awakened from Abigail Two to... Abigail One."

"A canine analogy. How flattering."

"I'm sorry," she said. "I did not mean...to offend you."

"No matter," I said. "So tell me this, doctor. Precisely what sort of action or expression from her would comprise a return of memory?"

"It would have to be...the recollection of a specific incident, unlike the one you just described...that had occurred...prior to the accident."

Although I was loath to utilize maritime vocabulary of any kind, I felt as if the good doctor had indeed taken the wind out of my sails.

178

Fifteen

As I had not seen nor heard from Sheriff Grimsby in quite a while, I was surprised to receive a telephone call from him one evening. I had recently returned to my abode following a splendid early dinner with Abigail and Balthazar. When my phone rang, I had been in the midst of rearranging the books on my parlor shelf into alphabetical order. Of course, due to my extensive library of fictional works, I had not invited Abigail over to my apartment.

"It is nice to hear from you again, Sheriff," I said. "May I ask the reason for your call?"

He growled quietly as I suspected he was of the opinion that I was not being entirely truthful. "William Octavian Butler."

I engaged in a short bout of throat clearing. "And why, pray tell, would you phone me about him? We have conversed before on the subject."

"Well..." Grimsby began. "I have a favor to ask of you."

"And what might that be?"

The good sheriff paused. "You see, Professor, since Butler is still a suspect in Ms. Bird's case, I have to ask him a few questions."

"And what is stopping you from accomplishing that task? You merely have to utilize the telephone."

"I wish it was that easy, Professor. I have to interrogate him in person."

"And how, may I ask, does this concern me?"

Again, he did not respond for a few seconds. "Well, according to regulations, the county has to pay his expenses, which means we have to get him here and put him up in a hotel."

"Good for him," I said. "He will no doubt be thrilled at the prospect of revisiting our magical metropolis."

"Oh, he's thrilled all right." I perceived a distinct edge of sarcasm

179

in the sheriff's voice. "He arrived here this morning and we got him a room at the Motel 6 and—"

"Oh Lord! Surely you jest. Said establishment is not worthy of housing pigs."

"Tell me about it. He refused to stay there. Threatened to go home." He was silent for a moment. "So, I was wondering…well… if you could put him up at your place?"

"Certainly not!" I said.

Unruffled by my exclamatory refusal, he said, "We'll pay you for your trouble, Professor. Just for twenty-four hours. Then he'll be on his way home."

The prospect of once again having to spend twenty-four hours with William Octavian Butler was not a terribly attractive prospect, although I did owe Felix several hundred dollars for unpaid rent. But it was not the pecuniary aspect of the arrangement that suddenly appealed to me, although any financial boost was welcome. I worried that if Butler stayed elsewhere, he might attempt to visit Abigail, and I did not wish for this to occur. It would be preferable if I were able to keep a watchful eye on him. Besides, I bore some fondness for Grimsby and was not averse to doing him a favor.

"Make it three hundred and I will grant you your request," I said.

"Really?" the sheriff said, perhaps surprised at the alacrity of my agreeable reaction. "Three hundred it is. Do you mind if I drive him over now? He's at the station and he seems to be getting kind of restless."

William Octavian Butler arrived at my domicile half an hour later, carrying the very same ancient, overstuffed duffel bag. I walked down the outdoor stairs to greet the famous author at the front stoop. He sported a pair of wrinkled cargo shorts and a T-shirt emblazoned with a mediocre lithograph of The Bard. Before greeting me, he stopped on the sidewalk to light a cigarette.

"Hello there, old sport," he said.

Forcing a smile, I said, "Greetings, William. What a pleasant surprise."

He grunted as if he found this difficult to believe.

"This whole goddamn interrogation shit is such a bloody hassle," he said. "I've nearly completed a first draft of my second novel and now I had to get on a goddamn plane for this pointless exercise." He patted his duffel. "In fact, I have a copy of it right in here. I think it's rather good."

"Your second novel," I said, with a trace of envy. "How very exciting."

He did not acknowledge my congratulatory remark. Perhaps he was hoping that I would ask to read it.

"What is the title, if I may ask?" I said. "I will certainly obtain a copy as soon as it is released. I do so enjoy your work."

"My tentative title is *A Man Named Horace*. What do you think? Do you like it?"

"Yes, very much," I lied. "Quite...*um*...catchy, as they say."

A moment passed as he contemplated my stammering reply. "By the way, how is Abby?"

"Making excellent progress, I am happy to report."

He nodded pensively. "Maybe I should pay her a call."

"I think that would be unwise at this time. She is still engaged in the process of re-orientation."

"Maybe she'll recognize me."

"I'm afraid there is little chance of that," I said. "I think it best that you stay away, William. I fear that it would only confuse her."

Oddly, he was not insistent and merely said, "Okay, if you say so." He blew a trail of smoke out of his nose. "By the way, Archer, thanks for agreeing to put me up for the night. Have you seen that godawful motel?"

"I have never actually ventured inside, for fear of contracting a disease, but I have observed the layer of a mud-like substance in the swimming pool on several occasions when passing by and I would not be surprised if said mud-like substance was, in actuality, fecal matter."

"Don't you folks have a goddamn health department?"

181

"We do, but the inspector is related to the owner of said motel."
He exhaled more smoke. "Soon as I finish this cigarette, we can
go inside, if that's okay with you. It's damn hot out here."

"Bit of a heat wave," I said.

He nodded. "Got any beer?"

"I'm afraid not."

The following day, I drove my houseguest to the police station
for his session of questioning, whereupon Sheriff Grimsby handed
me a check for three hundred dollars as promised. Prior to the interrogation, I bid an awkward adieu to Mr. Butler. Thankfully, he was
scheduled to depart Highland Falls in the afternoon, assuming he
was innocent, which I knew he was. As he was an impulsive, willful
sort of fellow, I worried that he would ignore my warning and visit
Abigail, should there be any intervening hours of inactivity during
which he was left to his own devices. Thus, I insisted on taking him
to the bus station myself and he gratefully accepted.

On my way back from the police station, I found myself with
some time between classes so I paid an unannounced call on Abigail.
When she greeted me at her front door, she was vigorously brush-
ing her hair, which was quite wet. I immediately noted that she was
wearing a silk robe, ostensibly of Japanese origin, the sheerness of
which afforded me an excellent view of the contours of her bosom. I
could barely take my eyes off this thoroughly appealing sight, though
I did my best, lest she conclude that I was ogling her. Yes, I had seen
her in a bathing suit before but this particular garb was revealing in
a far superior manner. Oddly, she was also wearing black galoshes.
After stepping into the foyer, I noted that the climate inside her
apartment resembled that of a tropical rain forest. As it happened,
a week of unseasonably sweltering weather had recently descended
over Highland Falls.

She gave me the customary cursory hug and said, "Please excuse
the informal nature of my attire, Archer. As you've probably noticed,
it's unusually warm in here."

"It is a beautiful robe. You look quite striking in it, Abigail. Quite striking indeed."

She blushed. "Thank you, Archer. So far, I've taken three showers today. My air conditioner seems to be broken."

Again she was a damsel in distress and I would have offered to repair her air conditioner, but I lacked the necessary mechanical skills, save for some ability to change light bulbs, and even that was a challenge.

"Have you perchance called a repairman?" I asked.

"Yes, but I guess many others in the town suffer from this same inconvenience. He informed me that it would take a week for him to inspect and repair mine."

"Bad luck."

"If you wish, I'll put on something more formal," she said.

"No, no, no, do not trouble yourself," I said with perhaps too much urgency. "I believe I can endure the sight of you in this attire, although I do not comprehend why you are wearing rain boots."

"My bathroom floor is quite wet from all the showers I've taken today. I don't want to slip and injure myself."

"I see," I said. "Very wise."

"I am afraid that my water bill will be astronomical."

We then seated ourselves on her sofa and I consumed several jellybeans that resided in a bowl upon the coffee table. As Abigail was aware of my penchant for confections, she maintained a variety of them throughout her apartment.

"If you wish to remove some of your clothing, please do so," she said.

I looked at her. Was this an invitation for a full or partial removal of my attire? Did she perhaps wish to engage in a sexual romp? Or was she simply concerned for my comfort? I was, after all, perspiring profusely.

Even after carefully studying her face—there was no blush to be found there—I could not discern the answer to these questions, so I merely unknotted my long paisley tie, (I no longer sported bow ties) and opened the first two buttons of my shirt. "Much better," I said. She looked at me appreciatively. "Great!" she said. "I was... concerned about your comfort."

As I stole a glance at her, I felt a surge of lust overtake me. After all, I was a young man with a normal testosterone level, or so my urologist had informed me. I contemplated moving toward her but I immediately decided that such an aggressive act would be premature, as I had not known the new Abigail for more than a few weeks. Perhaps she was merely in a lustful mood, one that would require no more than the attentions of any random member of the male species; or perhaps this was a misjudgment on my part.

The situation was indeed quite difficult to analyze so I eventually opted for prudence. I heard her sigh. A few moments of silence passed during which I offered her a weak smile.

Abruptly, she rose to her feet, appearing somewhat irritable, a reaction to the heat I concluded.

"May I refresh your glass, Archer? You are perspiring and it's important to keep yourself hydrated in weather like this. I wouldn't want you to suffer heat stroke due to lack of hydration. One must look out for the well-being of one's friends."

"No, thank you," I said.

"Then I'll get one for myself. I think I've had fifteen glasses of water since I woke up."

I groaned. When I had inched toward her on the sofa, her sudden rise to a standing position led me to believe that she was not desirous of engaging any further. Again, I did not wish to force myself upon her. I recalled sadly that she had again referred to me as merely a "friend."

"I simply can't endure this heat a moment more," she said after returning from the kitchen with her glass.

"Perhaps we might venture into your kitchen and thrust our heads into the refrigerator freezer for a few moments."

She laughed and sat down again. "I can just see that! How very funny!"

Though I had been jesting, I could not help but chuckle at the image.

She fanned herself with her palm. "I was thinking that maybe you would like to accompany me to town so I may buy a fan. I'd like that very much."

"Yes, of course," I said with a distinct lack of enthusiasm. I would rather have remained on the couch with her in hopes that something of an intimate nature might arise.

But Abigail seemed excited by her idea. "Okay then. I'll change into some appropriate clothing and then we'll go. I'll be quick about it."

In a monotone, I said, "Take as long as you require."

Apparently, she had detected the morose tone of my voice. "Is something wrong, Archer?" she asked.

"No, not at all."

Ten minutes later, she emerged from her bedroom clad in a pair of long shorts and a baggy T-shirt and we departed. While her spirits were high, I sulked as we walked down shady, tree-lined streets toward the hardware store on Main Street. But then, to my surprise and delight, she performed a gesture that thrilled me to my very core—she took my arm! Was this, I wondered, a sign of affection or was she merely fearful that, without the support of my elbow, she would trip over a badly paved area of the sidewalk? After all, she was a trifle clumsy.

Dean Fletcher's office resembled a florist shop that had recently run out of merchandise. The absence of any sign of his formerly thriving orchids gave the space a dreary ambience that, in spite of my complete lack of interest in flowering plants, saddened me, although the dean's face registered no visible sign of distress. There still remained a few small dollops of soil on several of the side tables, a tragic reminder.

The dean was scheduled to remove his belongings from his office in three days, and as we spoke, I glanced at the piles of boxes that stood atop each other in the room, surrounding us like the turrets of a castle. Yet he did not mention the absence of his orchids, for which I was thankful.

Moments before, I had been driving to the police station, for William Octavian Butler had completed his interrogation session with the sheriff and I had promised to convey him to the bus depot. It was during my journey to said precinct that Ms. Anastasia Goldfine alerted me via cell phone that the dean desired to meet with me as soon as possible As there would be insufficient time to complete both tasks, I telephoned Grimsby and told him of my dilemma, whereupon he assured me that he would deliver the esteemed author to the Greyhound depot himself.

The dean gave me a curious look. "Tell me something, Archer," he said. "How desperately do you wish to be dean of the department?"

I glanced out the window. On the quad, Frisbees were flying about like alien spacecraft, many of them crashing into trees.

I turned my attention back to the dean. "Quite honestly," I said, "I have very few skills in the art of administration. I will happily confess that my sole interest in the position was to secure an improvement in my deplorable financial status. Alas, I am finding it difficult to exist comfortably on the salary I am currently paid."

"I see," he said. "Yet you did have the clever insight to delegate your duties to Ms. Goldfine, while Eliot performed his obligations on his own."

I was surprised. "How did you discover this?"

"Ms. Goldfine informed me."

I nodded. "It is quite true. I utilized Ms. Goldfine's talents largely because I had no idea what I was supposed to do while the very apt Ms. Goldfine did. However, one would think that you would approve of Eliot's diligence more than my lack thereof."

Dean Fletcher studied my face, leaning forward in his chair as if he could not see me clearly from his former position. "Archer, if I understand you correctly, it appears that you would prefer that I choose Eliot for the position."

186

I stared back at him. "I had assumed that Eliot would be your choice anyway, Bob. After all, it was I who failed in my obligation regarding your beloved orchids."

"Nonsense," the dean said. "Ms. Goldfine also informed me that you made a supreme effort to nurture them throughout your term of office. I have a theory regarding the identity of the person who apparently poisoned them."

"And what might that be?"

"I believe that Eliot, in an attempt to sabotage your chances of receiving the position, was the culprit in the untimely death of my orchids."

I vigorously shook my head. "It was most assuredly *not* Eliot."

"How do you know?"

"Eliot is not a savage murderer of plants or, for that matter, any living species. I have come to like and respect Eliot very much over the past weeks, and I am certain that he would never resort to such puerile antics."

"Yet he desperately wants the position."

"It is quite true that he is an ambitious man. But this heinous act of subterfuge is below him. We have spoken of this matter as I, too, initially suspected him."

Dean Fletcher rose to his feet, and began to pace the room, taking great care to avoid tripping over the multitude of boxes that were scattered about. He stopped to look at me. "It may then come as a surprise to you that I had decided to choose you as my successor."

For a moment I was struck speechless. "I am indeed surprised and flattered, but I believe that you would be making an error in selecting me. You see, I have no particular ambition for the job. I would rather be spending my time pursuing other goals."

"Such as what exactly?"

"It has always been my dream to write an excellent novel," I said. "I have recently been encouraged by several people whose opinions I respect."

"I see," the dean reflected. "So in effect, you're declining the position?"

"Quite correct."

"Hmm," he said. "It is true that once the school year begins, the job will require attention and much of it will fall out of Ms. Goldfine's purview."

"Then Eliot is your man."

The dean wandered back to his desk chair, sat down, and stroked his chin. "You are a good man, Archer, and you're certainly worth more than the paltry salary you're currently receiving. As my last act as dean, I'll see to it that you are paid more handsomely."

I smiled. "That would be most welcome, Bob. I thank you."

He rose again and we shook hands. "I'll miss you after I leave this beloved campus, Archer," Dean Fletcher said.

"As I shall miss you," I said with great sincerity, "but I am certain we shall see each other again at various ghastly gatherings."

He laughed. "Well then, goodbye for now."

"Goodbye, Bob."

I got to my feet and made my way toward his door. Yet before I passed through it, the dean spoke. "By the way, how is your friend Abigail Bird doing?"

"Much better. Functioning normally at least."

"I'm glad to hear that. Give her my best wishes when you see her next."

"I shall be most happy to."

Later that evening, Constance and I dined together. As Professor Potter continued to suffer from his illness, Constance had been asked to remain as his substitute until he recovered. She invited Abigail and me to celebrate her good fortune at one of the town's more civilized taverns, a place unimaginatively called "The Tavern."

Because of my low tolerance for alcoholic beverages, I was planning to order a lager but Constance insisted I join her in imbibing a flute of champagne instead and so I reluctantly agreed, although the "champagne" consisted of a mixture of cheap white wine and club soda. We clinked glasses and I offered her my congratulations regarding the extension of her employment at Longfellow, to which she responded with a smirk.

"I believe we have another cause for celebration," Constance said.

"Oh? What might that be?"

"I think you know what I mean, Ishmael. Don't play coy."

"In all honesty," I replied, "I have no idea of what you are speaking."

Without answering my query, she lifted her glass and proclaimed, "To the new dean of the English department."

I followed suit and raised my flute, which was actually a chipped highball glass "Yes," I said. "To Eliot Altschuler!"

Constance's glass made it halfway to her mouth, a look of confusion etched on her face. "What?" she said.

"To Eliot Altschuler, the new dean."

"He appointed Eliot? That's not possible. He told me it was to be you. He promised me!"

"*Who* promised you?"

"Bob, I mean Dean Fletcher. I thought I had talked him into it."

Now I was confused. "Why would you attempt to talk him into it?"

"I thought you said you needed the money," Constance said.

I nodded. "I appreciate your kindness, Constance, and Bob was indeed prepared to appoint me, but I declined. Fortunately, he took pity on me and was kind enough to offer financial advancement, for which I was most grateful."

"That was good of him," Constance said.

"Yes. Besides, Eliot worked hard at the position. I merely watered the orchids as instructed. Ms. Goldfine performed every other duty."

Thereupon, Constance and I engaged in animated conversation. As we had invited Abigail to participate in our dinner, I voiced concern that she had not yet made an appearance and neither had she called or texted to explain her tardiness. I found this worrisome, for Abigail, in spite of her confusion regarding her identity, had once again embraced punctuality.

Filled with anxiety, I called twice and left several voicemails. After these went unanswered, Constance and I decided to repair to Abigail's apartment in order to make certain that nothing was amiss. We were relieved when Abigail opened the door to greet us. She appeared to be quite joyful at the sight of us as she ushered us in.

"You're early!" she said.

"Abigail dear, you were supposed to meet us at The Tavern," I reminded her. "An hour ago."

Abigail's brow furrowed. "That is not true, Horace. I do believe you and Lucinda were supposed to come here for cocktails at eight o'clock. We arranged it last week when I saw you buying Brie at the cheese shop in Brooklyn. Don't you remember? I invited several of our mutual friends—Leonardo and Alphonse and their wives—but they haven't arrived yet. We're going to hear about their recent trip to Bangkok and the marriage of their illegitimate daughter Eunice who, as you will recall, is afflicted with narcolepsy. Perhaps you forgot."

Constance and I exchanged a look, which I could best describe as a combination of shock and dismay. A cursory glance around Abigail's parlor quickly revealed the source of her delusion. William Octavian Butler's manuscript, the insipidly named *A Man Named Horace*, lay wide open on her coffee table.

PART FIVE

Sixteen

Ordinarily, I am not one given to anger, but my voice trembled with fury when I confronted William Octavian Butler by telephone the next day. I voiced more epithets than I had ever spoken in my entire life, a past record that included a diatribe aimed at my former wife Amanda Archer, née Blackstone some years before, following the transformation of my PhD thesis into ashes, although she had been absent at the time of my outburst. Butler explained that he had missed his bus and had decided to visit Abigail while waiting for the next one. Predictably, she had not recognized him, and he had left her apartment in short order, but had inadvertently left his duffel bag behind. He speculated that she had probably looked through it and had discovered his manuscript, which she had then at least partially read, most likely out of curiosity. He claimed that it had not been his intention for her to peruse it, although he admitted that he had mentioned it to her. But his explanation was of little mollification to me, as I had emphatically asked him *not* to visit Abigail. His subsequent request that I return his luggage via Federal Express, and his assurance that he would reimburse me for the expense, caused me to launch into yet another litany of epithets, characterized by a juxtaposition of the word "beetlebrained" with the word "simpleton," a slight redundancy, granted, but well worth the grammatical infraction.

"Was this manuscript your sole copy?" I asked, attempting to contain my rage.

"My only copy of the latest draft."

"Do you perchance have a copy of a previous draft?"

"No," he said.

"What a shame," I said. "Because said paper manuscript now resides quite thoroughly charred in a large trash receptacle commonly known as a dumpster situated in an alley behind Abigail's abode. It is accompanied by your computer, which sustained considerable damage when it met the sidewalk. Good day to you, you simpering, pompous thimblewit."

So apopletic was I from this confrontation that I poured myself a glass of wine to calm my overwrought state and consumed its contents in one long gulp. The bottle of wine, I recalled sadly, had been the very one that I had purchased on the day Abigail One had been scheduled to appear at my apartment for our first mentoring session. I had opened it somewhat ineptly with the corkscrew I had acquired at the supermarket on the same day, and consumed it from one of the same wineglasses I had purchased there. This upsetting recollection caused me to indulge in another glass.

Naturally, on the night of Abigail's relapse, Constance and I had immediately driven her to the hospital, although this required us to first convince her that Butler's characters, Leonardo and Alphonse, had suffered a minor accident and were themselves receiving medical care. Upon our arrival, she was sedated and admitted to the psychiatric ward for a repetition of the hypnotherapy. Dr. Partridge confirmed our speculation that Abigail had read a portion of Butler's novel and then fallen asleep, only to awaken as one of his characters.

If the hypnosis again proved successful, Abigail's present delusion would be erased from her memory, and Abigail would remain Abigail Two. I had feared that she might become an Abigail Three but Dr. Partridge assured me that this was unlikely to occur, as there had been no repeated brain injury to obscure her memory of herself as Abigail Two. She had merely taken a nap. This was, of course, a great relief to me, although I harbored some doubts. I called Balthazar to inform him of this new development and repeated Dr. Partridge's prognosis. He promised to come to Highland Falls as soon as he was able.

As Balthazar and I perceived, Abigail seemed to be making steady progress over the next few days. Dr. Partridge assured us that, barring any unforeseen developments, it would be no more than a week before Abigail would emerge from the pages of William Octavian Butler's novel. Nevertheless, I again found myself in a state of apprehension over poor Abigail's plight for I had grown quite close to her as Abigail Two and did not want our revitalized friendship to fade from her memory. On the fifth day of her treatment Balthazar departed, promising to return after completing several bypass procedures. After he left, I summoned the nerve to prove to myself that Abigail did indeed recall my identity.

"Do you know who I am?" I asked her.

She did not pause. "Of course, Archer," she said with a bright smile. "What an odd question. Why would I ever forget you?"

"Do you recall how we visited the art fair not long ago?"

"Oh yes," she said. "In Orangeville. How could one not recall all that horrible, horrible art?"

"Did I purchase something for you there? Do you remember what that was?"

"The lovely earrings, of course!" Then she frowned and gave me an odd look. "Why are you asking me these questions, Archer? Is it you who needs reminding? Has your memory of these events faded already?"

"No, of course not."

"I'm very relieved to hear that," she said. "For a moment I thought perhaps you'd hit your head and were suffering from a bout of absent-mindedness or temporary amnesia."

As she laughed, I breathed a sigh of relief for it appeared certain that we could resume our relationship and that I would not be compelled to begin anew and woo an Abigail Three. If that had proved necessary, I would have happily restarted our courtship for by this time it was clear to me that I was still in love with her regardless of the numercal reference that followed her given name.

Just after I had declined Dean Fletcher's offer of promotion, I had attempted to congratulate Eliot on his triumph but I had been unable to accomplish this in person for, as I was informed by Ms.

Goldfine, Eliot and Sandra had traveled to New York for a long weekend before classes resumed. On the day that Eliot returned to campus, I found him in his newly inherited office, filling the empty bookshelves with his vast collection of literary masterpieces, many of them bound in leather for, unlike me, he possessed the means to acquire these attractive treasures.

"Archer! How nice to see you! Have a seat."

I gazed around the room. There were no chairs present. "Where?" I asked.

"My mistake," Eliot said. "I'm having the old ones replaced, and I stupidly gave them to Goodwill before the arrival of my new ones. Pull up a box, my friend."

After a moment, I found one that supported my weight and lowered myself onto it. "I came to congratulate you, Eliot," I said. "I was hoping to come earlier, but you were in Gotham with your charming wife."

"I needed a few days off before assuming the dean's duties," Eliot said. "Quite a bit of work to be done now that classes have begun."

"Yes, I would imagine so."

"I hope there are no hard feelings, Archer," he said.

"None at all. You possess the skills I lack."

I then glanced through the door at Ms. Goldfine who was seated at her desk, arranging papers.

Eliot followed my gaze. "Unfortunately, the good Ms. Goldfine is, as usual, hopeless," he whispered. "It would be most helpful if she were able to aid me in my daily workload."

"Yes, well, perhaps you can train her."

"I doubt it. I'm afraid I will not have the time."

"During my brief tenure as dean, I found her to be most helpful in some matters," I said. "You may wish to reconsider."

Eliot looked at Ms. Goldfine as she continued her work. "Well, if that is your advice, perhaps I shall."

"In any case, hearty congratulations, *Dean* Altschuler," I said, extending my hand. "You certainly earned this promotion."

Eliot beamed. "'Dean Altschuler.' I must say, I like the way that sounds. But I insist that you continue to call me Eliot."

"All right…Eliot."

"Perhaps we can get together for a drink soon, Archer. I know Sandra would love to see you."

"That would be splendid," I said. "Anytime."

෴

Dr. Partridge released Abigail from the hospital a few days later and I motored to the medical facility to fetch her. She seemed quite elated to see me, for it had been a few days since I had last visited her. As I held my car door open for her, she paused for a moment and gazed at the entrance to the medical center.

"Archer, can you tell me why I was in the hospital?"

She had never asked this question before so I was uncertain as to the manner in which I should reply. The first time Abigail had undergone hypnotherapy, Dr. Partridge feared that her patient might inquire about the reasons behind her hospital sojourn, and had convinced her that she had been admitted for a routine physical, but perhaps the doctor had neglected to repeat the story on this occasion. I hesitated, but Abigail was intently studying my face so I knew that I would have to quickly invent some counterfeit explanation, yet I did not wish to prevaricate.

"You do not remember?" I asked.

Abigail contemplated. "No, I don't have the slightest idea."

"Well…it seems that you…suffered a lapse of sorts…several days ago in your apartment."

"What do you mean by a 'lapse'?"

"I am not sure," I said, relieved that I had avoided the need to fabricate an entirely bogus story. "Unfortunately, I am not familiar with the official medical terminology. The doctors determined that some minor tests were necessary."

Abigail nodded uncertainly as she stepped into my vehicle. "Do you mean that I fainted or lost consciousness?"

"I suppose. In a manner of speaking…"

"Hmm," she said. "I assume they concluded that it was not serious?"

"Yes."

Without further discussion of the matter, I snapped on my seatbelt and clumsily maneuvered the car out of the hospital's parking lot and onto Route 11. To prevent her from pursuing the topic, I switched on the radio. But momentarily she turned down the volume.

"How long have we known each other, Archer?" she asked.

I looked at her and wondered why she had made such an inquiry. It was a somewhat delicate question, to be sure. "I'm not precisely certain. Quite a long time, I believe. Why do you ask?"

"It just occurred to me that I have never seen your apartment."

"I am afraid it is not much to behold," I said. "Hardly a palace, I assure you. Quite dark and gloomy, in point of fact."

"Be that as it may, I would still like to see it."

"When?"

"I was thinking perhaps now."

This caught me by surprise but I was unable to formulate a credible reason to deny her request. Due to the enormous collection of fictional works that resided on my bookshelves, I feared that such a venture might be unwise. I would have to make certain not to leave her alone in my parlor where the shelves stood. Of lesser importance was the fact that, having been otherwise occupied for several days, I had neglected to straighten up.

"Oh my," she said when we entered my untidy apartment. "It looks like you haven't cleaned this place in weeks. I took you to be meticulous about cleanliness. This is very distressing," she said.

I looked about and beheld the chaos that characterized the interior of my residence. Fast food cartons were scattered about, dishes were piled up in the sink, and a layer of dust had accumulated on various surfaces. Moreover, the apartment bore a noxious odor that could best be described as that which emanates from rotting foodstuffs. Ashamed at the disarray, I said, "I am afraid that I have been otherwise occupied. I am usually, as you say, quite meticulous regarding tidiness, but alas I have lately neglected my housekeeping duties. For this I apologize."

Sniffing the air, she said, "My goodness! It positively reeks in here!"

"A result of food that has declined to the spoiling phase."

She wagged a finger at me. "Archer, you desperately need a house-keeper or a wife who will insist that you keep things tidy."

"Alas, I cannot afford a housekeeper, and the woman to whom I was once betrothed possessed no enthusiasm for cleanliness. Quite the opposite, in fact."

"How odd," she mused, scratching her head.

"Odd?"

"I was not aware that you had previously been joined in matrimony."

In point of fact, I had revealed to her a few details of this unsavory episode of legal bondage prior to her mishap at the glade but had not mentioned it after the calamity. "Perhaps I neglected to inform you," I said. "It is hardly a fond memory and, as a result, one of which I seldom speak."

"I see," she said. "In any case, I assume you must have far more expertise on the subject of the opposite sex than I do."

"Most of it unpleasant, unfortunately."

It was then, of a sudden, that a most interesting insight occurred to me. To wit: In all probability, the erasure of Abigail One's memory had left her with no recollection of any romantic entanglements from her past.

"I do not wish to enter private terrain, Abigail, but have you had many suitors in your life?"

She frowned. "None that I can recall. Isn't that odd?"

"Um—"

"Surely someone must have escorted me to my high school prom, although I do not recall my high school prom for some reason."

"Perhaps it was uneventful."

"I suppose so."

"So there has been...no one?"

"I guess not."

"Well, perhaps one day, a gentleman of superior intellect, excellent character, attractive facial features, and admirable kindness will sweep you off your feet, as they say."

I looked at her expectantly and she smiled at me, albeit with some measure of ambiguity. Apparently the subject was of no further interest to her, for she proceeded to make an optical survey of the room, rolling up her sleeves as if she were about to chop wood with an axe. "Now if you have no further questions regarding the history of my love life or lack thereof, shall we get to work?" she said.

"Work? What work?"

She placed a hand on her hip. "I swear, Archer, you can be such a...silly goose sometimes."

"I have little knowledge of geese, having never encountered one in close proximity, thus I do not know whether silliness is a state of mind that they possess, although I would guess not."

"For goodness sake, it's just an expression, Archer. By 'work' I meant the cleaning of this filthy apartment. Now, do you have a broom, a dustpan, and other such items?"

"I do indeed."

"A vacuum cleaner?"

"Yes, although it has a small hole in its receptacle bag."

"Cleaning products?"

"A few."

"And an apron? I don't want to soil my clothing."

"I believe so."

"Then get them this instant," she said in a playful tone. "I'll do my best to tidy up this horrific mess."

"You wish to clean my apartment?" I asked. "That is not necessary, Abigail. I will see to it myself, by the by."

In spite of my protestations, she insisted, so I reluctantly located my cleaning products, all of which resided in my pantry, and we both set about to make order among the chaos. Abigail flew about the place like a whirlwind and instructed me regarding which tasks I was to perform, checking from time to time to make certain that I was doing an acceptable job, scolding me when she found fault with my results. The process took several hours and when we had completed the task, my apartment was spotless. With a weary exhalation, she collapsed on my sofa, whereupon I repaired to my bedroom to change my dirty attire. As I was about to unbutton my shirt, I suddenly realized that leaving her alone in a roomful of books was a grave error. When I hurriedly returned to the parlor, I was distressed to behold her standing in front of my bookshelves, ostensibly admiring my collection of tomes.

"Have you read all of these?" she asked.

"Yes."

"You must be an avid reader."

"I am."

"What sort of books are they?"

"Mostly fictional works. Quite boring, I must say. Not of any real interest at all. Frivolous entertainments."

She pulled a novel from my shelf and perused the cover. It was an ancient paperback edition of *David Copperfield*, one that I had purchased at a used-book sale as a teenager. I was tempted to pull it out of her hand, but I desisted, so as to avoid any questioning by her regarding my motives for such rudeness.

"I confess that I don't read fiction," she said. "I have no interest in such entertainments."

"So you have said. It is a waste of precious time. There are so many other interesting things to do in life."

Admittedly, I felt a distinct uneasiness upon hearing myself utter these words and was somewhat angered at myself for my prevarication. Naturally I had never spoken such defamatory words regarding books before! Yet I felt a great sorrow for Abigail for she had once so enjoyed literature. Books had once given her such immense pleasure. Great novels had been her consuming passion, and I mourned the loss of her desire to write, for she had possessed considerable talent for it. Indeed, it had been this common obsession that had originally brought us together. I wished there might be some method with which to reawaken her interest without stimulating a delusional episode, but I knew that this would never come about. And so, I watched sadly as she returned the paperback to the shelf and suggested we take a walk.

᠀

Several days thereafter, I nearly tumbled off my bicycle when one of my pedals broke. I decided to take Mr. Williger up on his kind offer to repair my mode of conveyance and walked the unwieldy machine to my former student's dwelling.

When I arrived at the fraternity house, I was compelled to engage upon a circuitous route to the entrance, as the front lawn held an obstacle course of paraphernalia, such as beer cooling devices, athletic equipment, and lawn chairs. Following a series of knocks on the front door, a young gentleman, who sported a pair of ladies' panties on his head, greeted me.

Apparently, he recognized me as a professor for he hastily removed his improvised hat, although it was not my intention to mention the inappropriate placement of it. The young man was indeed familiar with my former student and informed me that Mr. Williger no longer resided at the frat house and that he had taken up residence in the town. He gave me the address.

Later that day, I stuffed my bicycle into the trunk of my car and drove to Mr. Williger's new address. I found him in the driveway, his head hidden under the raised hood of an ancient Buick.

I opened my trunk, removed my bicycle, and wheeled it toward him. The clattering must have alerted him to my presence, for he pulled himself out from beneath the hood and greeted me enthusiastically.

Looking down at my sorry two-wheeled vehicle, he laughed. "You still riding that thing, Professor?"

"Yes, and it nearly killed me," I said.

"I'll bet it did. Let's have a look."

At that, he squatted down on one knee and fiddled with several bolts, inspected the tires and pulled out a loose spoke.

"Can you repair it?" I asked.

Mr. Williger rose to his feet whereupon he stroked his chin. "Yeah."

"Excellent! I will be more than happy to reimburse you for the parts and labor."

He shook his head. "Nah," he said. "It's on the house, Professor."

"You, sir, are a prince among men."

Mr. Williger stared at me for a moment and rubbed his brow with the back of his hand. He appeared to be pondering something and I assumed it pertained to the possible reincarnation of my bicycle.

"Professor, I have a confession to make," he said, looking away. "I did a really bad thing. I fucked up, if you'll excuse my French."

"In point of fact, Mr. Williger, the epithet you have just utilized to describe the onerousness of your act is not of the French tongue, nor does it derive from that language. I believe its origin is Germanic or Dutch. The French have a quite different word to describe the act of intercourse." It did not appear that he had been listening for he stood there in silence. Momentarily, I grew impatient. "Pray tell, Mr. Williger, what is this wicked act of which you speak?"

My former student took a deep inhalation and closed his eyes before speaking. "I poisoned Dean Fletcher's flowers."

This admission seemed so preposterous that I wondered if I had heard him correctly, and required a moment to digest his words. "Why would you do such a dastardly thing, Mr. Williger?"

"I swear it wasn't my idea, Professor," he said, raising a palm as if he were taking a solemn oath of office. "She put me up to it."

"She? Who, may I ask, is this female personage of which you speak?"

"My girlfriend," he said. "Well, my old girlfriend. We broke up."

This confused me even more. "Again, you are not fully illuminating me, Mr. Williger. Who is this paramour of which you speak?"

"Sandra Altschuler."

I erupted with a guffaw. "That is patently absurd."

"It's true. It was her stupid idea."

"Assuming that this is not a fabrication, why would Sandra Altschuler, of all people, wish to assassinate Dean Fletcher's botanical specimens?"

"She told me it was just a prank. She had the keys to the office. I used bleach, in case you wanna know."

"Well, it was quite effective," I said.

"But later I found out her husband was up for the dean's job, so I figured she got me to kill the plants so the other guy wouldn't get it. I didn't find out until yesterday that the other guy was you."

"And how, may I ask, did you gather all of this information?"

"Everybody on campus knows about those frigging orchids, Professor."

He appeared to be so shaken that I was inclined to relieve him of his guilt. "No matter, Mr. Williger. As it happens, I did not really desire the job."

He immediately brightened. "Really?" he said.

"Yes."

He wrinkled his brow, most likely in confusion at my remark. "So you're not mad at me, Professor?"

"I am not, although I do not approve of childish nonsense such as this. and I mourn the tragic loss of plant life."

"Know what I think?" he said.

"I do not possess the gift of telepathy, Mr. Williger."

"I'm just guessing, but I think she found some other guy to fool around with. Maybe she wanted her hubbie to keep busy so she'd have more…free time, if you know what I mean."

I considered his speculation but found it somewhat lacking in logic. "Most likely, she simply wished to help him fulfill his ambition."

"Like I said, just a guess."

"Rest easy, Mr. Williger. I bear no anger toward you and I appreciate your honesty."

Thereupon, Mr. Williger, whose eyes had dampened, stepped toward me, and much to my astonishment, proceeded to embrace me.

During my drive back to campus, I pondered Mr. Williger's convoluted theory regarding Sandra's motive for destroying Dean Fletcher's colorful interior garden. She had never displayed any ill will towards me that I was able to discern. I had, however, observed that Sandra felt a palpable disdain for Eliot, a feeling that was confirmed by her sexual involvement with Mr. Williger. Perhaps my former student had guessed correctly—that she wished to keep her husband locked to his new desk late into the night in order to give her more freedom with which to pursue her adulterous affairs, which no longer included Mr. Williger. True, it sounded ludicrous, yet I must confess that my curiosity was piqued.

Seventeen

I will readily admit, albeit begrudgingly, that it was William Octavian Butler's second novel, or rather Abigail's reaction to it, that inspired me to create my own *oeuvre*, although my motivation was not derived from the content of the blowhard's fictional work, for I had not read it. As my tale was nothing more than a detailed accounting of certain recent occurrences in my own life, the formations of plot and character were undemanding.

I was unable, however, to determine the precise genre of the emerging work. Was it fiction or nonfiction? Perhaps this would depend entirely on the reader. To outsiders, it would be considered fiction; to others, nonfiction. In truth, it was a memoir, although my purpose in writing it was to present it to Abigail as a work of fiction. I was confident that she would agree to read it to please me. It was, you see, a deception of sorts and, although I am not a fellow given to trickery, I made an exception in this case for I perceived that the desired result would justify the means.

There were two protagonists in this tale—a fellow named Ishmael Archer, a professor of English, and Abigail Bird, an unmarried student with a master's degree in literature and a part-time job as a waitress. These two characters resided in a small town named Highland Falls, located at the foot of the Adirondack Mountains in New York State. Professor Archer was employed at an unexceptional institution of higher learning known as Longfellow College. The story commenced at Professor Archer's summer creative writing course, and concluded when the aforementioned Ms. Bird suffered a fall in a glade by the town's waterfall.

As my days were filled conducting lectures on literature and the grading of papers, I wrote late at night, often remaining awake until the early hours of the following day, my energy fueled by inspiration and copious amounts of strong coffee. I became a man consumed by a growing obsession, filling pages with words that came to me in such a cascade that my fingers could barely keep up with my mind.

During this intense process, I took frequent evening breaks during which I visited Abigail and proceeded with my courtship of her, a process that included the occasional jaunt to a restaurant or a movie or, occasionally, to a mediocre drama performed at the college. I needed this occasional hiatus, as my lower back was beginning to suffer the painful effects of prolonged hours of sitting in my poorly designed desk chair.

On another occasion, I happened to encounter Constance. I had been attempting to climb upon my bicycle, which Mr. Williger had repaired quite expertly, when she called out my name. When I espied her striding toward me, her arms yet again overladen with books and papers, I removed my helmet from my head and my body from my two-wheeled vehicle to greet her.

"Have you taken up the lifestyle of a hermit, Ishmael?" she asked. "I haven't seen you in weeks."

"I have undertaken a project of sorts and it is this that has kept me in my place of residence."

She narrowed her eyes. "May I ask what sort of project it is?"

It was with a certain degree of pride that I said, "I am currently in the midst of penning a book."

"That's great news! I'm so happy for you, Ishmael," she said, embracing me. "What inspired this sudden burst of creativity?"

As I did not wish to reveal the details behind my inspiration, I merely said, "Who knows from whence creativity springs?"

"So tell me. What's it about?"

I wavered. "You might call it a love story."

"I see. That's it? No further details?"

"Perhaps at a later date."

"Why are you being so mysterious?"

I shrugged. "The book is currently in its infancy. I will be glad to fill you in when it has matured."

"Okay, so when may I read it?"

"When I have completed it, of course."

"If it's fiction, don't let Abigail read it. We don't want to go through all that again, do we?"

"Do not worry, Constance," I said. "I am well aware of the consequences should Abigail read it."

Wishing not to field any further inquiries, lest I inadvertently reveal my deception, I climbed back onto my bicycle and carefully placed my helmet atop my head. "The muse beckons," I said.

"Don't be a stranger!" Constance shouted after me.

"I will see you anon," I said, and off I went.

The following day, Eliot stepped into my office as I was grading a stack of utterly atrocious essays regarding the character of Hetty Sorrel in *Adam Bede*. He reminded me of his previous offer to celebrate his ascension to the role of dean. I recalled the invitation but had assumed he had forgotten about it, as it had been issued in a casual fashion. Despite my excuses, Eliot was adamant.

"Don't forget, Archer, I'm the dean, ergo your boss," he said with a good-humored tone. "I therefore order you to be at my house this Thursday at seven o'clock."

And so I duly appeared at Eliot's house five minutes prior to the designated time. Owing to the demands of my writing venture, I had once again existed on little more than junk food for the last few weeks, so I found a hearty meal to be a most welcome relief from chips, cookies, and Cheetos. Sandra delivered a sumptuous repast. We toasted Eliot's success several times, although my glass was filled with Sprite rather than champagne, for I wished to remain alert for the remainder of the evening in order to write.

At one point, Eliot excused himself and ambled into his garage where he kept his wine. Sandra and I smiled at each other pleasantly as he disappeared into his makeshift above-ground wine cellar.

"I have come upon an interesting coincidence, Sandra," I said. "It appears that we have a mutual acquaintance."

"Oh? And who is that?"

"A young gentleman by the name of Mr. Williger."

If she was startled, I was unable to perceive it in her expression. "I don't believe I know him. Is he one of your students?"

"He was. He has since graduated."

"Nope, don't know him."

"Yet, he claims you are quite well known to each other."

Taking a sip of her wine but keeping her eyes on me, she said, "I'm sorry, but the name escapes me."

"Such an alibi is ineffectual, Sandra. The fact is, I happened to catch sight of you and Mr. Williger in your convertible on the day of the Highland Falls art fair. You were parked in the shade not far from the Porto-Potty."

She blushed. "Did you happen to see—?"

"I'm afraid I did."

For a moment Sandra did not speak. "Well, that's pretty goddamn embarrassing. Were you spying on me, Ishmael?"

"Most certainly not! I was merely approaching the portable commode to relieve my bladder."

"Oh Christ," she said, placing her palms over her eyes. "You won't tell Eliot I hope?"

"I shall not breathe a word as I do not wish to cause any distress, yet I have a question which I would like you to answer truthfully." I paused for a moment. "Please tell me precisely why you engaged Mr. Williger to murder Dean Fletcher's orchids."

"He told you that?" Sandra said, outraged. "Dammit!"

"Yes, he did indeed inform me of this deplorable act, for he felt a great deal of guilt about it."

Sandra sighed and looked away. "I did it because I wanted Eliot to get the job as dean."

"Yes, I deduced as much."

"I apologize, Archer," she said. "I'm really sorry that I fucked things up for you. It was awful of me."

"Never mind that. I did not really wish to have the position anyway."

"Oh," she said, surprised.

I decided to be bold. "I do not know if I believe Mr. Williger, for he is not terribly astute at times, although I do have some fondness for him. In any case, he speculated that perhaps you wished to assure your husband's success so that you would have more freedom with which to carry on more...shall we say...clandestine activities."

"Certainly not!" she said. "That's an awful thing to say, Archer. What a low opinion you must have of me."

"Trust me, I do not wish to judge you, Sandra. You are free to do as you like. I am not a Puritan. I am merely positing a theory put forth by your former paramour."

She placed her wineglass on the table. "I killed the orchids because I knew how much that job meant to Eliot," she said. "He's a very ambitious man. I want him to be happy. I love him, Archer. My extramarital affairs are a thing of the past, I assure you. We're trying to patch up our marriage. That was the reason we went on that romantic jaunt to New York a few weeks ago. We stayed at the Plaza and spent much of our time in bed. I swear to you, that is the God's honest truth."

Although I was not interested in learning more about their sexual escapades in a bed at the Plaza Hotel, her face told me that she was being truthful. I must confess I felt a trifle embarrassed at having accepted the incorrect conclusion espoused by Mr. Williger. I was about to apologize to Sandra when Eliot stepped back into the room with a bottle of Pinot in his hand. "How about another glass, darling?" he asked Sandra. "It's your favorite and who knows what it may lead to later."

As Sandra smiled provocatively at her husband and eagerly extended her glass, Eliot handily popped the cork and winked at me.

&

Shortly thereafter I completed work on my book, all seventy pages of it. I struggled over attaching an appropriate title and, after a few hours of contemplation, finally chose a simple one that I thought would adequately summarize its subject matter. I titled it, *All About Abigail.*

Once it was fully edited and devoid of spelling, punctuation, and typographical errors, I printed it and placed it in an attractive plastic folder in order to create a more impressive presentation. Of course, I did not consult Dr. Partridge, for I knew that she would attempt to forbid me from giving it to Abigail, an act that had been my entire purpose in writing it. My goal was to inspire her to return to her identity as Abigail One, just as she had taken on the identity of a character from Butler's novel. This, I theorized, would cause her to reveal her past feelings or lack thereof for me. Of secondary importance, my strategy might bring back her love of literature as well as her gift for writing. In all modesty, I must confess, I found the notion quite ingenious.

"What is this?" she asked when I presented the finished manuscript to her the day after I had completed it.

"It is a short...book...a story actually...that I recently finished writing," I said.

"That's wonderful, Archer. I'm ever so very happy for you."

"Thank you, Abigail. I hope you will enjoy it. I plan to dedicate it to you, for I think of you as my muse."

She seemed astonished at my words. "Truly?"

"Yes."

"That is such a lovely compliment," she said, placing a hand over her heart. "I'm at a loss for words, Archer."

"I would not have written it were it not for you."

She smiled. "What inspired this sudden burst of creativity?"

"Why *you* did, of course."

She frowned. "Is this a fictional book, Archer?" she asked, with a trace of displeasure. "I do believe that you recently told me that you had written several novels in the past but, as you know, I haven't had the inclination to read them, for which I hope you will forgive me."

"Yes," I said. "It is indeed fiction. Although I know you do not care for this genre, I would like to hear your opinion of it all the same."

"All right," she said, with a tepid smile. "I suppose that would be all right, but I don't believe I've ever read a fictional tale."

"That does not matter. I think you will find it to your liking."

"Well...okay. Do you mind if I read it now while you are here? It seems quite short."

"Please do."

It was with a degree of hesitancy that she flipped open the cover. I watched her intently as she turned the pages, demonstrating her amusement by letting forth an occasional chuckle. She even became tearful at one point, which I interpreted as a promising sign. In all, it took her an hour. When she had finished, she placed it on the coffee table without a word.

"Did you enjoy it, Abigail?" I finally asked her.

"Oh yes," she said. "But to be honest, I'm a little confused, Archer."

"Oh? And why is that?"

"You said that this was a work of fiction."

"I did indeed."

She frowned, picked up the manuscript again and quickly thumbed through its pages. "But if it is a work of fiction, why didn't you change the names of these characters? Why did you choose to name the characters Abigail Bird and Professor Ishmael Archer? Did you perhaps lack the imagination to come up with fictional names?"

"No."

She paused. "Nonetheless, Archer, I think the story is quite fanciful."

"Does any of it feel familiar to you, Abigail?"

She frowned. "No," she said. "Why would it?"

I pressed on. "The Abigail in the book took a creative writing class that the Archer character taught."

"Yes. It seems that this Abigail was most interested in becoming an author."

"But you are not?"

"I believe I've told you several times that I have no interest in it."

"You have."

It then occurred to me that I had never actually witnessed Abigail's past transformations into fictional characters, so I did not know whether they were immediate or gradual. Perhaps if I departed and then returned the next day, she would assume the character's identity. Maybe she needed to slumber.

Yet, I decided to remain with her and probe further into the matter. "And how did you find the section where Abigail successfully climbs the rocks at the glade by the waterfall?"

"She was most daring and impetuous."

"And her attendance at the art fair with Professor Archer?"

"Very entertaining."

"And the character's obsession with the reading of literature?"

"Interesting but hardly an engrossing detail."

Perhaps she noted my expression of dismay for her next words were, "You have a remarkable imagination, Archer."

"Thank you," I mumbled.

Now I was confused, not to mention thoroughly disappointed. How could this be? It made no logical sense to me. If she had been transformed into Anna Karenina, Daisy Buchanan, and the woman in Butler's novel, why had she not taken on the identity of Abigail One as she was portrayed in my story?

"Were there any parts of the book that you particularly enjoyed?" I asked eventually, not knowing what else to say.

She gave the matter a moment of thought. "Yes. I liked the part in which Professor Archer attempts to catch the Greyhound bus. That was very suspenseful and quite romantic."

"Hmm," I said.

"Also, I thought it was so very sweet of Professor Archer to gently wipe the drops of strawberry ice cream that had fallen on Abigail's dress. I liked that very much. It was so chivalrous of him. I was very touched."

"And the accident at the glade? How did you find that?"

"Most tragic! That poor young lady."

"Yes, quite tragic indeed, "I mused, scratching my head, not yet ready to concede defeat. "Perhaps you should take a nap, Abigail."

She gave me a look that contained equal parts mirth and confusion. "A nap?" she said. "Whatever for, Archer? It's ten o'clock in the morning. I woke up no more than two hours ago."

"You look a bit tired."

"I assure you," she said, "I am wide awake."

I sighed deeply. Now I worried that I had inadvertently caused poor Abigail's identity problems to worsen. Certainly, her level of confusion was now elevated. Perhaps I should have altered the names of the characters. Yet, had I done so, Abigail would no doubt have been transformed into whichever name I had chosen for her.

I was tempted to consult Dr. Partridge, in the hope that she would be able to enlighten me about the bewildering failure of my strategy, but I did not, for fear that she would become angry at my recklessness.

Not surprisingly, I was unable to sleep that night. How could I have been so utterly foolish as to think that I, a professor of English could begin to comprehend the science of delusion, hallucination, and identity loss? I was neither a neurologist nor a psychiatrist; I knew nothing of the intricacies of the human brain and even less about the effects of traumatic brain injury. Yet, I had taken it upon myself to conjure a deception that I had hoped would magically result in a positive effect and give rebirth to Abigail One. In short, I was an addlepate of the highest caliber.

As I lay on my bed, staring at a sinuous crack in my ceiling that threatened to cause the plaster to collapse, most likely on my head, I repeated in my mind the events of the day, dwelling upon each of Abigail's specific reactions to my interrogation. Yes, there had been some suspense involved in my inept attempt to reach the bus station during a torrential downpour, but she had not actually *witnessed* this scenario. What did that mean? As for our initial attendance at the Highland Falls' art fair, the only occurrence she seemed to enjoy was a minor moment in which I had cleansed her dress of an errant dollop of strawberry ice cream. Her tumble from the rocks had simply been, in her word, "tragic." It was as if these incidents had all happened to someone other than herself. There was simply no logic to be found in the matter.

Impatient at my frustrating inability to attain a state of slumber, I rose and repaired to the kitchen, where I explored the depths of my half-empty refrigerator and, after discovering nothing of interest there, finally indulged in a stale bag of kettle corn. I brought this item to my desk and, for no particular reason, switched on my computer and proceeded to locate the file that contained my story, *All About Abigail*.

As I idly read through it, taking little joy in the process as it had been such a resounding fiasco, I considered deleting it in its entirety, but it occurred to me then that perhaps something could be salvaged. In all modesty, I had to admit that it was written quite splendidly and, as a romantic story, it might well appeal to a publisher of some reputation. Of course, I would have to alter all the names and expand it, but neither of those alterations would require a great deal of effort. I already knew the story.

But then I stumbled upon a section of the book that nearly caused my eyes to pop out of my head. With mounting exuberance, I perused the segment in question again. I was both astounded and profoundly uplifted by the words—or rather the lack thereof—and, in order to ascertain whether this was indeed the same version that Abigail had read earlier that day, I hastened to my coffee table upon which the manuscript sat and let my fingers flip hurriedly through the pages.

જ

As I had predicted, my inept meddling in Abigail's case did not please Dr. Partridge, but her displeasure was soon assuaged by my momentous discovery of the previous night. On my way to the hospital, I had called Balthazar, who had arrived at Highland Falls that morning, and requested his immediate presence in Dr. Partridge's office. Although I did not detail the nature of my fateful discovery to him over the phone, I assured him that it was of considerable import.

"Are you sure…about this, Professor Archer?" Dr. Partridge asked. "There was absolutely no…mention of this episode in your story?"

"Quite correct."

"Nor did you duplicate the…strawberry ice cream cone incident during your visitation to the Orangeville art fair?"

"I attempted to, but there were no ice cream vendors to be found on the premises. And of course there was no guarantee that she would once again dribble ice cream onto her dress as she had before."

"Quite extraordinary…Professor," she said.

But Balthazar seemed puzzled. "Let me see if I have this straight, Ishmael. You wrote a story about you and Abigail, which was actually a memoir but you presented it to Abigail as fiction."

"Correct."

He appeared irked. "That was probably a mistake."

"Agreed. Although in light of this revelation, perhaps not."

"And after she read it, you asked her to tell you which parts she had enjoyed the most?" Balthazar continued.

"Correct."

"And she told you that one of her favorite episodes in the story concerned a strawberry ice cream cone that she had enjoyed at your venture to the art fair in Highland Falls prior to her accident."

"Correct."

With every question, Balthazar's voice became increasingly animated. "Yet this episode was not present in the manuscript that she read yesterday?"

"Correct!"

"You are certain of this?"

"I am," I said. "Thus, my conclusion is that she has remembered that occurrence from the time before her accident."

"That's...utterly amazing!" Balthazar said, then turned to Dr. Partridge. "In your opinion, doctor, do you believe this to be a breakthrough?"

Dr. Partridge glared at me. "Professor, I am still very...angry at you for taking it upon...yourself to indulge this whim...without first consulting...with me. I had told you before...that such revelations... might be traumatic for Abigail."

I attempted to project a degree of shame. "I know, doctor, and for that I apologize, but you have not yet answered Dr. Bird's query."

Dr. Partridge looked first at Dr. Bird and then at me. "It may be premature...for me to say this...but yes, this certainly might...be a breakthrough."

PART SIX

Eighteen

Sadly, Abigail's curious breakthrough involving the strawberry ice cream cone appeared to be nothing more than an anomaly, for there were no further remembrances regarding her life as Abigail One, although on one occasion, prior to a dinner date, I happened to witness her examining both pairs of Algonquin earrings as they sat upon her vanity. Her brow was wrinkled, seemingly in perplexity, which led me to believe that perhaps she was in the process of recalling the purchase of the first pair during our outing to the Highland Falls art fair. It seemed such a long time ago, as if I, too, had lived a previous life.

As I sat languidly in her parlor, waiting for her to choose her attire, she held both sets of earrings up for me to behold. "Which pair of these do you think I should wear, Archer? As you can see, they're quite similar except for the colors."

"The pair with the crimson stripe matches your socks," I said.

"You're always such a wizard when it comes to clothes, Archer."

"Thank you. It is true that I have a certain fashion sense. But why do you suppose you have *two* pairs of them, Abigail?"

She studied the earrings as if they were rare breeds of insect life. "I really don't know. I recall that you bought this pair for me when we went to the art fair in Orangeville, but I am at a complete loss regarding the other pair. How bizarre."

"Perhaps I purchased them for you at an earlier time. Perhaps at another art fair."

A pensive look appeared on her face. "But we did not attend another fair," she said. "Besides, although they're quite attractive, a person doesn't really need two nearly identical pairs of earrings of Native American provenance, if that's really their true origin, which I

218

doubt, not that I'm an expert in such things. Yet it was very thoughtful and kind of you."

"It was my pleasure, Abigail." When she had put them on, I said, "They look quite striking on you."

She gave me a look that appeared to display affection, or at least that was my interpretation. "Thank you, Archer."

As she stood before me with the earrings dangling from her lobes, I was transported back to the day upon which I had bought her the first pair. A moment later, my thoughts turned to the day of the second purchase. Had her reactions on both occasions not been the same?

Happily, Dr. Partridge had been quite correct in her prediction that, in spite of her amnesia, Abigail Two was essentially the same delightful, charming young woman she had been as Abigail One. Had she loved me then? Would I ever know the answer? The question gnawed at me. Was she developing romantic feelings for me now? The profound passion I held for her had never dissipated, not even when she had been Anna Karenina or Daisy Buchanan, although her delusion regarding Butler's character was somewhat irritating. More importantly, Abigail Two's lack of interest in literature was no longer of any great significance to me, for I had come to the conclusion that a shared interest is not a vital component of love. If a man is obsessively captivated by the sport of baseball and his mate is not, this should not prevent him from loving said mate. After all, books are but stories that contain another person's view of existence. I do not mean to denigrate literature, for much of it contains profound perceptions of human life and I shall never forsake my fascination with the classics. But sadly, upon reflection, I realized that I had spent most of my days living vicariously through the characters in these tales—I was not Fitzwilliam Darcy, Amory Blaine, or D'Artagnon—and it was a welcome relief to finally exist in a world of reality in which Ishmael Archer was the protagonist, and the story was that of his own life. Abigail had awakened in me a certain depth of feeling of which I did not previously know I was capable.

But then, several days thereafter, a most troublesome chapter in the story of Ishmael Archer commenced. That afternoon, in desperate need of a container of shoe polish, I ventured via automobile to an establishment on Elm Street that sold such merchandise. Although it was February, the weather was most pleasant and required only a light jacket. The recent snow had turned to slush, and beads of water dripped in a steady rhythm from the icicles that had formed upon branches.

I was motoring down Walnut Street, some three blocks away from my destination, when I encountered a sight that nearly caused me to lose control of my vehicle—Abigail was walking down said avenue with a young gentleman. At first, I thought my eyes deceived me— perhaps this woman merely resembled Abigail, a doppelgänger but it increasingly became apparent that such was not the case. As my car approached them, I slowed a little. I was thoroughly distraught and did not know quite how to behave in a situation such as this without causing embarrassment.

The gentleman in question was several inches shorter than Abigail, quite thin and lanky, perhaps in his thirties. Beneath his baseball cap, emblazoned with the logo of the New York Yankees, I could discern a stubbled beard. His cargo pants and wrinkled sweatshirt suggested a man possessed of no particular sartorial taste or grooming, yet the two of them appeared to be engaged in animated conversation. They were not, however, holding hands or otherwise physically engaged, to my considerable relief.

When I arrived at the first intersection, I impulsively performed an illegal U-turn, an act that resulted in a raucous cacophony of honking cars, and drove slowly back down the street until my vehicle was about twenty yards behind the two. Were I to again drive past them, Abigail might notice my automobile, and I did not wish to be thrust into an awkward situation requiring me to remove myself from my car and interrupt their conversation.

Yet, I was beside myself. At the next intersection, I turned right and, once out of their range of sight, sped back to my apartment.

Who, I wondered, was this fellow? Where had they met, and what was the precise nature of their relationship? Abigail had mentioned nothing to me regarding an affiliation with another man. Had she deliberately kept this information from me and if so, why? For how long had this association been going on? When had it begun? Was he a colleague from her job? A customer? Someone she had recently met at the local Starbucks? Had they shared a bed? If not, were they about to? Whoever the gentleman was, this situation would not do. As a confirmed pessimist, I feared the worst.

I do not know why it took me so long to realize it, but at that moment it occurred to me that Abigail would not remain forever without a true paramour. After all, a woman had certain…needs. Perhaps she wished to marry and produce offspring. We had never discussed these topics.

Yes, it was indeed time for me to stop delaying my declaration, for the prospect of losing her was inconceivable. I could dillydally no longer, come what may.

&

That evening, I hied myself to Abigail's dwelling. Of course, I was quite fearful that I would find her in the amorous embraces of the young gentleman, but I could no longer delay. In order to fortify myself for this worrisome mission, I had imbibed half a glass of wine.

To my relief, when Abigail appeared before me in the doorway, she was not clad in an ensemble that could be considered seductive—she was attired in a pair of yellow flannel pajamas emblazoned with images of chimpanzees, and a pair of fuzzy red slippers. As she opened the door and ushered me inside, I glanced around the room for signs of the interloper and was relieved to find no visible evidence, not that I was quite certain exactly what it was I was looking for.

"Why, Archer!" Abigail said. "What brings you here at such a late hour? Not that I am unhappy to see you."

In point of fact, it was only seven o'clock, but I made no

mention of this. "I must speak with you, Abigail. On a matter of some urgency."

"You look so serious, Archer," she said. "Is there something unpleasant you wish to tell me?"

"Not at all. I hope you will find it most agreeable."

She studied me. "Yet, you appear somewhat…nervous. You seem to be fidgeting."

"I assure you, I am quite calm." In truth, my stomach felt as though it were housing a family of moths that had recently ingested an overdose of amphetamines.

"Oh. Well, please do come in and make yourself comfortable."

I had come to Abigail's residence with two purposes in mind— the first, to determine the depth of her relationship with the young gentleman; the second, to finally declare my feelings for her. But as I gazed at her, I decided that the long-awaited declaration should take precedence. The identity of her mysterious companion would be irrelevant if she rejected me.

I settled upon her sofa. Then I patted the area beside me, an indication that I wished for her to sit there, to which she readily complied. Although my mind was conflicted, I suddenly felt the strong urge to revise my strategy by prefacing my remarks with a forbidden subject. Generally, I am not a man given to impulsiveness but on this particular occasion, I found myself possessed of an over-whelming desire to begin my declaration with an honest revelation that would expose the true duration of my love and adoration for Abigail. In retrospect, I believe I simply wished her to know that my courtship of her had predated the one in which we were currently involved. And, as Abigail had observed, I was indeed fidgeting.

I boldly took both her hands in mine. For a few moments, I paused.

"Abigail, I have something of great import to tell you."

"All right," she said. "By all means, please proceed."

"Do you remember reading my story not long ago?"

"Yes, of course."

I hesitated again, knowing that Dr. Partridge would certainly disapprove of what I was about to say. "Do you perchance remember a part of the story in which the Abigail character consumes a strawberry ice cream cone at the art fair and spills a few dollops on her dress, which are then removed by the Archer character?"

"Why, yes! I found it a most touching scene, as I told you."

I drew a deep breath. "The part about the strawberry ice cream cone does not in actuality appear in the story."

Abigail frowned. "Of course it does."

"No, it does not. I promise you. I reread the story several times and found nothing relating to this scenario."

I observed the bewilderment in her eyes. "Well, perhaps I simply imagined it in some way. I don't know. A dream, perhaps."

"No," I said. After a moment of silence, I added, "This event actually took place at an earlier time."

She laughed, as if I had just told her a mediocre joke. "Had that been the case, I'm sure I would have recalled it."

"You did! In point of fact, this episode did indeed take place and it was *you* who spilled the ice cream, and it was *I* who wiped it away with my pocket handkerchief."

"You jest, Archer," she said. "That's impossible."

I sighed and decided on a different approach. "Do you remember the part in which the Abigail character suffers a fall from the rock staircase at the waterfall?"

"Yes," she said.

"And that she hits her head and falls unconscious?"

"Yes."

"Well, that too actually occurred."

"Oh yes? To whom?"

I gripped her hands tighter. "To *you*."

Again, an expression of bafflement overtook her visage. "Archer," she said in a firm tone, "I am not finding this at all humorous."

"It is not intended thus, Abigail. I am being perfectly serious. The fact is, you suffered what is known in medical terminology as a

223

traumatic brain injury some months ago after falling from the afore-mentioned rock wall."

"No, this is most assuredly not true." Then she narrowed her eyes at me. "Archer, have you been drinking alcohol?"

"Of course not! I assure you, I am quite sober."

"Perhaps you have taken a mind-altering drug of some sort then?"

"Absolutely not!"

"A severe blow to the head?"

"No."

"Perhaps it was something you ate?"

"Negative."

Her face flushed and her eyes commenced to display signs of anger. "Then why are you speaking such utter nonsense?"

"It is not nonsense, Abigail," I said. "As a result of your head injury, you were in a coma for several weeks and when you awoke you had no memory of your past life, nor do you at present."

At that, I felt her body stiffen and she pulled her hands out of mine. I could feel her ire mounting. Perhaps I should then have ceased my narrative, but I found myself unable to do so and continued. "In your past life, you were a dedicated reader of literature and wished to become an author. We first encountered one another at a creative writing class that I conducted."

"Archer, I wish to change the subject," Abigail said. "I am finding this imaginary tale of yours quite disturbing."

"You did not recognize me when you awakened from the coma, nor did you even know the identity of your father."

"I beseech you to stop at once! I did not take you to be a liar!"

Yet still I persisted. "The reason you have two sets of Indian earrings is because I bought you one set before your coma and the other afterwards."

Abigail clapped her hands over her ears and commenced to hum a tune. "Enough of this!" she said.

Rather than remove her hands from her auditory organs, I raised my voice. "Abigail, you must believe that I—"

"STOP!" she said, rising to her feet. As I had never witnessed her in a state of wrath, I was taken aback.

"I believe, though I am not certain, that during this pre-coma stage, you held some romantic feelings for me," I said. "I had great romantic affection for you at this time and I still love you with—"

But I believe that she did not hear my words for her hands remained over her ears and my declaration produced no effect. Blinded by rage, she removed one hand and pointed at the door.

"I would like you to leave now, Archer," she said.

"Did you not hear what I just said?"

"No, I am no longer listening to you."

"But—"

"Get out!" she said. "I believed that we were friends, but clearly we are not. I no longer know what to think of you!"

"Abigail please…I just told you that I—"

"Get out of my sight, Archer!" she said. "How many times must I say it? I cannot bear this cruel nonsense anymore!"

"Abigail, please believe me when I say that—"

"GET OUT! GET OUT!"

"Abigail, I beg you, please be reasonable. I did not mean to upset you. You must believe that I have no reason to lie."

Abigail's visage was now deeply flushed; a vein stood out on her forehead; her hands trembled. I made an attempt to calm her by taking her hand, but she withdrew it and marched to the door, which she then opened. "Leave me now and never come back. This is a cruel, cruel joke and I do not know why you are acting in this way. Your behavior is… reprehensible! I do not wish to ever see you again."

"Please calm yourself," I said.

"I will not! How many times must I repeat it? Leave me this instant. NOW!"

Mournfully, I stood up and trudged to the exit, but then I turned to face her one more time. "Abigail I—"

"Goodbye, Archer."

And then she slammed the door shut with so much force that I thought it would remove itself from its hinges.

&

Utterly forlorn, I stood before her front door and listened to the sound of her weeping. My cardiac organ was pounding with such force, I feared it would exit my chest. A moment later, I heard the distressing sound of a lock engaging from within the house. What foolishness had I perpetrated? Why had I surrendered to impulse? Why had I persisted in the face of her mounting anger? Had I lost my mind? Of course, I desperately wished to re-enter the premises for the purpose of apologizing and perhaps even consoling her, but I did not wish my reappearance to increase the level of her rage. The damage had been done and could not be erased. My conclusion was that it would be most prudent to allow her time to calm herself. As I walked down her front stairs, it was necessary that I hold the bannister, for I was nearly blinded by optical liquidity and did not wish to lose my balance and topple into a hedge. Once safely at the curb, I robotically opened my car door, stepped into the driver's seat and drove away into the night.

I did not know how long I had been driving, nor was I even aware that I was on Route 11, until I noted the "Welcome to Orangeville" sign that stood on the side of the road, its letters somewhat obscured by black swaths of graffiti. I did not really know my way around Orangeville, for I had not been there often, but on a whim, I exited the highway and proceeded into the small neighboring burg. Had I continued on Route 11, I would most likely have gotten hopelessly lost.

Though it was only eight o'clock, the avenues of said burg were deserted and the stores were closed. Having no particular destination, I motored randomly down the streets, one of which took me to an establishment called Doolittle's Olde English Tavern, which I presumed to be a place that served alcoholic beverages. Though I was not desirous of consuming liquor, I felt an urgent need to relieve my bladder.

To my surprise, Doolittle's Olde English Tavern possessed quite a pleasant ambience. Soft lighting emanated principally from an antique chandelier that hung above a long polished mahogany bar and an assortment of oak tables. A grandfather clock ticked annoyingly from one of the corners and a row of nineteenth-century portraits of British nobility graced the walls. The bartender wore a red-striped vest and a bow tie. Even the bathrooms featured antiquated fixtures, and the gender identification signs on the doors were simple brass renderings of men and women dressed in old-fashioned attire—top hat, tuxedo, and cane for the men's lavatory; hoop skirt, wide-brimmed hat, and bodice for the ladies' room.

Following my journey to the lavatory, which was impeccably clean, I contemplated departing but instead settled myself onto a bar stool at the elbow of the bar, for I did not wish to sulk and pace within the solitary confines of my oppressive domicile, and peaceful slumber would surely be impossible.

My seat afforded me an excellent view of the other patrons who were present—a well-dressed elderly gentleman conversing with the bartender, a youngish couple, each absorbed in their cell phones, and a blonde woman clad in a business suit who smiled at me as I sat down. To my left hung a black-and-white photograph of Big Ben.

"What'll it be, mate?" the bartender asked in a British accent.

"Are you, by chance, Mr. Doolittle?" I said, for no particular reason.

"No. There is no Doolittle."

"How curious. Perhaps your establishment derives its name from Mr. George Bernard Shaw's delightful play *Pygmalion?*"

"No. Don't think I ever saw it," he said after a moment of contemplation. "So what can I get you?"

I gave the matter some thought, "Well, perhaps, good sir, you might be kind enough to suggest a suitable libation that would magically quell the intense distress of a man who has suffered the loss of the woman he dearly loves because he voiced to her something that angered her greatly, whereupon she ordered him to depart her abode posthaste."

After a moment of open-mouthed silence, the bartender gave forth a whistle. "Good Lord, that was a bloody long sentence."

"I am given to verbosity on occasion. My apologies."

He waved it off. "Well… the appropriate drink would depend on whether you want to be relieved of your sorrow or wallow in self-pity."

"The latter."

"I'd suggest wine then. Preferably red."

"So be it."

As it happened, he was quite correct. After two glasses of this beverage, I was even more desolate than I had been an hour before. Yet I ordered another.

I was so consumed by thoughts of a dismal nature that I failed to notice that the aforementioned blonde female had dismounted her bar stool and materialized beside me. She, too, was consuming wine.

"Hard day at the office?" she said.

As this was none of her concern, I considered remaining silent but did not wish to appear rude. Thus I replied with a curt, "No."

"Death in the family?"

"No."

"Dog died?"

"No."

"General angst about the state of mankind?"

"Of course, but that is not it either at the moment."

She drummed her fingers on the bar. Evidently, having reached the conclusion that I was not interested in conversation but not yet ready to surrender, she said, "Is it animal, vegetable, or mineral? Maybe we could play charades."

I did not offer a response, yet she possessed a kindly face and a pleasant smile and, having consumed two glasses of the grape, I was somewhat inebriated.

"Sorry, I didn't mean to intrude. I'll leave you to your sulking. Enjoy your—"

"A woman," I said. "It concerns a woman."

She nodded sagely, mounted the stool beside mine, and introduced herself as Carlotta Engelwing, C.P.A., whereupon I informed her that my appellation was Martin Chuzzlewit, D.D.S. "It's usually about a woman," she said. "I should have guessed. Silly me."

As I did not wish to enlighten her regarding the curious reasons behind my recent tragic encounter with Abigail, for these would more than likely cause Ms. Engelwing, C.P.A., to question my sanity, I merely said, "I am afraid my paramour has jilted me."

Ms. Engelwing smiled and touched my hand. "Welcome to the club, honey."

I frowned. "There exists a club? How curious."

"You're funny."

"That is not my intention," said I. "I am not generally thought of as a man of great wit."

"So you had an argument with this woman?"

"Indeed," I said. "I attempted to enlighten her about something that she did not wish to hear. Her reaction to this was most unpleasant. It was entirely my fault, and now I sorely regret my actions. She grew angry, ordered me to depart the premises, and informed me quite emphatically that she did not wish to see me ever again."

"Does she love you?"

"Alas, I do not know."

"Why?"

"She has never indicated it. She refers to me as a 'friend.'"

"Have you ever tried to put the moves on her?"

"If by 'moves' you refer to sexual advances, the answer is no, I have not."

"Why not?"

"Because, dear Ms. Engelwing, I am not that sort of fellow."

"So you're not normal, you mean?"

"For your information, I am perfectly normal," I said. "It is, as

229

they say, a long story. May we please move on to other pastures?"

She nodded. "Well then, let me ask you this, Martin. Have you at least asked her how she feels about you?"

"Alas, no."

"Why not?"

"I am afraid that cowardice, derived from several previous disastrous entanglements with members of your gender, has prevented me from inquiring about it."

"You know what I think?" she said.

"What?"

"I think you need to grow a pair of balls."

I gave her a questioning look. "If you are referring to testicles, I already possess the correct number, which I believe is two, and I do not wish to further burden my undergarments with a third. Secondly, I do not think this is even remotely possible."

She was silent for a moment, as if she was awaiting a punch line. When one was not forthcoming, she said, "I think you know what I mean, Martin."

"I do indeed. But as I was telling you before regarding my *affair d'amour*, I cannot, at this time, inquire about my would-be paramour's feelings for me or lack thereof because the young lady in question just made it abundantly clear that she does not wish to see me again in the future."

"Maybe you should just call her and apologize."

"I dare not for I sense that this approach would cause her to anger even more intensely."

"Well, as they say, Martin, time heals all wounds."

I made a disparaging sound with my nostrils. "With all due respect, Ms. Engelwing, I am afraid that I do not subscribe to banal proverbs such as that one. They are mostly incorrect."

She shrugged. "Just trying to be helpful."

"I am aware of that," I said. "Please do not take offense."

"None taken."

It was then that I felt a distinct signal from my gastric organ that regurgitation would be an imminent possibility, which was confirmed when Ms. Engelwing told me that my face appeared to possess a somewhat greenish coloration. As this sensation commenced to increase in urgency, I tumbled from my stool and, with my hand covering my mouth, made it to the commode, where I proceeded to vomit with more than a little intensity.

As I was too light-headed to safely convey myself home, I temporarily abandoned my automobile in the parking lot, for the bartender had been kind enough to summon a taxi. This journey cost me dearly for it was a fifteen-mile trek. As I did not possess sufficient currency, I was compelled to knock on Felix's front door for the purpose of borrowing the difference. He was happy to lend it to me as I had recently settled my rental debt, but when he inquired about my unusual inebriation, I assured him that I would illuminate him at a later date regarding the cause of my sorry state of being.

I slept fitfully that night, my mind awash with thoughts of the crisis I had stupidly brought upon myself. The following morn, I awoke with a headache of such considerable severity that I would have happily submitted myself to a guillotine in order to be rid of the agony, although I was reasonably certain that no one in Highland Falls or the surrounding areas possessed such a macabre instrument of decapitation. Instead, I consumed several tablets of a medication known as Tylenol, which somewhat relieved the pain.

Physically as well as emotionally sickened, I canceled my classes for two days and lay abed, attempting fruitlessly to occupy my mind with reading, but I found it nearly impossible to concentrate. As Ms. Engelwing had suggested, I contemplated placing a call to Abigail but soon dismissed this notion, for I feared that she would not be pleased to hear from me while she still harbored such profound displeasure, and I would not be able to endure another confrontation such as the one that had occurred the last time we had been together. Most likely, she would not answer the phone. Balthazar called me to inquire about his daughter's wellbeing, but I did not advise him regarding our recent dispute. I merely told him that she was quite well. Constance also called, but I did not reply to her voicemails.

Two weeks passed and I began to lose all hope of reconciliation. Although I resumed my classes, teaching was now an entirely joyless endeavor, and my demeanor was decidedly grim. Yet whenever I encountered Constance or Eliot, I produced counterfeit smiles of varying mirth and attempted to act as if there was nothing amiss.

Not wishing to appear utterly foolish, I resisted the temptation to make an appearance at Phil's Rib and Steak Emporium for fear that Abigail might ignore me, a fate that would leave me with no alternative but to sit alone whilst consuming a foul concoction from Phil's menu. There was also the possibility, albeit remote, that she would throw water or some other liquid in my face.

Nor did I encounter Abigail in town or on campus. Perchance she had taken a romantic holiday with the young gentleman or fallen back into the embraces of William Octavian Butler. The mere visualization of such a horrid scenario caused me to lay awake at night, and I sometimes wished that I had simply maintained my former solitary life rather than engage in a romantic involvement with a female of the species, for at least my former lifestyle—uneventful and unfulfilling as it had been—had held no possibility of emotional turbulence. Returning to monkhood had its appeal.

But I digress.

On several occasions, I drove past Abigail's apartment building but I did not espy her, for all her curtains and blinds were closed. As I did not wish to appear too pathetic, I abstained from any further surveillance and, from that time on, avoided motoring down her street.

Nearly every night, as I lay abed, recounting every minor detail of my last encounter with Abigail, I wished that I had conducted myself in a different manner. Why had I not silenced myself upon witnessing the onset of her fury? But, as some say, one cannot put toothpaste back in the tube, although on one morning, I attempted this exercise with a container of a dental cleanser named Colgate and found that it was not entirely impossible.

A month passed with no word from Abigail. More than a few times, I dialed her phone number, but I never made it past the sixth digit.

On several occasions, I encountered Constance, and although I was tempted to seek her advice on the matter, I refrained, sensing that she would most likely berate me for having confronted Abigail with the details of her past life. I was well aware that I had horribly misjudged the situation and did not wish to suffer through a scolding.

Instead, I found myself confiding my woes to Felix. He was not a denizen of the so-called ivory tower and ergo the only acquaintance of mine who possessed some knowledge of the ways of the world, especially in regards to the fair sex. After all, Felix had grown up in a family populated principally by women and was the father of two daughters. However, much to my chagrin, the most perceptive analytical response he was able to muster was a Greek adage that roughly translated means: "Who understands women? They are all crazy!" Yet, I sincerely enjoyed his company and we set a date for a discussion of Hemingway's *Green Hills of Africa*, an event at which he promised to introduce me to another Greek alcoholic beverage known as Metaxa.

Nineteen

Apparently, Felix was overeager to begin our scheduled book discussion because I received a knock on my door an hour prior to our scheduled meeting. This had transpired before, and I admit to having been somewhat perturbed by it. Punctuality dictates that one appears at the precise appointed hour, not after, and certainly not an hour before. (My philosophy regarding punctuality dictates that ten minutes is the limitation for an early appearance.) In any case, I had been in the midst of cleaning my apartment in preparation for his arrival, and the ear shattering cacophony of my second-hand vacuum cleaner nearly prevented me from hearing his rapping. But when I opened the door it was not Felix who stood there.

"Hello, Archer," Abigail said in a voice that seemed to contain some degree of annoyance.

"Abigail" was the only word I could muster.

"May I come in?"

"Yes, of course!"

She followed me inside and proceeded to pace while I lowered my anatomy onto a chair and watched her. I noticed that she was wearing Wellingtons and carrying an umbrella. There had been precipitation earlier in the day but it had since ceased. I felt my heart flutter, as if a ventricle was fanning my ribcage. What was she doing here?

Before speaking, she stopped abruptly in the midst of her journey from one end of the room to the other, and held my gaze for nearly ten seconds, although it felt like an eternity. "I've missed you, Archer," she said. "I have missed you very much."

I was momentarily taken aback by her admission, for it was unexpected, although, of course, encouraging. "And I have missed you," I said.

"It's been a month, Archer."

"Not to nitpick, but in point of fact, it has been precisely thirty-eight days, seventeen hours and…" I glanced at my watch. "Forty-seven minutes."

"How have you been?"

"Miserable," I said. "And you?"

She did not immediately reply. "I, too, have been miserable. The prospect of never seeing you again was… unthinkable."

"For me as well."

"I had hoped that you would call or visit me, but you did not."

"If you recall, you were quite livid when last we encountered one another," I said. "I believed that you did not wish to hear from me ever again, as you rather pointedly insisted."

"Yes, this is true, but I had hoped that you might overlook this dismissal eventually and forgive me for my outburst. Are we not friends?"

Friends. There was that word once again, that disconcerting term that I so despised. I stole a furtive glance at her, hoping that she would elaborate but alas she did not, thus leaving me in a state of profound disappointment.

"Yes," I said. "We are indeed…friends."

"Good. I am happy to hear that."

"But I—"

Before I could finish my sentence, she experienced yet another ill-timed sneezing fit, most likely a result of the dust that had been emitted by my vacuum cleaner. I handed her my pocket-handkerchief, and she blew her nose.

Anticipating her words, I said, "Yes, you may take it with you in order to rid it of mucus." She looked at me quizzically. I then realized that I had spoken these words to Abigail One.

"Shall we take a walk?" she said.

"Yes, if that's what you wish."

"It's a bit dusty in here and it's irritating my nostrils. Have you been vacuuming?"

"Yes."

"You really should buy a new vacuum cleaner, Archer. It makes no sense to pull dust out of the carpet only to spread it elsewhere."

"Quite true."

Grabbing a coat from the rack that stood beside my door, I ushered her out into the somewhat chilly air, noting that she brought her umbrella along. We descended the stairs and proceeded to stroll down the sidewalk. Periodically, drops of water from the trees dripped on our heads, yet she did not open the umbrella. My state of mind was most anxious and I surreptiously glanced at her several times in an attempt to interpret the expression on her face.

"Is there any particular place you wish to go?" I said.

"No. Just an aimless stroll."

I gazed upward and beheld several foreboding clouds. "It may rain again. You were quite sensible to have brought an umbrella."

"If it rains, we can share it," she said.

I turned to her. "Departing from the conversation regarding possible precipitation for a moment, I thought you might be amused to know that following our argument, I was so desolate that I found myself at a bar in Orangeville where I consumed three glasses of wine and subsequently vomited several times in the lavatory."

"That is so very touching," she said. "Not the vomiting part, though."

I nodded. A moment of silence ensued. "Abigail, may I ask you a somewhat personal question?"

"You certainly may, provided it doesn't concern that loathsome tale you told me on the evening of our quarrel."

I decided not to contradict her. "It does not."

"Then by all means proceed."

I hesitated. "Just prior to our last meeting, I happened to espy you strolling down your street with a young gentleman. At this time, I was driving to a shop for the purpose of securing a container of shoe polish, for my footwear had become disgracefully scuffed. I do not wish to intrude, but I am curious regarding his identity."

She reflected on the subject. "I believe you mean my cousin,

Archibald. My father brought him along to visit me. He informed me that I had not seen my young relative in ages. I'm afraid I had quite forgotten him."

Much relieved, I nodded and mouthed the word, "Oh."

Moments later, we found ourselves wandering into an unpopulated playground that boasted a seesaw, several swings, monkey bars, and a slide. This sight reminded me of my youth, for my mother had sometimes escorted me to such places, hoping that I would engage in play with the other children. But I found such sport tiresome and always preferred to read while the others cavorted. Ah, youth!

As we continued our walk, I spotted a wooden bench and thought perhaps Abigail and I might sit upon it for awhile, but it was quite damp so we exited the playground and strolled once again down a tree-lined street with no particular destination.

"May I ask you a question, Archer?" Abigail said.

"By all means. Ask away!"

"Did you perhaps assume that I had...a romantic interest in Archibald when you saw us together, since you did not know that we are related?"

"I confess that the thought had crossed my mind."

Before continuing, Abigail looked down at her shoes. "And did this assumption upset you?"

I steeled myself. "I will admit that it did."

Abigail scrutinized me as if she had something of great significance to utter. "Archer, do you perhaps...have some affection for me that... exists beyond mere friendship?"

A few seconds passed before I was able to croak out the word, "Yes."

"Then why have you not informed me of this before? Why did you give me no reason to think it?"

"I wanted to, Abigail," I said. "But, alas, I was fearful of rejection. It has always been thus for me as I have in the past suffered great humiliation in the pursuit of the fair sex, a complex that commenced in the eighth grade, when I was spurned by a comely young lady by the name of Heloise Chuckerman. Later, when I attended high school, my prom date—a pretty lass by the name of Alexandra Fernspiegel—cruelly deserted me for another young fellow, a cretin, I might add. It has, as they say, been downhill from there regarding other affiliations, including my disastrous marriage and the two experiences that followed.

"I am sorry to hear that, Archer. You poor man."

"I appreciate your sympathy," I said. "But perhaps if you had offered me a signal of sorts that *you* had emotional feelings for *me*, I may have acted."

"But I did!"

"When?"

"Did I not kiss your cheek once?"

"Yes, but—"

"Do you remember when I wore that revealing Japanese garment?"

"I do indeed."

"Were you not stimulated?"

"Yes, but—"

"When we attended the cinema and I wept, were you not moved enough to console me, although, in all honesty, the film was rubbish?"

"Yes, but—"

"Archer, it was *you* who gave *me* no—how did you put it?—signal. I believed that *you* merely thought of us as friends."

"But that is how you referred to me as well."

"And how was I to refer to you? We were not related by blood, nor were we lovers."

"You have a point."

"Archer, I don't mean to insult you, but you are quite thick-headed, " Abigail said, "and much too analytical."

"Alas, you are not the first person to have made that observation." Sensing that this was indeed an opportune time for me to declare my feelings for her, I said, "My dear Abigail, I wish to tell you that I do feel quite an—"

But once again I was unable to finish my sentence. Abigail had been swinging her umbrella in front of her legs, not unlike a person afflicted with blindness searching for obstacles. Given her occasional tendency toward clumsiness, I feared that she might trip over it. As if reading my thoughts, she then withdrew it from her path. This came as a relief, but immediately thereafter she came upon a raised flagstone on the sidewalk and tripped over that. As I was standing a foot in front of her, I quickly turned and caught her before she toppled to the firmament. Of a sudden, she was squarely located in my arms. Our faces were no more than three inches from each other, our noses nearly touched and I was able to take in the sweet scent of her breath, which had a minty quality that I recognized as toothpaste. Without forethought or analysis of this happenstance, I kissed her on the lips and was delighted to perceive that she was most receptive to the coupling of our facial orifices.

"Oh, my dear Abigail," I said when our lips separated, thus allowing us a moment to breathe, as if we were two whales rising above the surface of the sea in order to inhale oxygen prior to plunging back down. "I do indeed have great affection for you, a feeling which one might even designate as love, a word defined in the dictionary as 'a profoundly tender passion for another person.' I have been in this exact state of mind for—"

But Abigail did not allow me to finish. Her arms encircled my waist tightly and she pulled me toward her until our lips once again engaged.

"Oh my goodness," she said. Her eyelids were fluttering, and her face betrayed a dreamlike quality. "How delightful!"

"Most pleasurable indeed."

"I have never experienced a kiss before, Archer. Perhaps we can perform it again?"

Oh joy. Oh rapture! I was beside myself with euphoria, the likes of which I had not experienced since my parents presented me with a leather-bound edition of *Remembrance of Things Past* by Mr. Marcel Proust for my ninth birthday.

❧

We strolled arm in arm toward my apartment, stopping periodically to engage in a passionate kiss, uninhibited by passersby. I felt as elated as a teenager, although as a teenager I had seldom been elated. When we arrived at my domicile, Abigail took my hand and led me into my bedroom, whereupon she pushed me gently onto the bed, which, to my great relief, was bedecked with freshly laundered sheets and pillowcases. Naturally, I had expected her to join me on the bed, but instead she politely excused herself and entered my bathroom, which, as good fortune would have it, I had thoroughly cleansed hours earlier in expectation of Felix's arrival. From the bed, I heard the sound of water shooting through the showerhead, which was followed by the lilting tones of a song that Abigail commenced to sing in a voice only slightly off-key. At least half an hour elapsed before she emerged, her body completely unclothed. I lay upon the bedspread, as wide-eyed as a frightened owl at the sublime beauty of her physical person, and of a sudden my mouth became as arid as the Kalahari, although I have never in actuality ventured there.

"Archer, do you not intend to remove your clothing?" she said with a lustful half smile. "Did you think we were about to take a nap?"

How had I overlooked this obvious necessity? At her suggestion, I rapidly began to remove my trousers but stopped at the knee when I realized that I would first have to rid my feet of my shoes, which I then proceeded to do. I placed them neatly beneath a chair, folded my pants, and began to fold my shirt when Abigail, who was now sensually reclined on the bed, said, "Do you think you might do the folding business at a later time?"

"Yes, of course." Recklessly dropping the rest of my garments to the floor, I approached the bed and lay beside her. We locked in an embrace and at once our eager hands flew about one another's anatomy.

"I must warn you, Archer," she said, interrupting our epidermal exploration. "I am a virgin."

Of course, I knew this was untrue as she had certainly engaged in carnal activity with William Octavian Butler and perhaps others that may have preceded him, but of course she did not recall these events, for they had occurred prior to the onset of her delusion.

"I shall keep that in mind and be gentle."

We then continued our sexual fondling with mounting fervor but in the midst of this she again brought the festivities to a halt.

"Archer, do you by chance own a condom?" she said. "I may wish to one day give birth to a child, but I do not wish to conceive it today."

This gave me pause. "I believe I do indeed, my dearest, but, alas, I have not engaged in sexual activity for quite some time, and I fear that the expiration date of said items may have passed."

As I had not planned ahead for this event, I was momentarily at a loss. "Let me see," I said, reaching into my night table. I found nothing in the way of rubberized male birth control, so I excused myself and hied to the bathroom where I frantically pulled out drawers and opened cabinets but again found nothing. In the midst of this fruitless exploration, there was a rather ill-timed knock at the door.

"Who the devil might that be?" Abigail said with some irritation.

"I do not know," I said as I continued to rummage through my medicine cabinet. "I most certainly shall not answer it."

"Excellent decision."

But the rapping did not cease and in fact grew louder so, with a growl of annoyance, I threw on a robe and opened the door. It was Felix. He appeared to be quite perturbed.

"Felix, although it is always a pleasure to see you, this is perhaps not the best time to—"

"Where have you been, Professor? I came by half an hour ago but nobody answered the door."

"My deepest apologies, Felix," I said. Thereupon, in a soft voice, I offered him an abbreviated version of what had transpired between Abigail and me and within moments his face made the transformation from anger to joy. He slapped me on the back several times and shook my hand, offering me his congratulations.

At that moment, Abigail called from the bedroom, "Archer, what's taking you so long?"

"I shall return shortly, my dearest."

Felix winked at me and turned to leave, but as he was about to depart, I stopped him. "Felix, do you perchance own a condom of recent vintage that I may borrow?"

"Yes, I do, my good friend," he said with a laugh. "But a condom is not really the kind of thing a person *borrows*. I sure the hell don't want it back. You may have one to keep."

"Perhaps two? It has been quite some time since—"

"Two it is!"

"Please, make haste. My damsel awaits!"

A few moments later, with condoms in hand, I returned to the bed where I struggled with trembling hands to pry open one of the packages. Once appropriately outfitted with said item, I proceeded to engage in feverish copulation with my beloved Abigail. As there is no way in which to describe this act without mimicking lurid passages from a genre of fiction known as erotica, I shall abstain. Suffice it to say, nearly every muscle in my body ached by the time our bout of carnal gymnastics had reached its climactic conclusion. To my relief, two aspirin tablets dispatched my discomfort.

Bliss, the likes of which I had never experienced, overtook me, and those I encountered on campus observed that I appeared to have a perpetual smile on my face. One day, I found myself skipping to class, a form of childish propulsion that caused an emanation of laughter from several students and members of the faculty who passed me on the quadrangle. Engaged in reveries, I toppled off my newly refurbished bicycle four times and collided with foliage twice. I informed several people of our budding romance—Constance, Eliot and Sandra, Balthazar, and my parents—all of whom were more than pleased upon hearing the news.

Abigail and I spent every night together, which required us to transport ourselves from one apartment to the other. This commute soon became tiresome. After some discussion, we decided that she would relocate to my somewhat larger apartment, a suggestion that I immediately perceived as somewhat problematical due to the vast number of novels that I possessed. It was Mr. Williger who constructed an elaborate locking system that would prevent anyone other than myself from opening the cabinet doors and this solved the predicament.

As my mattress was a single twin size and thus too small to comfortably accommodate two bodies, I purchased one described by the merchant as a queen size, though I doubted it was meant exclusively for female monarchs. Fortunately, neither of us was beset by the plague of snoring, so we slept quite soundly in each other's arms. I only introduce this topic because my former wife, Amanda Archer, née Blackstone, possessed a snore that resembled the cacophony produced by a dozing plow horse, not that I have ever been in the presence of such an animal during its slumber. Yet, I would imagine that after an arduous day of pulling a plow through hard soil, a horse of this sort would sleep quite soundly.

But I digress.

One night, Abigail suddenly awakened and switched on the light beside our bed, thus waking me as well. She sat up, whereupon she drew her knees to her body and placed her arms around them.

"Is something amiss, my dearest one?" I said as I placed an arm around her shoulders. She then rubbed her eyes with her charming little fists.

"I had the oddest dream, Archer. I can make no sense of it."

"Was it perchance a nightmare?"

"No, not really. It was not unpleasant at all."

"Pray tell, my dear," I said.

She hesitated for a moment. "It was most bizarre, my beloved. I dreamed that I was a foreign lady of some sort, a Russian I think, and I believe there was a man who had a racehorse as well."

I waited for her to continue. "And…?"

She frowned pensively. "I'm afraid I do not remember anything beyond that, my darling."

Before responding, I gave the matter some deep thought. I most certainly did not wish to explain from whence this dream had likely originated, lest it upset her in the same manner in which my previous revelation had done so many weeks ago. I merely voiced the opinion that her dream was indeed quite odd. And so, after a moment, she switched off the light fixture and we both lay back down and continued our slumber.

Twenty

To my considerable surprise and overwhelming gratitude, it was Felix who was kind enough to lend me the necessary capital with which to make my purchase. Constance accompanied me to the appropriate place of business, which was located in the magnificent downtown area of Syracuse. After much vacillation, I settled upon an item of exceptional beauty and was somewhat taken aback and highly amused when Constance successfully convinced the merchant—a garrulous, unkempt gentleman by the name of Seymour Oukenblitzen—to reduce the price by one-third. She accomplished this magical feat of persuasion by carrying on a rather flagrant flirtation with the old gentleman.

But once again, I became tragically analytical and therefore, per my usual tendency, indecisive. Several seemingly perfect opportunities arose, yet I found myself unable to perform my appointed mission, for I was not entirely certain of its outcome. Alas, we had never discussed it. Perhaps Abigail considered our affiliation to be no more than a casual romance. Perhaps her feelings were not of sufficient depth for us to venture to the next stage. Or was I simply overcome by senseless apprehension? And so, once again, I dillydallied. I knew, however, that it would have to take place without too much delay because Mr. Oukenblitzen's business establishment had a thirty-day refund policy.

One day prior to this expiration date, I escorted Abigail to an overpriced restaurant in the nearby township of Frickenhausen, where we consumed various foodstuffs, piled into lopsided towers or presented upon plates striped with colorful sauces. The portions were miniscule, their flavor dominated by garlic, and when dinner had concluded, I felt my appetite to be barely diminished. Our waiter—a humorless and somewhat arrogant fellow, who unnecessarily introduced himself as Joseph—informed us that a particular dessert with an unpronounceable French name was, in his words, "to die for." When I asked him whether he would be inclined to rescue said dessert from a burning building, thus risking his life for its preservation and possibly dying in the process, he snorted and walked away. Following dinner, I desperately wished to follow my unfulfilling gourmet repast with a Twinkie but was unable to locate an establishment in the area that stocked them.

Fortunately, I had imbibed a glass of wine during our repast and the consumption of said liquid had succeeded in stimulating in my person a degree of boldness and daring.

It was late April and snow flurries had afflicted the area three days prior, but this night was clear and unseasonably temperate, so Abigail and I strolled hand in hand along the streets, admiring the stars that shone in the sky, this being the usual place for orbs of this type to perform their illumination.

On our journey through the restaurant's parking lot, I noted that my slight inebriation, and the boldness that had accompanied it, were beginning to dissipate. An empty parking lot had certainly not been my first choice of romantic locales, but no more than ten feet from the location of my vehicle, I impulsively fell upon bended knee before Abigail.

"My goodness! Are you all right, Archer?" she said with some alarm. "Did you fall down?"

"No. I performed this lowering of my body on purpose."

"Why?"

"I must ask you an important question," I said.

"Can this not be done without the knee bending?"

"Yes, of course, but I wish to be formal. This is as I had rehearsed it."

"You *rehearsed* this?"

"I did indeed. Many, many times."

Following a search of my pockets, I extracted the small blue velvet box from my tuxedo. Of course, by this time, Abigail knew what was about to transpire. Her expression displayed great tenderness that was tempered by a hint of amusement.

After a few moments of fumbling, during which I nearly dropped the box, I managed to open said velvet container, whereupon I displayed its contents before her.

Abigail put a hand to her mouth. "Oh my!" she said. "It's wondrous, Archer! I am nearly blinded. Look how it sparkles!"

"I specifically requested one that sparkles."

"I believe you are about to ask me to marry you."

"Quite correct," I said. "How did you perceive this?"

"You must admit there are more than a few clues. The knee bending, the ring... But are you aware that you are kneeling in mud?"

"Yes," I said. "But never mind that."

"Okay. Please procced then."

I took both of her hands in mine and cleared my throat. "Abigail Bird," I said. "I, Ishmael Archer, have loved you dearly for quite a long time. Longer even than you may know."

"As have I, you," she said.

I wished to say more regarding the depth and duration of my love for her, but a chill wind had suddenly arisen from the east. To add to this unpleasantness, the knees of my trousers were indeed quite caked with mud and I could feel the stain spreading northward, so I abbreviated my proposal and said, "Abigail Bird, will you have me, Ishmael Archer, as your husband?"

"Yes, of course! Of course! A thousand times, of course!" she said with great excitement.

"Then you will have me?"

She laughed. "Did I not just say that?"

"I suppose you did. I just wished to confirm it."

And then, with no further ado, I slipped the ring upon the correct finger and noted with some considerable delight that it fit her digit perfectly and would therefore not require adjustment.

"Now, please do stand up, Archer," she said.

"Excellent idea."

As she had suggested, I rose to my feet and fruitlessly attempted to brush the mud stain from my trousers, an exercise that only succeeded in making my hands muddy as well. Without placing my dirty hands upon her, Abigail and I then embraced, whereupon she promised to launder my soiled garment, although I explained that this was not necessary and that I would be glad to perform this tedious task myself for it was I who had created the stain. As they were rented tuxedo slacks, she then suggested that it would be wiser to deliver them to a dry cleaner, and I agreed that this would be preferable. Following this controversy, our lips met and I perceived that her breath reeked with the odor of garlic, but I suspected that mine did as well. For a moment, I contemplated the idea of pinching my nostrils shut but this would be less than romantic and severely complicate the process of breathing.

Garlic aside, this was the most memorable moment, the climax, as it were, of the story of Ishmael Archer.

It was a magnificent summer day that produced a fragrant breeze and a cloudless sky that an unimaginative author would likely describe as either azure or cerulean, possibly even sapphire, beryl, ultramarine, lapis lazuli or just plain blue. Wildflowers of assorted colors had sprouted in the meadows of the foothills and the ice packs had melted from the peaks of the Adirondacks. Dean Altschuler and Sandra, both of whom were delighted for me, had been kind enough to insist that the event and subsequent festivities take place in their enormous backyard. Fearing that there might be precipitation, they had leased an oversized canvas tent under which a number of round tables were placed. At their insistence, a wedding photographer and a person known as a DJ had been employed, although I was loath to suffer through stilted wedding photos and dancing. Abigail and I were married on a scenic bluff twenty feet away from the tent, an event that was accompanied by the college's chamber ensemble, which played a romantic Bach concerto with surprising competency. A retired Methodist minister by the name of Horace P. Elderberry officiated. I had never met the gentleman—apparently he was a friend of the Altschuler's—but thankfully he did not invoke the name of the deity once during the ceremony. I had chosen Eliot to be my best man; Sandra, who Abigail had befriended, acted as her bridesmaid. Following the ceremony, we strode down a makeshift aisle between the seated guests, some of whom stood up to shower us with uncooked rice pellets, a pagan practice that, as I later discovered, had originated with the Egyptians and was meant to ensure that the newlyweds enjoyed luck, prosperity, and a successful crop, although I had no intention of taking up agriculture. As we ducked this starchy attack, Abigail squeezed my hand tightly. She looked utterly glorious in her wedding attire.

Acceding to our wishes, the aforementioned affair was a small informal gathering, attended by no more than twenty people. Balthazar, who sported a splendid custom-made tuxedo, took on the role of co-host. My parents flew in from New York, both of them overjoyed that I had finally met a woman who was superior in every way to Amanda Archer, née Blackstone, whom they had both intensely disliked and had, in fact, warned me about. Prior to the wedding, Abigail and I had visited Mother and Father and the three of them had greatly enjoyed each other's company. (During this sojourn, my parents informed me that my former grade school companion, the taciturn Mr. Jerome Duckworth, resided in Palm Beach, Florida and was currently employed as a motivational speaker. Ha!)

Bob Fletcher and Constance arrived together as they had officially become a couple, although they had no plans to tie the proverbial knot. Under Bob's tutelage, Constance had become a devoted and proficient golfer and the two of them had recently returned from a week's vacation in Palm Springs, a city that boasted a number of superior golf courses. They were both deeply tanned as a result of their trip to this desert outpost and filled with joy and good wishes for us, the newlyweds.

After some vacillation, I refrained from inviting Dr. Van Buren or Dr. Partridge, as I feared that their presence might cause my new wife some confusion. Six months prior, Dr. Van Buren had published a scholarly paper regarding Abigail's unique delusion and, as a result, Van Buren Syndrome had become the accepted name of the disorder. Although his documentation of her case had received great acclaim, he had confessed to me that he was somewhat conflicted about having a disease, albeit a rare one, named after him. I had also been tempted to invite Mr. Williger, as he had been most kind and generous to me, until I recalled that his presence would no doubt place both he and Sandra in a somewhat uncomfortable position. Of course, I invited Felix, who performed a Greek dance and threw some plates at a tree, as was the custom in his homeland. I discovered later that said plates were part of a prized set of some considerable value that Sandra had inherited from her late grandmother although she did not appear in the least upset at their annihilation. Ms. Anastasia Goldfine arrived in the company of a man who I judged to be at least fifteen years her junior. I did not inquire as to their relationship for that would have been discourteous, but apparently he was not a relative. Also present were several of Abigail's colleagues from Phil's Rib and Steak Emporium.

As father of the bride, Balthazar offered up a superb oration that contained several amusing reminiscences from Abigail's youth and concluded with a heartfelt declaration of love and admiration for his daughter as well as an expression of affection for me, his newly appointed son-in-law. It was a most emotional speech and Abigail placed her head on my shoulder and wept. My father followed this with a violin rendition of La Vie en Rose, a performance that oozed with profound sweetness and aptly demonstrated his proficiency as a musician.

After the wedding repast had concluded, Abigail insisted that I dance with her, although in my case dancing was more of an aimless arrhythmic shuffle. She was rather talented at it, though, and I took great pleasure in watching her gyrate sensually, although at one point she nearly fell off the dance floor. I gathered from the intimate manner in which Eliot and Sandra danced that they had recaptured their love for one another, which made me quite elated. To my surprise, Ms. Anastasia Goldfine moved about the dance floor quite energetically, her arms flailing, her feet keeping pace with the beat of the music. Later in the evening, Felix engaged us in a Greek folk dance called the *Kalamatiano*, which required us to form a circle and kick our feet. Though I was thoroughly inept at it, I found it most agreeable, partly because I had, by that time, consumed some alcoholic fortification, but not enough to cause a repetition of my regurgitation of several months before.

Although I generally do not care for social events of any kind, I found this particular one to be most pleasing for it meant that Abigail and I would spend the rest of our lives together. I was deliriously happy.

Following our honeymoon in Venice, Italy (a journey to literary graves, although my preference, was obviously out of the question), Abigail and I pooled our resources (mine had increased thanks to Dean Fletcher) and rented a small three-bedroom domicile on the outskirts of Highland Falls that afforded us an excellent view of the foothills and an extra room for any ensuing progeny that might require separate quarters. We leased a small truck and enlisted the aid of Mr. Williger for the process of relocation. He was most gracious and refused remuneration, although, when he was not looking, I secreted a fifty-dollar bill under the base of a plastic model of a girl in a hula skirt that adorned the dashboard of his car.

Once all the boxes were situated in the parlor of our new house, I was eager to begin the process of unpacking, but Abigail claimed exhaustion and retired for the night. For some reason, I was possessed of considerable energy as well as a desire to rid the premises of the plethora of cartons that occupied most of the room. The majority of the boxes contained my books, which now included ten hardcover copies of *All About Emily* (I had changed the names of the characters), which I had expanded into a novel that had recently been released by a well-respected New York publisher. Although sales had been decidedly mediocre, I was gratified by a fair degree of critical acclaim and was determined to write another novel once things had settled down in our household.

While Abigail slept soundly in our bedroom, I began the arduous task of removing the contents of the aforementioned boxes and attempted to decide where they would go. Having conquered most of this work by midnight, I found that I still possessed enough energy to begin unloading some of Abigail's belongings, although I refrained from attacking the boxes marked "Clothing," for I had no idea how she wished to organize these items. And so I began with a small carton marked "Miscellaneous." I was halfway into unloading its contents when I came upon an unmarked manila envelope that was lodged beneath an assortment of empty file folders and magazines. As the envelope was Abigail's personal property, I resisted the temptation to open it, but curiosity eventually got the better of me. Inside the envelope was a slightly faded manuscript, the title page of which read, *Miss Brighton's Most Ardent Wish By Abigail Bird*. As the date had been typed in the upper margin, it became clear to me that this was the short story Abigail had written prior to her accident, the sample of her writing that she had intended for me to critique at our first mentoring session. Of course, I knew that she would recall neither the origin nor the existence of this manuscript, a fact that caused me to wonder why she had even packed it. Perhaps she had merely dumped the contents of a drawer into the moving box without bothering to sort through any of it. Or maybe she had simply not noticed it amongst the other paraphernalia. I myself had long since forgotten about it. But now, here it was, laying in my hands, which were filthy from the day's labors. Eager to discover the nature of Miss Brighton's most ardent wish, I turned the title page and commenced reading.

Miss Brighton's Most Ardent Wish

By Abigail Bird

As the weather that day was most pleasingly temperate, Miss Amelia Brighton, the eldest unmarried daughter of Lord and

Lady Brighton of Kent, decided to consume her afternoon tea out of doors, on the well-manicured lawn that swept before her ancestral home like an endless green blanket. She had recently completed her lessons for the day so she had taken with her a new novel written by her favorite author, Miss Jane Austen, who resided only ninety miles away. The local vicar's wife had recommended it. But as she took the book in her hands and began to peruse the opening page, she found that she was unable to concentrate, for her mind drifted to thoughts of her tutor, Mr. Ian Ambler of London. Recently installed at Dudley Manor, Mr. Ambler had been educated at Oxford, where he had studied Literature, Greek, Latin, History, Philosophy, and the Art of Woodcraft.

He was quite a tallish man, no more than four years her elder, who wore ascots of a peculiar nature and spoke with an excess of verbiage, though she found this appealing as she was given to the same tendency. He was, in a sense, quite handsome but his demeanor seemed more similar to that of an older man. She believed that they had much in common, most notably a consuming interest in literature. Therefore, it was a shame that she was required to learn such tiresome subjects as Greek and Latin for which she would never have much use, although the art of woodcraft was blessedly absent from Mr. Ambler's curriculum. Woodcraft was not an art that most women engaged in, certainly not women of Miss Brighton's station.

But Mr. Ambler also suffered from an excess of reserve, which she found most troublesome. In a very short time, she had developed a great fondness for him, and although they had spent most of their mornings engaged in the pursuit of higher learning, which was the purpose of his tenure at Dudley Manor, they occasionally passed the time in the garden or the salon discussing literature and other topics of common interest. Yet he did not seek out her company as she had hoped, nor did he initiate assignations or conversations. It was always she who proposed such pastimes. And, although she was grateful for his company, she was beginning to wonder if he had even the slightest affection for her. Did he perhaps feel it improper for a tutor to consort with his student? Would her strict parents disapprove of such boldness on his part? Was he in love with another woman? Was he merely timid? Or was he a simpleton?

Yet it was true that she herself was somewhat wary of engaging with a man, for a suitor whose original intentions had been matrimony, had recently spurned her. Did Mr. Ambler perhaps sense this? Was he aware of it? After all, there had been gossip.

Whilst strolling in the garden the day before, she had deliberately allowed her hand to swing quite close to his, hoping that he would take it in his or at least touch it. But he did not react to her hint of intimacy. Nor did he kiss her when, on several occasions, she had deliberately put her face close to his. She longed for him to give her some small signal that he felt some affection for her but he did not. As she too was afflicted with timidity, she was unable to demonstrate a display of passion. Besides, propriety demanded that the man initiate a gesture in that direction.

Over a short time, she began to feel the stirrings of love for Mr. Ambler, yet he still appeared to be oblivious to her feelings. She found this state of affairs most frustrating. How, she wondered, could a man be so appallingly dense? Had he suffered a previous rejection that kept him from requiting her love? Alas, she was too meek to inquire, as perhaps this information may have been of a personal nature and she did not wish to intrude upon his privacy. Moreover, such an inquiry would most assuredly not be ladylike and Miss Brighton prided herself on her excellent manners.

Then one day, much to her delight, he performed a small act that gave her reason to hope. It was a subtle gesture but she felt that it had been more than mere kindness. At her request, they had visited a small annual festival that was held by the peasants in the town. As they wandered about, she stopped at a vendor and purchased a cold liquid-like confection that she ate from a bowl. They sat side by side on a bench while she consumed it.

"It is a most tasty treat, Mr. Ambler," she informed him. "I believe they call it ice cream soup. Do you perchance have a sweet tooth?"

"I do indeed, Miss Brighton," he replied. "Yet I have a preference for cupcakes, chocolate ones that are called Hostess."

"What an odd name," she mused.

"I also enjoy another victual that is made of a crunchy cheese variety. I find these to be most appealing in their taste."

"Such a coincidence! I too enjoy a variety of cheese!" she exclaimed, wondering how the conversation had meandered in this peculiar unromantic direction. "I have not, however, sampled one of a crunchy type."

He turned to observe her. "Hark," he declared. "You have spilled a small drop of your liquid confection upon your blouse."

"Goodness me!" she remarked. "I can be quite the clumsy oaf at times."

"Please allow me to remove it from your person," he offered. And then, much to her astonishment, he removed a handkerchief from his coat and swept away the drop. It was a most bold act for it required him to touch her anatomy, which he had never done before. She interpreted this small gesture as an awakening of his love for her and she felt at that moment an odd excitement sweep through her loins. He loved her! She was certain of it.

But as the days passed, Mr. Ambler performed no further gestures of this nature although she remained certain that he would. One morning, prior to her lessons, her dear father, Lord Brighton, informed her that Mr. Ambler had been suddenly called away to London to attend to his mother who had fallen ill and that most likely he would never return to Dudley Manor, and that another tutor had been engaged to continue her education, an elderly widow by the name of Miss Violet Trousdale. Devastated by this woeful news, Miss Brighton hied herself to her bedchamber and copiously wept until the tears soaked her pillow. She remained there for several days, desolate and forlorn. Would she ever find another gentleman of Mr. Ambler's quality and attractiveness or would she remain a spinster for the rest of her life?

Her heart was broken as if it had been severed in two by a sharp blade. She never saw Mr. Ambler again.

How delightful, I thought! Such an excellent lampoon of the literary style of the era! Clearly, my new wife, or rather the previous version of my new wife, Abigail One, had had an impressive talent for parody. Woodcraft indeed! Utterly hilarious! If Miss Jane Austen were alive today, she would have appreciated this superb spoofery.

As I perused the story again, I began to notice a few oddities contained in the unfulfilled liaison between Miss Brighton and Mr. Ambler that reminded me of my early relationship with Abigail One. The dollop of a confection that had besmirched her clothing had occurred in reality with the strawberry ice cream at the art fair. There was also our common affection for literature and her description of Mr. Ambler's attire, reserve, and verbosity sounded quite familiar.

On yet another reading, I became aware that the initials of Amelia Brighton were identical to those of Abigail Bird and those of Ian Ambler were the same as mine.

My mind raced and my heart fluttered. Had Abigail, in writing the story, attempted to inform me in a subtle way that she loved me? Had this been her motivation for writing this tale of unrequited love? Yes, I decided. Yes, indeed! Yes, yes, yes, a thousand times, yes! She had never really intended for me to be her mentor—that had obviously been a ruse! How alarmingly dense I had been—thickheaded at not perceiving her feelings for me and even more so in not reaching the obvious conclusion immediately upon reading the story no more than ten minutes before. Abigail One had loved me all along! My cowardly diffidence had been for naught!

Thus enlightened, I placed the manuscript back in its packing box, taking pains to secrete it beneath the other detritus, and tiptoed to the bedroom, where I quietly shed my clothing and slipped into my pajamas. Abigail was slumbering soundly and I gazed adoringly at her as a barely audible whimper escaped her lips. Quietly, so as not to awaken her, I pulled the covers back and climbed into the bed. A few strands of her hair had fallen into her face and I gently pulled these back and tucked them behind her ear. Then I moved closer to her, so that my entire body touched hers, and placed my arm around her slender waist.

Acknowledgements

Whom, I wonder, shall I acknowledge this time around? My old college English professor who encouraged me to become a writer without mentioning the possibility of starvation? My agent who encouraged me to make the book more marketable without telling me how? My editor, who pointed out that it might have been wise for me to have paid more attention when my teachers were explaining grammar? Or to the cumbersome Dewey Decimal System, now, sadly, no more than a vague memory among those of a certain age? Nah.

Since *The Strange Courtship of Abigail Bird* is the story of two people whose lives are utterly consumed by classic literature, I think it appropriate to pay homage to those who love to read, that noble minority of souls who still look to books for engaging stories and endearing characters, for clever turns of phrase, for the joys of well-wrought interior monologue.

They say that we booklovers are an endangered species. I think not. My meanderings throughout the maze of social media have led me to believe that reading is indeed quite alive and prospering. One can easily find a plethora of those dedicated to reading on Instagram and Tumblr; Goodreads reaches twenty-five million people, twice as many as the previous year; book bloggers abound; Facebook offers hundreds of groups dedicated to a variety of books, not to mention countless author fan pages, many with thousands of followers.

Amazon's cybershelves contain the largest collection of books in the history of the written word and the retail giant has given birth to the most innovative approach to reading since the invention of typesetting. Thus, thanks to Amazon, I may now travel with hundreds of books without increasing the weight of my suitcase by more than a few ounces, giving new dimension to Stephen King's famous observation that "Books are a uniquely portable magic."

259